# (The) Diamond Planet

R

This book is a work of fiction. Any resemblances to actual persons or events, living or dead or purported to be dead, is entirely coincidental.



The quote attributed to Joan Didion comes from her essay, "7000 Romaine, Los Angeles 38," originally printed in *The Saturday Evening Post* under the title, "The Howard Hughes Underground."

*Yuuyaraq*, a keyword appearing in (The) Dragooned, is a Yup'ik expression for "the way of life [as a human]." The author uses this word to provide the setting with the membrane of authenticity, and trusts its usage does not come across as too Anglo. Readers of Alaskan aboriginal descent, as in many adjacent cases, have full authority to cringe.

*"He is the last private man, the dream we no longer admit."*

**—Joan Didion, 1967**

# (The) Cracksman

***Jacob Pulkkinen, 29***

***Most recently employed by Jiffy Lube***

***Average monthly income: $802.44***

***Income this month: $1,056.83***

***Malibu, California***

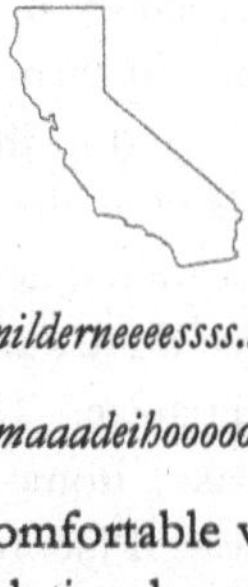

"*Hannannawoohmmmmmilderneeeessss...*"

"*MmmmMmmmMmmmmaaadeihooooohhoooo...*"

Jacob Pulkkinen, so comfortable with disabling the Hytex 230CC Home Security Solution he can operate unconcerned as to what kind of noise he's making, is humming, badly, Madonna's late 1984 hit *Like A Virgin*, which for the present moment he incorrectly believes was sung by Cyndi Lauper.

"*Diddahmmm...hhm... tillaaafunuuuu...*"

*What ever happened to that lady*, he's alright to wonder despite having his eighties pop starlets all turned around. Is she the type to burn out and serve time on some boring richwhite crime like tax evasion, or is she the cool old lady predisposed to performing a benefit concert draped in a rainbow flag? Has he stolen from her house yet? Does she live in Malibu? No, there's no way. He'd never have left without checking the platinum plaque.

*"Tryyyying to avoiiiiid… a malpractice suuuuuit…"*

Tossing the Hytex 230CC interface in the spacious backyard deck's infinity pool, Jacob has started singing the adjacent Weird Al Yankovic parody *Like A Surgeon.* This he also doesn't realize.

What can any Home Security Solution hope to do when the family it is designed to secure gladly tells anyone where they are at any time. Home security is a myth in the Instagram age. Jacob follows the entire Otterlake clan twice over and knows half of them, immediate and extended, are on their private island in the Anambas archipelago (to say their private island *is* the Anambas archipelago), and the other half are scattered across a handful of European resorts so exclusive there's no epithet the Instagram story stickers may recognize. The latter counts step-matriarch Irene Otterlake, ironic because all this extra home security bullshit was, if Jacob has it correct, her idea.

Jacob never revisits what's already been burgled. A break from the norm if criminologists know what they're talking about. Apart from seeing the look on Grand Duchess Otterlake's face when she sees her Home Security Solution so easily rendered a Home Security Problem, he can't picture himself driving all the way back down to Malibu even if he were guaranteed a second score as straightforward as this first one. There are cameras, of course, and Jacob makes sure to wave at the first unit greeting him as he clears the sliding glass door. Light's on, but he's positive no one's home.

A second camera watches the short, artistically slanted crack of transition between the sliding glass and the rec room—if the Otterlakes know any distinction between work and play; if the Otterlakes know what work is. Jacob's roommate is paid forty-grand a year to review the footage on these useless things. As in he's paid forty-grand to sit in a basement office three-hundred miles north of here and *pretend* to review the footage on these useless things while instead designing AutoCAD models and browsing his weird porn (anime stuff). This is what's actually protecting these people, and this is why Jacob does a Fortnite dance for the camera in the billiard hall. They'll laugh about this when Jacob gets home.

Malibu property of this persuasion is built to miraculous, arrogant dimensions. Sensible architecture begins and ends in unsensible ways because shelter is the fifth or sixth priority. Take the blown glass chandelier above and on top the ground floor living room, the abject hazard that stretches down to kiss the mirror white tiles and blurs the line between chandelier and sculpture. It fractals outward at hazardous angles and frosted light like a frozen grenade. Would be real fun to kick to pieces, Jacob thinks, then remembers these intrusive thoughts are what separates the attempted burglaries from the successful. He's similarly tempted by the liquor bottles cabineted behind the brushed steel bar. The Otterlakes would consider anything also carried by Total Wine beneath them, surely. Any one of those potions would get Sotheby's hot and bothered. At the same time they must be liquor bottles in quantities so miniscule they can be itemized on the individual level.

Suspect material. Best not touch.

Jacob rounds the bar anyway, because spots like this carry a hidden valuable the part-timers don't even think to think about. These people are always gifting each other extravagant versions of basic tools, and if his intuition is correct, the bottle opener he's now rolling in his palm is plated in some precious metal. White gold, canary gold, chartreuse gold. Clark Buys Gold would be very interested no matter the subgenre of gold. Best of all? Gifts like these are totally off the books. He bets right now, zipping the bottle opener away in his coat, the Otterlakes won't notice this missing for months. If ever. They may forget they own the house.

At the far wall, by a modular staircase rendered in the tradition of Manhattan fire escapes and blasted in bright baby blue, is a painting bigger than Jacob's bed. Why it must be that big when all the artist did, to Jacob's philistine eyes, was smack the canvas with reds and peel off the painter's tape laid down at fanciful angles. If it's on this wall in this house, however, it must be worth as much as the property itself. Jacob's gloved fingers find the stretcher and pressure a crease in the canvas.

At this level, homes have their own names. They are destinations more than somewhere a child would grow up. The Otterlake's primary Malibu escape property is dubbed Harriot and is the only one the clan uses in the orthodox sense. The rest, numbering some seventeen properties along the coast, are either leased out or left unattended apart from scheduled deep cleanings. Speculators anticipate a boom somewhere in the next fiscal. How prodigious of the Otterlakes to have added seven properties to their portfolio just the year prior.

They're nothing special, apart from the architecture. Jacob's already checked.

*So what is someone sneaking around one of a multibillionaire's dozens of properties looking for*, Jacob hopes a documentarian will ask him decades down the road. And he'd tell them, rubbing his hands as people with a lifetimes of examples must do before answering, that what you're after is the master bedroom. No matter the income level, there's just *ways* all of us behave, *man*, priorities all of us share. Our most valuable things are in the place we spend the most time. Sure, maybe there's a safe in the garage (in this case there is not) but that only means the good one is in the walk-in-and-around closet. Don't waste your time with the living room tchotchkes and don't you dare concern yourself with the media room. Jacob doesn't care how nice the projector is or if the Otterlakes have a PlayStation 7. Irene Otterlake keeps her pearls in the bedroom, just like your own mom.

The fire escape staircase isn't as noisy as Jacob had prepared for, taking his careful first step with landmine-testing precision. It's just the standard variant of wealthy art tacky. If one of those Koons dogs is in this house, somewhere, Jacob's seriously gonna consider crushing it in is hand like a Pepsi. But he won't actually. Professional. Documentary-bound. YouTube worthy. Meet The Guy Who Stole From The Elite For Years Before Getting Caught.

"… A virgin… *hey*!"

The *hey!*, by complete sonic coincidence, is genuine.

Seems Jacob's stepped in something without his noticing. A security feature? Dye packs? Now he's getting his anti-theft measures confused. Against his own advice Jacob clicks his LED flashlight and checks what he's been dragging across the impeccably polished lightwood flooring.

Of some persuasion, animal shit.

Vermin? That's where Jacob's mind goes, for how small a mass he's been painting on Harriot's pants. Guard dogs know better than to shit where they work, and they know where guard dogs of lesser conviction end up if they do. Butterfly farm upstate. He sits at the end of an obnoxiously large couch (seriously, this thing could seat eighty people) and checks his boot. Something he'd normally only do once he was out, but the Otterlake security system has proven so lax Jacob figures he could take a nap and still be out before the sun.

Yup, that's a skid mark, all right. And that blemish he's seeing on the floor right next to the pink iron spiral staircase (what the fuck) must be exhibit B. In a home as untarnished as Harriot Jacob thinks he could spot a flea in the dark. And there's quite a bit of rodent shit on this floor. The Otterlakes haven't been away from this house very long. Three weeks at the maximum. Last in here was Tucker Otterlake, nephew once removed to the Otterlake patriarch and guy who only uses Harriot as a supply port on his way out to Hawaii. Which he last did, again, three weeks ago. Has the mice problem in California gotten this bad? Three weeks of not replacing the glue traps means they're sprinting about without fear of human retaliation, liberally shitting wherever their ass happens to be at the time, growing four times the size Jacobs expects and scampering out from the throw blanket he's sitting right next to.

"*Fuckfuckfuck!*" Jacob stutters, a man who would say he's got no problem dealing with mice if maybe a girl asked him. To be fair, he was ambushed. The shape rolling under the mink blanket was about as big as the ghost of the mink that would be more than justified coming back to haunt the blanket's owner. It scampers out from underneath and embarks onto the corner of the couch, its little heart beating so fast Jacob can see the silhouette throb without giving the form light.

When he does, he reveals a blueish-gray chinchilla.

*Oh, okay,* Jacobs can sigh. *There's the culprit. God damn these things are cute.* Against his own burglary advice Jacobs squats, making himself small, inviting the frightened puffball thing to come closer. He pretends there's some kind of food clawed in his hand. The chinchilla gathers itself and bounds over, sniffing his leather fingers.

"Come here, buddy."

Jacob doesn't know the proper way to handle a chinchilla and settles on gripping his new friend upright like a can of beer. His little paws hold onto Jacob's forefinger, a little shocked to be manhandled but calming down in a short minute. *Someone's pet escaped* is what Jacob assumes first, and leaving such an innocent little thing unattended for three human weeks is just how he expects out of touch maniacs like the Otterlakes would treat their animals. Irene probably had this little dude's parents made into a hat.

As of right now, Jacob doesn't know what he's gonna

do with this chinchilla. What he does know is the fur is pleasant to the touch and he's pretty confident *he* could shit on the floor without consequence. Harriot has opened up for him and waved a ghostly hand like *here, man, come take the silver, you earned it.* And he's worried if he just let this little guy go he'd accidentally step on him later. We don't want *that,* "*do we, little buddy,*" Jacob starts to say before getting a hold of himself.

On the pink iron spiral staircase (still doesn't sound right) Jacob feels himself very nearly step on something. Something cushiony enough he can sense a foreign object and stop himself before applying any serious pressure. A second chinchilla.

Jacob gets to the top of the stairs now double-fisting chinchillas. *Where's the party at?* No but seriously he does need to let these guys go somewhere. The sink, maybe—can they get out of a sink? Oh, you know what, Jacob has a capital idea. He'll keep his eye on the *third* Chinchilla, hiding underneath the long, long dining room table and running out when Jacob's boot makes a noise, and see if it runs right back to the pen. It better: if he stays holding these two much longer he'll start wanting to give them names. *Raoul.* Yeah, that'd be good.

Someone left a light on in the kitchen. Cleaning staff are known to do this. Gives the impression the homeowners are nearby and signals to each other who's recently been around. A trick of the trade he remembers from his housekeeping days. Housekeepers don't stay overnight, however, and Jacob thinks nothing of the light but a decent place to put the chinchillas down and gather himself. He realizes only after spotting the sixth chinchilla that he's let himself get wrapped up in completely superfluous chilla -wrangling. This isn't his problem whatsoever, delightful as these little dudes are. *So tell us about the fuzzy cashmere rodents.* No documentarian's gonna want that scoop; that will do nothing for their thesis. *Oh, but that time you broke into the Otterlake's Malibu residence—the shitdamn Harriot—and went inside their bedroom safe only to find incriminating documents revealing the families dark secrets. Tell us about* that, *greatest thief of all time.*

Jacob's gotten thoroughly distracted. Here's why you don't love in this business. He rounds the doorway to the kitchen and, unprepared, noticing too late what he should have already noticed, finds the fridge thrown open, its contents tossed onto either the ground or spacious island, pilfered by a young man currently shoveling mango slices in his mouth with Game 7 Lebron James intensity. The chinchilla in Jacob's right hand (Raoul) makes a squeak. The boy's head snaps to the left so fast Jacobs expects him to fall over dead.

Jacob bolts the other way, making a rookie mistake in the stress of the moment: going somewhere he hasn't already been. From the outset his exit was back the way he came. As solid an option as one can hope for: single room access, spilling out to a back patio inaccessible anywhere but the interior. In any case, a smarter place to be making than the frosted glass skybridge he now finds himself crossing, his clumsy hands putting chinchilla to kangaroo pocket, gripping the cable railing and slingshotting his clumsy body to the midpoint.

It's not that he means to stop here or that stopping in this circumstance is at all the wise thing to do. No, it's the very idea of a skybridge in a house that gives him uncharacteristic pause. Fucking Malibu. A skybridge is the sort of fixture a home needs to be built *around*, this in spite of the fact it can only service two points of the home by nature. What the homeowner gets in return, apart from a skybridge and all the self-assured significance, is a central point of observation which knows no contemporary. For instance, a view back down into the kitchen, where Jacob can see the young man with the mangoes hasn't moved and has not stopped eating mango blades.

Half a crescent of mango hangs from his mouth. His eyes seem to forget what he was supposed to be looking at and he starts to giggle. The chinchilla bounding out of nowhere onto the kitchen island sneaks towards the scent of fruit, reminding Jacob he's nursing two in his hoodie. Oh, and it looks like there's another two on the skybridge. The young man bites his crescent in half and waves the rest at the chinchilla, which rather than take the bait instead sniffs at the glass Tupperware. God, even the Tupperware smacks a putrid degree of luxury.

"*Mango?*"

Is he asking Jacob or is he asking the chinchilla. He's looking at neither so it's impossible to say.

"*Mango? Mango? Mango? Mango? Mm? Mango?*"

Okay, he's asking the rodent. The rodent seems to say no.

"*Ahahahaha fuckin' you do you man like it's whatever.*"

Jacob checks his Instagram for which Otterlake this could possibly be. Another intruder? The world's his oyster in a way it's not Jacob's, then. What, did he go and try all the funny candy behind the bathroom mirror? Actually, now that Jacob thinks about it, his behavior is not unlike that ayahuasca trip his roommate (not the porn one) took last Spring. Attention is measured in seconds or hours. In his mind he's been offering this chinchilla a mango slice for three days.

*"Where's your fuckin' like brothers and sisters or whatever the hell y'all are to each other like I think I saw you or fuckin' like your brother or something in the bathroom a second back like."*

Aw, poor guy.

Acknowledging he should really just take advantage of the situation and find that master bedroom, Jacob feels a pity not unlike driving by roadkill-in-progress. His wants are in line with burglars of all sizes—your stuff. He doesn't want this puppy dog to be worrying about his pets. What probably happened, Jacob's now thinking, is this guy, rendered by his drug cocktail to a state of purehearted immaturity, unlocked the cage on his dozen-and-counting chinchillas and will not realize the error of his ways until the next morning, when's he turning Harriot upside down to find all his expensive rat things. Time to make the call, Jacob.

*"Where your friends? Mm? Brothers and sisters?"*

"I got two."

The young man twists his neck, uncomfortably if he were sober, up at the skybridge and grins, "ah hell yeah you got the fat one hey bring 'em down I gotta feed 'em this granola or whatever."

Responding not at all how someone would upon finding an intruder in their home, twice over, the young man goes adventuring through all the brushed steel cabinets for the aforementioned granola or whatever. Not a box of molded corn syrup to be seen; the Otterlake food stocks are surgically prepared and grouped in the ways only professional, contracted teams operate. Jacob should've figured Irene isn't down here chopping those carrots herself—hold on, was that cabinet actually a mini fridge? That quiet little frill somehow infuriates Jacob worse than the painting downstairs.

Going back across the skybridge, down the narrow stairs, and back around to the doorway, Jacob plops the chinchillas down on the kitchen island. The three—no, five—rodents congress around the open glass dish of mangoes.

"Mm yeah go crazy yeah these are from where the fuck they grow the good fruits like Belize or Bali or somewhere humid I dunno."

"… Is that so."

"Ever been to Belize man we got this thin strip of beach down there with some bungalows whatever you call them when it's like a bunch of people own them at once."

"Timeshares."

"OH I'm thinking of Isla Mujeres man fuck's wrong with me."

Innocent mistake. But the Otterlakes do probably also own that thin strip of beach down in Belize.

"Oh shit, it's the fat one!" he says, forgetting this Chinchilla being the fat one has already been established. He seizes the little guy with both hands and kisses the top of his head. "This one is Liv's favorite and she wanted to name him like something fat but I don't think she had anything good."

"Raoul?"

"*Ahahahahahahahahahahaha!*" he makes kookaburra noises. Here's when Jacob realizes this is most probably Cameron Otterlake, only child of patriarch Nigel Otterlake and heir to the largest independent fortune in North America since the Rockefellers. Trying a failing to feed a dozen chinchillas and tripping balls.

"Are you the only one here?"

"*Aaaggghhh* yeah it's me here like I thought I heard the door downstairs a minute ago but nah it's been pretty quiet y'know."

*Hmm*, Jacob hmms. "Where's the master bedroom?"

"Way upstairs ah hell nah I never sleep up there I'm worried the stars will come down or the moon'll explode cuz I'm looking too hard."

"All the way upstairs?"

"Shit dude I like sleeping on the *couch* right like you can sprawl out on the motherfucker when I'm up there man I think about the moon exploding dude it really freaks me out."

Noted. Jacob's about to head back on the skybridge but he stops in the doorway one last time. "Hey, you wouldn't happen to be Cameron, would you?"

He spends a comically long time chewing a mango slice. "If somebody has to be."

It's good to be burgling again. Jacob feels a warmth in his heart witnessing his master bedroom safe theory proven correct yet again. Keeping the thing behind the long winter coats is so amateurish he can't believe *the* Otterlakes do it too. A retail safe, no less. Schlitter's 2010 ACS12000, a model notorious for the loud clacking made by the dials. This is the kind of safecracking foley one expects from a movie, where the *cliclicliclic* intonates for the audience how safecracking works. This isn't Jacob's first ACS12000. In fact there's a 2002 model he practices on back home. Schlitter had made zero significant design tweaks in those five years; the snake is charmed nigh-subconsciously and the door pops open.

Huh. That's not Benjamin Franklin. He thinks maybe it's safe to make a call.

Unzipping his crossbody bag, shoulders glad to be rid of some penetrative heavy cargo, Jacob sets Suzy on the nightstand. A local cellular data jammer, dimensions of a VHS tape with heft beyond its size, co-developed by his roommate. What for is unclear. That guy has covert calls to make. Something to do with his torrenting network. Jacob didn't ask, nor did he ask to borrow Suzy in the first place.

"*Jakey*?"

"Do they still have Mao on the Chinese money?"

"*You took my fucking box, shitass.*"

"Answer the question, dude, I'm looking at like half a million Mao's."

"*Fucking… yeah, he is, but Mao's on all the Yuan. Gimme a color.*"

"Watermelon Sour Patches."

"*A hundred? Yeah that's like fifteen bucks. How much are you looking at? Also, where are you?*"

"At the Otterlake house in Malibu."

"*You aren't narrowing it down. Those guys own half the West coast and a quarter of the East.*"

"The one where they stashed *half a million Yuan* in the bedroom."

"… *Still probably haven't narrowed it down. It's a stable note. Bet you most of their cash isn't American.*"

"Get excited, loser, we're gonna move houses."

"*Get the money here without going to Otterlake-sponsored jail. We'll talk to my crypto guy.*"

"Speaking of, the house is called Harriot. I'll need you to scrub the footage when you get the chance."

"*Dude, nobody checks those. And bring my box back!*"

*Click.*

Now would be a good time to call it a night. Jacob is unprecedently lucky to have gotten Cameron, of all Otterlakes, for reasons that would take too many tabloid links to explain if someone asked. Even if that record-setting jackass somehow remembers this happening in the morning it's not like the things Cameron Otterlake says happened have legs. Cameron Otterlake says a lot of things happened. Cameron Otterlake said he found a tarot card at the bottom of the ocean (the King of Cups). The United States Coast Guard found him sitting in an inner tube drifting two miles off the coast of Palm Beach clutching the king of hearts.

And that's hardly the most recent breakdown of his—Jacob's favorite occurred one year ago, near to the day; Cameron's attempt to buy the Playboy Mansion out from under current owner Daren Metropoulos. With what money? Kids like Cameron Otterlake aren't brought up to think about those things. In all likelihood Cameron did have the personal spending power to get his mansion. But Daren wouldn't sell, not even when Cameron offered to pay 16% above market value. Cameron would whinge to anyone who would listen, which in his case is most people he's ever known. Kids like Cameron Otterlake aren't raised to think anyone might not give a shit about their stupid mansion dreams, and in fact may feel nothing but contempt towards a pampered twerp whose idea of a bad day is failing to secure the boob palace despite putting up nauseating levels of cash. When TMZ tried the door at the Otterlake's East Central Park property, Cameron not only answered but let the crew inside, offering 50-year scotch to the interns so long as they listened to him complain about Daren Metropoulos for what ended up being three uninterrupted hours.

How did he work his one-sentence complaint into a TMZ exclusive, three-hour interview? He didn't. By hour two he was, as celebrity psychologist Dr. Antonio Esposito diagnosed, spiraling. Jacob's not sure spiraling is a medical term.

Out from the master bedroom, across the skywalk, down the steps (watch for chinchillas), down the pink iron spiral stairs (it's growing on him), Jacob studies through the darkness a human-shaped blob of sludge spread eagle on the tectonic couch, having gathered as many chinchillas as it could before plopping down and letting the little fucks have their lay of the land, crossing over its back and nestling at its legs. Looks to Jacob like a plague body dumped in the sewer, devoured by rats. He has yet to spy a light switch anywhere on Harriot's spotless walls.

He asks the body, "You want the lights on, man?"

"*Mmmmmmmmm…*"

Uncharacteristically courteous of him, but it only occurs to Jacob right now that he's in the audience of a celebrity.

"They say you should keep the lights on if you're gonna have a trip, y'know."

"*Mm.*"

Not an answer, but Cameron's cognate enough to stretch out a hand until he finds a chinchilla head, stroking slowly.

"Well, I'm gonna get going, Cameron. Take care—"

"AND GOD SAID."

Chinchillas dart away from the noise in all directions. Humming to life, slowly and beautifully like the house-lights of a lavish concert hall, Harriot's ceiling yawns in soothing yellows.

"And there was *ahahahahahahahaha.*"

Should've guessed it would be something stupid.

"And what turns them off?" Jacob asks.

"Fucking I dunno man I can't do shit in this house you could do whatever the fuck you want man you could kill me."

"What did you take, exactly? If I can ask."

"Mm?!"

"What-did-you-take?"

"I been looking all over the house and the plane for my sweater but I don't think I took it with me when I left like it may still be back wherever I left it."

"Was it shrooms?"

"Is a COP asking—"

"I just assume the Otterlakes have access to the best shit in the world."

"OH! Okay yeah nah I don't like those they taste weird."

"They, plural?"

Cameron doesn't answer. Jury remains out but Jacob, having only this thimbleful of direct correspondence with Cameron, does not realize how normal this behavior really is. "Hey, man, I don't wanna pull you out of your journey but, if I may *ground* you for a sec, I'm finding your pets all over the house."

"Oh they can be here dude it's cool."

"... It's just one of them might get hurt falling off the skybridge—"

"*Where's the fat one*?!"

"Raoul?"

"Yeah!"

"On your stomach."

Raoul is on his stomach, fat enough to be recognized amongst the herd. Cameron brings Raoul up closer to his neck. "I mean Liv wanted to name him Monchie but I like Raoul tho like he's really friendly and if you wanna pet him he just sits there and lets you do it."

Very true—and something he's already said. Raoul just sits there and lets Cameron do it.

Jacob asks, "And who's Liv? Is she your girl?"

"*Ahahahaha* yeah I dunno I guess pretty much yeah like we've been seeing each other for a minute now or something like that whenever my cousin's thing in Tahoe was. I was gonna invite her here sometime soon cuz she'd told me she wanted a chinchilla when she was little so when I got here yesterday morning I thought like '*oh shit imagine she walks in and there's just so many of them*' and I called the pet store south of here like '*ey gimme every Chinchilla you have*' which was twenty-six."

"Is she someone I'd know about?"

Cameron doesn't answer this but the answer would be

maybe. Olivia Achenbach, third daughter of the Achenbach family, is rich in the normal, boring way. The Achenbachs are cabin royalty, controlling over half of the vacation rentals dotting the shoreline of lake Tahoe, including the entirety of Nevada's claim. On top of this, her father, Nigel Achenbach, is the President and CEO of the next-gen jet ski manufacturer WaterNife. Forbes dubbed WaterNife the "Tesla of the Seas"—what was supposed to be a compliment but instead beckoned several days of mockery on Twitter and elsewhere.

Olivia's oldest sister, Joann "Joey" Achenbach-Clement, is more likely to be recognized than her sisters, being the co-hostess of popular HGTV renovation series *Cabin Rescue*. A typical home and garden program remarkable only for a recent scandal wherein Joey's male co-host was found to frequent alt-right message boards. For the latest season he's been replaced by Amber Scott, the secret Property Sister of the famous Property Brothers and a woman who, to the shock of millions of HGTV viewers, exists.

Apart from her high school diving accolades and decently compelling bikini photos there's little to nothing Olivia Achenbach has done that would implore Jacob to follow her on any social channel. But if the Otterlake network would allow her and Cameron to "pretty much been seeing each other for a minute now or something like that [sic]", then the Achenbachs pass the bar dividing the merely wealthy from the Elite. Jacob will have to make a point of robbing from them at a later date.

While Jacob was spacing out, Cameron had gotten up, Raoul perched on his shoulder, humming *bumbumbumbum-*

*bum-bumbumbum-bumbumbumbum-bum-bumbumbum* up the pink iron spiral stairs. In truth he'd been *bum-bum-bumming* for a while so inconsequentially Jacob hadn't bothered to commit the tick to narration. Perhaps a song Cameron wasn't remembering with enough accuracy. Jacob would never be so inaccurate with his own humming, he thinks.

The lowest level of Harriot hits Jacob with something cousin to nostalgia. He remembers creasing that stupid paining and thinking about kicking that stupid half-chandelier-half-sculpture-all-disgusting to knives. His hand unconsciously fondles the gold-plated bottle opener in his coat, slithering through the folds of Yuan. Jacob's already thinking about the drive back up north, the way he'll plop down on the couch with a beer in hand and 500,000 Yuan on the floor and coffee table, telling his roommates about finding Cameron Otterlake shroomed the fuck outta his mind cuddling a couple dozen chinchillas, all while he does a departing pop & lock move for the security camera. *You got served.*

Right at the sliding glass door, gloved hand on the handle, Harriot roars in surround sound. Some of the dark spots in the ceiling, what Jacob had assumed were lights, are in fact speakers placed with surgical consideration. In the crack of strings and rumbling drums there's not a hint of unwanted reverberation. How naïve of Jacob to suggest Harriot is only *like* a concert hall.

Finding the source takes pacing the whole house a second time, dodging the stampedes of chinchillas who take the sudden burst of music as something hostile. Turns out where Jacob needs to be is the second floor, perpendicular to the stairs and through what he'd thought was a big closet. Instead he finds an immaculately sculptured listening room the likes of which he thought only Rick Rubin had. The back wall looks to be entirely records, with one of those rolling ladders he's only seen in libraries. The ceiling curves gently up and sharply back down at the black leather couch standing on thin steel legs, the one Cameron lies across with his feet sticking up and his head bent to a right angle at his chest.

"*What is this?!*" Jacob hollers over the song, a war hungry orchestral screed prepared to die.

"*Hm?!*"

"*What—is—this?!*"

"*Music!*"

"*No, what's the song?!*"

"*I have no fucking idea but it's cool!*"

Shit. If there's a noise complaint, Jacob is fucked. Harriot isn't shoulder to shoulder with its neighbors like some stretches of Malibu but you'd be surprised how little it takes for people who live here to think someone's being disruptive. Maybe you wouldn't be surprised.

Cameron adds, "I'm just trying to hear the end part like I heard this at this thing Nigel sponsored and it's so fucking tight like hold on it's coming up listen to this."

Jacobs says, "After this you mi—"

DUNDUNDUNDUN

Jacob says, "… After—"

DUN DUN DUN

"A—"

DUN DUN DUN DUNDUNDUN DUN

"… After—"

DUUUN DUUUN

"So after—"

DUUUUUUN DUUUUUUN DUUUUUUN

"You mi—"

BWOOOOOOOOOOOOOOOMMMMM…

"… You mind if… okay, you mind if I throw something on?"

*Must be shrooms*, Jacob is all too confident to think. Cameron has that agreeable eagerness only seen in people who think, over the course of one hour, they've figured everything out. His nerve ending have been sanded numb. Anything could happen. Jacob could kill him. Wordlessly Cameron flings an arm around violently at the shoulder and Jacob takes this to mean he should go through the records.

He should've known the Otterlakes wouldn't disgrace their distinguished record collection with Cyndi Lauper, who he still thinks did *Like A Virgin*. He searches the Cs fruitlessly until thinking maybe Cyndi did that song when she was in a band like how Gwen Stefani didn't so *Spiderwebs* under her birth name, so he Duckduckgos the answer and discovers it was actually Madonna, feels stupid but glad he hadn't told anybody, navigates down to the Ms, and is shocked to find the Otterlakes do have Madonna on vinyl.

"Ever listen to this lady?" Jacob makes conversation while bullshitting his way through loading a record.

"We got like all the songs here but nah I don't think so unless she's on the radio or something nah I dunno."

"You listen to the *radio*?"

"I don't like making choices sometimes."

This is the best imaginary friend Cameron's ever had. Jacob is introducing Cameron to promising, untreaded ground, like eating mangoes inside the listening room and the greatest hits of Madonna. Despite this listening room having "all the songs[citation needed]," it seems Cameron's listened to a morsel of a morsel. And he's still only listened to as much, because he keeps getting up to restart *Like A Virgin*.

Likewise, Jacob's learning things about Cameron Otterlake either too boring or too frightening for the tabloids. He hates dogs, apparently, and one time paid out of pocket for every dog-bearing guest of the Paris Four Seasons to stay somewhere else. A military helicopter once landed on top of Everest so he could have technically summited, but Jacob has to let him down with the reality that the Alaska mountain is Denali, not Everest.

Shame he doesn't like dogs, because Jacob would compare talking to Cameron with talking to a pampered golden retriever. Full of interests and little else, chasing fleeting pockets of dopamine. Very cute. Very stupid.

"It's funny you say you don't like choices," Jacob says,

searching fruitlessly for a Daft Punk record the Harriot listening room does not have.

Cameron says, "they got rid of the apple skittles but I bought a couple tons of them before they got rid of them," which has nothing to do with anything they've been talking about, but since this has already proven itself a pattern of cognition Jacob is not thrown off.

"But you *chose* to be *here*," Jacobs speaks up over the thumping bass of *Like A Virgin*'s opening. "Without anyone *knowing* you're here. Am I right?"

"Well yeah like the security agents don't like it when I go off on my own so I gotta like do it in *secret* y'know. I was up in London because I had to meet with Irene and the cousins and the stepcousins but it sucked man everyone's fucking looking at me all the time. Fucking hell. So, so, so, like, yeah, so like, I got in touch with Steve who's the pilot and told him '*hey, take me back to the Malibu house*' and he says '*ooh, sorry sport, I need clearance from your mother or father before we take off*' and I say '*uhh no you don't I'm a grown ass man and this is my plane.*'"

"... Is that the end of the story?"

"This guy was playing spoons at the airport! Like fucking crazy the spoons were clacking so fast—"

"Forget it." Jacob takes the other side of the couch Cameron gives up when the song piques his interest. "Is anyone on their way here?"

"Shit I was gonna maybe fly Liv over here but I dunno I think I kinda like being on my own. Just kinda hard to fucking DO because everyone needs me to be somewhere all the time. Go fuck themselves I say."

Jacob asks, "Who's watching you?" out of fear there's some secret security measure he hadn't considered before now.

"My family all the time."

"I know how you feel," Jacob says.

"Yea?"

"I… in the *abstract*, I know how you feel. Overbearing parents and all that. But you know everyone would like to live the way you do."

"Nigel says that" Cameron says, calling his dad Nigel.

"But… you *do* live the way you do. Like, *you're* that guy. If you wanted to disappear, I mean, you very easily could."

Cameron's bopping his head, too occupied to respond.

"I'm saying," Jacob peels Raoul off the floor and pets him gently in his palm, "if you don't wanna be seen in London, or at whatever jackass function the Otterlakes need to be seen at—"

*"Touched for the very first time!"*

"… I'm just saying, if you want something, who's permission are you waiting on? Ever? You're an Otterlake. It wasn't my impression you guys *wanted* anything. You just get—well, not the Playboy Mansion—"

"—wait how do you know about that—"

"—But if you wanna fuck off, then fuck off. Y'know? Take Madonna here: she's experiencing something new, but on a level plebians would understand. You could be like the ultimate virgin. Further than Malibu, man, you can just vanish. Rip the antenna off your plane. Most rich people we don't even know about. Us normal people. But not you guys."

"I caaaaaaan't, dude, Liv likes Raoul and I can't leave him here or he'll starve or fall of the bridge or the other one will gang up on him for being fat."

"I thought he was Monchie."

"She wants one of the dudes to be Monchie. OH! And one of the girls needs to be Amanda. *That* one can be Amanda. If it's a girl. Go check if it's a girl."

Surprising himself, Jacob says, "I'll take care of Raoul, man, you go do your thing."

He might actually want to keep Raoul on some selfish level.

At a point Cameron stopped answering. This stage of a trip is something Jacob's roommate calls the Siesta. The final stage of cognizance before the patient clocks out for the night and, ideally, wakes up with a fresh perspective on themselves and the world they're so lucky to live in. For someone like Cameron that feeling must be titanic. Not that Jacob's ever going to know. He leaves Cameron in the listening room, once he realizes he'd stopped to hang out an inadvisably long time.

He pounds down the bizarre stair choices one last time and, Raoul held over his shoulder like a baby, departs Harriot back out the way he came. The nighttime sky of only a little bit ago is mixing into a milky blue.

When he gets back to his car he can't rip off his ski mask quick enough. He wipes thin sweat from his face and fixes an old scarf on the dashboard, gently placing Raoul on top. Then he sets off down the unending taffy stretch of Malibu, unaware at this time what he's really done tonight. Burgled a house, yes, but that fact is less significant than being the man who, intentional or not, inspired Cameron Otterlake to run away, and in doing so throw the Otterlake family into gradual but eventually permanent disarray.

Also, did he forget Suzy?

# (The) Mediaries ♀

***Irene Otterlake, 63***

***Two-time Miss Europa winner***

***One-time Miss Universe winner***

***Average Monthly Income: $322,300,711***

***Average Monthly Income--after taxes: $322,300,611***

***Step-Matriarch of the Otterlake Family***

***Monte Carlo, Principality of Monaco***

The *Parata*, Monaco's annual running of the rarest and most beautiful motorcars in the world, is often though not by choice a funeral procession. Given the risk innate to motor-sports, it's more inevitable than possible a significant driver will die the way *he* or *she* or one year *they* lived, and at that point it would be insensitive not to dedicate the next year's *Parata* to their memory. Such was the case this year, honoring the deaths of Monaco's very own Cesaire Favreau, as well as the four American drivers victim to what would come to be known as the Talladega Incident.

Since the first running of the *Parata* in 1946, the Otterlake family has proudly counted themselves among the most generous benefactors. They could comfortably be *the* biggest, mind, but the late patriarch Quentin Otterlake felt a bit of humility was due. Made future negotiations with parallel benefactors "fall down the throat," a clumsy drinking metaphor which simultaneously broadcasted the late patriarch's status as a teetotaler.

This year's event begins two days after the advertised opening flag, citing inclement weather. The rain had stopped fourteen hours ago, but still the sky is murkier than Irene Otterlake would prefer. Ruined the colors—especially for Ferrari, her favorite manufacturer because she just loved the way sunlight cooked over their sanguine finish and because she didn't know a lot about cars. It seems to her the Japanese manufacturers thrive in these conditions, the way their cool earthtones dance under the ocean spray. Though the Datsuns and the Mitsubishis better resemble farming equipment than sleek sportsters (she would never say this out loud) market research has demonstrated their appeal to the younger demographic. What that appeal is, precisely, Irene couldn't say.

Maddie, one of Irene's three personal assistants working today and one of twenty-six Irene currently employs, is standing to her right. She knows as much about cars as her boss but earns a hair's width per month, and as such her unspoken fondness for the Datsun 240c parked underneath the Otterlake's Monaco property is entirely believable.

"Magdalene," Irene waves to her right, getting Maddie's name wrong so severely she invents a new personal assistant, "is that one down there a part of the show, do you know?"

"I… believe so," Magdalene (she only started two weeks ago and still fears correcting Irene, ever, would reflect poorly on her) says, pretending to check her tablet. "Is something wrong?"

"No hate in this heart, but if we're going to be photographed, I would just like our best and our brightest up front."

It wasn't up to any one benefactor which cars ran in the *Parata* and it certainly wasn't in Magdalene or even Irene's authority to have anything altered. If the personal assistant formerly known as Maddie has it right, the lineup was determined by order of arrival. "I'll see what I can do, ma'am," she answers anyway.

"What's that third one?" Irene asks.

"Third one?"

"Ferrari, and Lamborghini, and the third one. What's the third one?"

"You may be thinking of Porsche, ma'am."

"There it is. Have *that* one replaced with one of *those*. An old one if it's possible."

*"Old… Porsche… Trident…"* Magdalene jots a useless note on her tablet. Here she applies two massively helpful bits of advice she'd received while in training—one, always offer a solution instead of a correction. *What "third one," there is no "third one" you idiot,* a less astute PA may have been dying to say. But Magdalene's been trained to catch

her tongue and knows how to answer the question as if Irene is just about to on her own. Two, always add to the request. In truth Magdalene had made up the Porsche Trident. That's not a real car. That's the ignorant product of her confusing hood ornaments between the Porsche and the Maserati. However, Irene wouldn't know this and will never take the time to learn, and the goal is to demonstrate how you've internalized the request and are prepared to deliver. So, one Porsche Trident coming right up.

Irene has separated herself from the few dozen VIP connections she's supposed to be making, if only spiritually. A security detail posted in the hotel across the road watches the heiress through binoculars and relays with the second security outfit based one floor above their wealthy and paranoia-curious employer. Truthfully Irene has never liked crowded rooms, even if the breath she's sharing is that of people born into a greater GDP than some small countries or, and she only recently learned this about her own fortune, the entire state of Michigan. Every now and then and almost always at the inconvenience of her business partners, Irene needs a floor to herself, and a young woman standing to her right taking notes.

When she'd entered the Otterlake family she'd been horrified to discover her new husband employed zero women. Anywhere. In any stage of familial operation. For Christ's sake, the *housekeepers* were men, and that sort of thing doesn't happen unless you mean for it. Then she learned this was court ordered because of something to do with a prominent business partner of Nigel Otterlake's, something or other, but that business partner was found dead in Kuala Lumpur two summers ago and now the

Otterlake family is fifty-percent women operated.

The pool of personal assistants she'd brought to Monaco reflects her femme-centric employment ordinance. Supporting her this weekend is the enthusiastic greenhorn Magdalene Watson (Madeline Shoon), the multitasking mastermind Tatiana Willus (Tina Oswald), and admittedly her favorite of the entire fleet, the steadfast veteran Lucy Gideon (she got this one right). So much did she like and trust Lucy that she'd let her in on the plan to eventually replace all her personal assistants with names easier to remember. Alliterated names. *Rebecca Roswell.* She doesn't exist—*yet*—but saying it out loud strangles her lips to a smile.

"Rebecca, Ma'am?"

Irene doesn't answer.

At the exact moment Magdalene was typing out the fake name of a fake car, Lucy Gideon, lead of the Personal Assistant outfit and Irene's favorite, was preparing for her weekend with the matriarch, a personal ritual which included a half dozen yoga poses struck in private—in this case the secondary sitting room closed off by sliding doors made of wood salvaged from a sunken man-o-war—and a half baggie of cocaine. She'd very nearly recanted her business with yesterday's Parisian dealer when he called the baggie a hit of *Belushi,* not only for mocking the death of who she assumes was a good man, but debasing the art of drug incorporation with his gratuitous arrondissement jargon. She was however fine with calling it a baggie.

Immediately following her three-minute Balasana, Lucy vacuums up her drugs right from the receptacle and cools down with a less disciplined windmilling of her arms. She'd found through years of experimentation that using right at the apex of her pre-shift ritual had a way of holding her in that stretched-out euphoria. Refixing her hair bun nice and painful (it helps her stay focused) she mumbles the day's itinerary. Memorized.

Brilliant. At the turn of the hour, Maddie first knocks, clicks the door, then enters. A three-step entering method Lucy had instructed her to perform that gives the person on the other side time to prepare themselves. One never knows what could be behind that door, but it's the responsibility of a Personal Assistant to give them due warning. A small buffer with which what they're doing may be adjusted to something more flattering. Entirely useless in this instance because Lucy is still gripping an empty bag of cocaine between her fingers.

"Gideon," Maddie says (Ms. Gideon is too formal but she would still like some respect), "Mrs. Otterlake wants a different car parked outside?"

"Are you asking me?"

"No, I just... it's the boxy one. Pearl white, center with the windows out there, number 53. She wants something else, something nicer."

"In the suite directly across from ours, Maddie, the organizers are preparing to speak with the documentary team. Take it up with them and remember to introduce it as a request of the Otterlakes."

"Okay—oh, and my name is Magdalene now."

"Is it?"

"She—she called me that, it's too late to correct her."

Oh. Probably is, then. "Tina's with Mrs. Otterlake?"

"Uh, no, nobody is. Not right this second."

Dammit. "Her *brother*, still?"

"Last I spoke with her. I'll stay with Mrs. Otterlake! You finish up whatever you're doing—"

"Across the hall, please. I will stay here."

A nod, and Magdalene twists back around and clicks out of the suite. Lucy, with her own tablet, shuts the man-o-war behind her and joins Irene at the window.

"Magdalene is getting that number 53 sorted out," she assures the matriarch who, frighteningly, cringes at the thought.

"The longer I look at it the more I appreciate its… attendance. It's got a pop art appeal."

"Absolutely, ma'am."

"When I was your age I was driven through the streets of Geneva in a topless soda can. I couldn't tell you the make and model but it was old and did belong to the then mayor."

"I could find that out for you, if you'd like."

"This was after winning Miss Europa, my first time. You could not see the road for all the roses thrown."

"I've seen the pictures, ma'am, you were stunning beyond words. Did you want me to cancel that lineup cha—"

"We haven't had a winner since, you know. It seems the *jury's* tastes lie everywhere *but* Switzerland. You know they accept women from Morocco? I'm not suggesting anything about… I just thought we all agreed where Europe starts and ends, is all."

"Took the words out of my mouth, ma'am. About that car—"

"I thought about sponsoring a more involved national scouting. I'm afraid Switzerland could have and should have won so long as we checked every hill and valley but I don't think the representatives are interested."

"The current sponsorship program could stand to have its budget increased."

"Current sponsorship?"

Yes, Irene. As Lucy already knows and in fact organized herself, a pageant scouting program sponsored by Irene Otterlake already exists for the country of Switzerland and has for the past two years. Lucy knows better than to interrupt the matriarch with this information and instead presents a simple fix that would only require an approval on the part of the Otterlake duchess, which is immediately approved thereafter. She's *good.*

"So you would like the number 53 to stay, Mrs. Otterlake?"

"… No, move it."

Across the hall, the acting Magdalene is waiting for a break in the shockingly sappy interview to speak to sappy interviewee Ivan Salas, a *Parata* organizer. The suite's been stripped of all its furniture to make room for all the necessary filming equipment. Box lights and no less than four cameras and two reserve cameras and sponsorship banners situated in every conceivable frame and an Amazon jungle's worth of cords which the gaffer gaffs down like his life is on the line. Outside of the frame the lights are low and the blinds are pulled.

"I see the children at the sidelines and I imagine myself at the same age, you know, Graz, nineteen sixty-one. I imagine they feel what I did when they see a motorcade of this magnificence and I like to think we give them something to dream of."

Cut.

"Wonderful stuff, sir," the man behind the camera says, "it would be great if we could get the same thing with a few more pauses. He can read your comment back to you."

"You've written that down?"

"Yes, sir."

"Excuse me," Madgalene butts in and goes brutally ignored.

"Pause where, would you say?"

"Riiiight at 'something to dream of.' But slowing down the whole thing would be excellent."

Ivan says, "about the question regarding the ban on French manufacturers."

"Yes?"

"I'd just like to change my answer. If we can take care of that right after this."

"We should have time."

"Request from Mrs. Otterlake, sir."

The entire production halts. The gaffer pauses mid-gaff and looks up at Magdalene. She wasn't prepared for an audience. "… Just that…" she begins, "she's asked for the number 53 to be moved."

Ivan clarifies, "the Datsun?"

"If that's the number 53, yes."

"That's a classic Japanese rally, what's wrong with it?"

"She's not a fan."

Flummoxed, Ivan Salas, one of three performing this interview, waves at the other two sitting out of frame as if to suggests someone needs to go tell someone to find whoever has the keys. Or four men who can push half a mile. "Tell Mrs. Otterlakes the Dukes gladly honor their ladies."

Alright. Whatever.

The man behind the camera asks, "that's it?"

"Yes, that'll be all, you can get back to the shoot. Sorry for inter—"

"Does Mrs. Otterlake have a comment on Cameron?"

The room groans in surround sound. Whoever that is, Madgalene thinks, he's obviously disliked. Cheap looking suit, argyle sports coat, expensive looking sunglasses hung from a cheap looking dress shirt, the question asker makes himself obvious, standing from his chair and clicking the light on an audio recorder, clutched at his hip, Terminator red.

"I can't speak for Mrs. Otterlake," Madgalene insists. She's said these words exactly, so often, enough to be what her action figure would say when you press the button on her back.

"No comment on her missing son?"

"I can't speak for Mrs. Otterlake."

"You just did, you said what she said about the car. You can't say what she said about her missing son?"

Magdalene excuses herself from the suite and nearly breaks down the door across the hall.

The personal assistants of Irene Otterlake have developed a system of nonverbal gestures so as not to disturb the matriarch with information they mean only for each other. A roll of the shoulder, for instance, means something Irene has asked for cannot be located. Fastening one's belt a notch tighter means they're running out of time, and the opposite means they have plenty. Almost all of these were created by Lucy Gideon, something she's proud of if only in private.

At the door (Lucy glances at every opening and closing

door to keep tabs), Magdalene runs a hands under her jaw and scratches the skin under her chin, briefly making a choking sign across her throat. This means an emergency is developing.

Silently, out of view of Irene, Lucy returns a tense nod and points behind herself to the other room. Magdalene makes for the man-o-war doors, pretending to check her tablet and look busy.

On the other side she finds Tina, furiously typing away at her personal phone instead of her tablet, which she's tossed on the leather armchair by the window.

In an undesired departure from the infantry, Tina isn't feeling up to working today. Her brother was umpiring a little league baseball game this morning, Chicago time, cut short by a sudden downpour not helped by his appendix exploding at the top of the third inning. He'd gone under the knife an hour ago, Chicago time, and Tina's predisposition to worrying has resulted in calling both her sisters three times each in the past four hours, Monaco time.

Shutting the doors behind her, Magdalene asks "is this a good time?"

"No."

"We have a situation."

"Well join the club, Maddie, I'm on forty minutes without an update."

"It's Magdalene."

"No it's not?"

"It is now. Long story." And she leans with to whisper,

*"Cameron's missing."*

"The kid?"

"That's all I know. Can I see the log?"

Tina doesn't have a free hand to point at her tablet and kicks in the general direction of the armchair. "Can you be quiet, though? I'm on hold."

Makes zero sense but sure. The Personal Assistant infantry's rotation of responsibilities includes logging the location of the Otterlake family's most unpredictable heir, a request from all the way at the top. Cameron had no-showed the family's much-anticipated attendance at Wimbledon two years ago, prompting the seldom-heard-from Nigel Otterlake to request a continuous log for his son's impromptu adventures. One might say this is the easiest part of the job. Just copy and paste the flight logs of Cameron's plane, the history on his credit card(s), which property he's using and what time of day he opened the doors. With all this in mind it seems impossible the young man *could* go "missing," but it should be noted the Personal Assistant who dubbed this the easiest part of the job suffered a mental breakdown three months ago. She hasn't been heard from since and her direct deposits have remained static in her bank account, which for some reason the Otterlake payroll administrators can see.

Alright, then. Looks like his plane landed at Crux Airfield two days ago, Magdalene is seeing. That's the landing strip the family uses when staying at Harold or whatever they name their houses. From there the plane was… docked? Stored? At the private hangar. Conveniently it seems the pilot lives an hour away and the copilot took an

Airbnb assuming Cameron would want to be somewhere else really soon. Cameron entered the house a little after two and left again ten minutes later, taking the Lamborghini Urus from the garage, returning two hours later with six cardboard boxes poked full of holes. The next few door notifications are just Cameron moving in the boxes. Then nothing for the next thirteen hours until, oddly, a backdoor notification a quarter past two in the morning.

"Tina, *Tina*, over here," Magdalene insists with a furious waggle of her wrist. Tina doesn't answer, pacing the other side of the room in a tight semicircle and getting nowhere with the receptionist on the other end.

"Tina!"

"*What*?!"

"Someone broke in the house."

"Which house?"

"The Cali house."

"Narrow it down, *Mag*, they own half the fucking state."

"*Keep it down.* Cameron's in the Malibu house—the one they actually use—and I'm seeing a guy in a ski mask breaking the door down."

Tina drops the phone from her ear. A receptionist squeaks from the other side but doesn't get a word back. "So he's dead," she says.

"Hold on, hold on. Okay, I'm seeing… he leaves. Ski mask leaves fifty-one minutes after the break-in… has this been reported? Shouldn't the security system have called the cops?"

"You would know. How'd you find out he's dead?"

"We don't know he's dead, I just heard from the reporter—"

Feeling eyes burning on her neck, Magdalene turns and finds Lucy standing at the open man-o-war doors, blood drained from her face, Irene also glancing past her shoulder.

Horrifyingly, Irene is the first to speak. "Who is dead, now?"

"Oh, I heard about this," Lucy jumps on quick, still as a corpse. "Louge competitor, from town. Killed during practice just yesterday. Shame. A friend of one of the drivers today. Apparently his Alfa Romero's livery is in tribute."

"Ah. Lovely, then."

"Yes, it's a point of conversation among the reporters. *Magdalene*," Lucy lacerates, "can you tend to Mrs. Otterlake for a moment."

"Right," Magdalene says, handing Tina's tablet over and pointing sharply at the screen. Lucy trades her tablet in kind, muttering something about going over the dinner plans. Really it would be best if *Tina* took the shift with Irene, but Magdalene froze and didn't find suggesting so appropriate.

Slowly, Lucy pulls the doors shut and snaps her finger. A balloon pop. "*What is happening.*"

"I don't know," Tina says.

"What, Madd—*Magdalene* didn't tell you? Who is dead?"

"Check the tablet. Magdalene said Cameron was at the Malibu house. Harriot. Did you know?"

"—I knew there was an *intruder*, but the police didn't say Cameron was… Christ, he's dancing."

All Lucy knew before now was a man had entered the Otterlake's seventeenth Malibu residence just before sunrise but didn't seem to take anything. Police had responded to a noise complaint and found suggestions that an intruder had been in the house earlier. When they arrived, however, the intruder was gone. He helped himself to the fruit in the kitchen and let loose the pet Chinchillas whose existence was new to Lucy. Still an ongoing case.

"Cameron was in the house, Magdalene said?"

"Yeah, what she said. I haven't seen the footage."

"Why haven't you seen the footage, that's your fucking task this week!"

"Because my brother might be *dying*, prick!"

"Oh, you didn't hear? Word at the salons is everyone might be dead this season!" Without her Belushi, Lucy would be absolutely fuming right now. But if she wasn't ready to deal with this issue quickly and covertly, she wouldn't be Lucy Gideon.

Her process in these circumstances is another personal invention; one she calls Spoke-to-Wheel. She'd need only identify and cross-reference enough effects to eventually arrive at the cause. She lays both Magdalene and Tina's tablets on the coffee table (sourced from the remains of an old Genoa temple) and begins to pace against the grain of her coworker. Spoke one: Burglar arrives at Harriot. Two, Burglar leaves without taking anything. If Cameron were dead his body would be found but all the police reported to her was an unkindness of rodents. And the footage does not show the burglar leaving with a body or leaving with any urgency period. This means Cameron either *didn't* leave Harriot—which seems unlikely—or he left in such a way that he didn't trip the cameras. This would suggest, to Lucy, that he wanted to leave without anyone knowing.

"Tina, you spoke with the pilot when Cameron landed, yes?"

"Tina."

"What? Yes, I did, he said Cameron was high or something and the copilot drove him to the house. That's all I know."

"Do you know how many cars are currently housed in the garage at Harriot? Apart from the Urus."

"It's just the big one. Is that the Urus? It's the big one. That and the nephew's bikes. Tucker."

Lucy leans over the table to review the footage. Harriot, despite its size and exuberance, has only one formal entrance—the front. One could enter through the patio doors, as their surprise friend from the previous night had done, but that would mean crossing over the shrubbery and a six-foot fence, as he must have also done. But Lucy has a theory: these cameras account for who is using the doors to enter and exit. There is no camera for the garage and the camera for the front door…

"… Does not trigger unless the car enters or exits from the *left*," Lucy has begun relaying to Tina, "so if Cameron were to intentionally exit from the right and, most important, use the small form factor of the bike, he could leave without alerting the security system!"

Pause, for this crack to sufficiently impress Tina.

Tina isn't impressed. She says, "better idea."

"Oh, whenever you're *ready*, then."

"Call his phone."

… Right. And Tina couldn't do this on her own, so Lucy finds herself without something snappy and authority-asserting. Only she has Cameron's personal number. Problem is it's on the tablet she'd handed off to Magdalene.

"… Some murderously boring colleague of Nigel's," Irene is in the middle of telling Madgalene, who isn't sure whether this should be written down, "and that startup from San Fransisco. It sounds absolutely Star Wars—I told Nigel not to bother."

"Satellites can do a lot these days," is all Magdalene can muster.

"Control the weather? I don't care how many you'd like to shoot up in the air, they're not stopping a tornado."

As soon as Magdalene was alone with her, Irene

groaned at the sight of a possible storm cloud and began ranting about a hypothetical weather control program she'd rather the Otterlakes have no stake in. All Greek to the Personal Assistant. She prays this is the end.

"I've never seen a tornado in person," oh god, "and we do have that lovely old plantation house in Louisiana. I've had it remodeled a few times. Do they have tornadoes in Louisiana?"

"I believe so, ma'am."

"It can't be *too* much of a problem. That house has been there since Buffalo Bill's time and has seen nothing but an awful rat infestation some seasons ago."

"Couldn't be. It's a beautiful house." Magdalene's never seen this house. She's celebrating her twenty-second anniversary of knowing it exists.

Irene rubs her lips in thought. "… If it *will* rain," she says, "I'd like to have been *on* the boat, at least."

"Shall I have it prepared for you, ma'am? We can send a bottle down from the hotel, or I—"

"The champagne in this room is terrible."

The matriarch is referring to the bottle nested in a sweating bucket of half-melted ice (Lucy would encourage thinking of the ice as half-frozen but she would digress). Frenchword Decadesago, whatever the calligraphy is trying to say. Point is Irene Otterlake doesn't like it and what she doesn't like must cease to exist.

"—Or I can get you the onboard cellar log."

*I can also get you the status update on your perhaps murdered stepson*, an intrusive thought smacks against the inside of her skull. If that shlubby reporter in the argyle sports coat got the news, it's only a matter of time before Irene does, and learning about it from a French tabloid would be a failure of her Personal Assistants so massive at least one of them will be jobless by sunset. Probably Tina. She and Lucy already agreed some months ago that, if need be, Tina was the sacrifice.

"Should we invite the organizers, do you think—"

*"They're busy!"*

"Quite busy," in comes Lucy, sliding around and in-between, swapping out her and Magdalene's tablets so fast the latter doesn't notice her biometric login won't work. "You've done everything you need to do, Mrs. Otterlake, I think Magdalene's suggestion is just perfect. I could have Tina escort you down to the lobby if you'd like. Your security detail—"

"Tina?"

"Yes, Magdalene and I have itinerary co—"

"I thought her name was Tatiana."

"Correct, ma'am, excuse me. Tatiana can bring you down to the security team."

"It would be wise to soak up *some* of this," Irene agrees. Her personal assistants can breathe. "I don't know when I'll next make it down here. Let alone when the sun is out."

(Tatiana) is quick on the rebound, leading Irene Otter-

lake to the suite doors and letting her out first, trailing close behind. Lucy messages a bodyguard waiting one floor above to momentarily block the door to the suite across the hall. When they arrive at the lobby, Tatiana's to relay a secondary motion to the security escort waiting downstairs—clear the sidewalks down to the harbor, let nobody within thirty meters, let no one speak to her, lock the harbor when she boards, open that one Cab Sab she likes. They know the one.

The two remaining personal assistants let the suite be still for some precious seconds. And of course it's Lucy Gideon who snaps the duo back. "We're calling Cameron's personal cell."

"Oh, good idea."

*Beeeeeep.*

*Beeeeeep.*

*Beeeeeep.*

*Beeeeeep.*

*Beeeeeep.*

*Beee—*

*"Uh hey yeah this is uh yea y'know ahahaha I'm not at my phone right now.*

*"OH! Uh leave a message or whatever almost forgot."*

Now would be the time to leave that message, only Lucy is static at the other end, ferociously gnawing away at skin on her bottom lip. She ends the call.

Magdalene's eyes pan from the phone to Lucy several

times. "You're not—"

"He doesn't like us, you know."

"Why not?"

"We work for his stepmother, whom he already resents for helicoptering him as a, quote the raven, grown-arse man. I had called him four months ago. Introduced myself and my title. And he hung up on me. What I'm saying is locating him was never going to be easy, yet I was praying we could confirm he's…"

"… Alive?"

"Sure."

"Could he be with someone we could call instead?"

Occam's Razor. This is why, Lucy thinks more and more these days as she gains favor with the Otterlakes and finds herself drifting further from the thought process of regular people like Magdalene here, it's often best to buy your cocaine from a Parisian who calls it Belushi.

"His partner," Lucy's careful to phrase.

"I didn't know he was dating someone."

"I'm not certain they know either," she explains while searching up a contact, "but he's sweet on the youngest Achenbach daughter. Camping royalty. One-time Olympic diving candidate. Irene's less than fond of her. Finds their source of fortune *inelegant*."

*Beeeeeep.*

*Beeeeeep.*

*Beeeeeep.*

*Bee—*

"*Hello?*"

They'd been so primed for another failure Lucy forgets to answer immediately. She and Magdalene high-five for some reason. "Hello, Olivia, this is Lucy Gideon, assistant—"

*Click!*

Lucy's still. "What the—"

"What happened?"

"She hung up on me!"

Both of them trade answers. "She doesn't recognize your name?" Magdalene offers.

"Who hangs up just because they don't know a name?"

"She's not… *not* famous. I'm seeing right here her Instagram has a million—oh, is this what Mrs. Otterlake means when she says *inelegant?*—"

"You try. Your phone."

Magdalene drops it and nods. She's been passed an urgent responsibility by whom best constitutes an idol in her career. From day one she admired Lucy Gideon's immediacy, her punctuality, her immaculate form with the Balasana. Would it be responsible to also admire her frequent dependence on, her phrasing, *drug incorporation?* Y'know what, sure. It's working.

*Beeeeeep.*

*Beeeeeep.*

*Bee—*

"*Yeah?*"

"Otterlake family business, please do not hang up *please.*"

The line goes clickless. They have a bite. "My name is Magdalene; I work for Mrs. Irene Otterlake. Cameron's mother. Stepmother. Excuse me. We're uh… we're having some trouble getting in touch with him. When was the last—or rather—have you seen Cameron recently?"

"*Uh… I spoke with him this* morning…"

Huzzah. She fist pumps in Lucy's direction, signaling a strong lead. Sweet confirmation, Cameron is not dead. That or he did not die as long ago as they were led to believe. Either or would give them options.

"Great! Thank you."

"*Mhmm.*"

"And wh—"

*Click!*

Astonishing. "She hung up again!"

Lucy wonders aloud "what is her deal?" and slams a number into her own phone. "Was it a poor reception, on her end?"

"No, I was about to ask where he was—"

"Hi, Otterlake family business, still," Calling Olivia

back herself, Lucy's plastic niceness overpowers the thought. She switches to speakerphone so in the event the call is dropped a third time there will be a witness. "My apologies for bothering you, if you're busy."

*"Hm? No, I'm just hanging out."*

"Are you."

*"The other one said, 'thank you,' and, like, I thought we were done. What's up with Cameron?"*

"We were hoping you might find out for us. If it's no trouble. We're just having technical issues and cannot get ahold of him."

*Click!*

"Again. Again, Madgalene—*she hung up again!*" Lucy makes a motion like she's about to spike her phone on the carpet but only threatens so. "Watch the lines," she instructs Madgalene, depositing her phone in the junior PA's remaining phoneless hand. "I need to... *do cardio.*" In a huff, Lucy disappears behind the man-o-war doors, and a moment later Magdalene hears the faint rhythmic thud of jumping jacks.

Here would be the worst time for the newly christened Tatiana to get that call she's been waiting on restlessly for the past hour. Right at the most critical moment of Irene Otterlake's transfer to the journalism-proof yacht, at the point where she would pass the matriarch off to the dozen men making up her first-response security detail, in the *middle* of the hotel lobby, the building that despite being owned wholly by the Otterlake family accepts tourists and civilians without prior clearance and as a result is currently swamped with *Parata* attendees, many of which counting themselves proud practicians of tabloid journalism—this tradeoff that if successful would mean Irene never gets word about her possibly dead stepson yet carries the highest level of risk in the entire land-to-sea transference operation.

That *would* be the worst time to take a call. So it's a good thing it didn't happen there. Instead Tatiana took that call in the elevator headed down. Now, this is actually the *third* worst place, in ontological order. For scholarship's sake the second worst place would be the revolving door in the lobby.

"*Tori?!*" she opens with an urgency that spooks Irene out of her Mediterranean slippers. "*Yes*—no, yeah, nah, yeah this a good time."

*Is it, though,* Irene finds herself wondering. Personal indulgence of this magnitude is something she suspects the ever-reliable Lucy Gideon would beat out of her subordinates. How she wishes it were her in this elevator, right now, rather than the diligent but often scatterbrained Tatiana. She's giving the latter adjective a real workout, here.

"… Okay, and that's good? That's bad? Do you know?"

As brief as it feels now, there was a time in Irene's life where she could and frankly relished taking off on her own. She remembers crushing sand beneath her feet in Bangkok, decades ago, spinning in a circle and seeing nothing but her once-longer hair drift into view. In that moment she felt alone in the universe and all the warmth of all the stars belonged to her. She thinks about her first husband's beach house at Sullivans Island, a seaside community hugging the edge of South Carolina, where the day didn't begin until the sun had already found its apogee and a good time for a smoke was whenever her fingers may brush the iron patio table. She thinks of the drive-thru at Wendy's. Really she's open to thinking of anywhere but this current diving bell of medical updates.

"Was he sedated? I don't wanna imagine him feeling all these tubes—oh, okay, gotcha. Antibiotics?"

*How long ago was this elevator installed,* Irene thinks. Certainly the building is older than the invention of the elevator, but her question mainly concerns the technological advancements made since. Her question is whether faster elevators could be deployed.

"I'd like a note made for the concierge," Irene declares, then is relieved to see Tatiana power on her tablet to make it so. She keeps her neck presented to the wind, clutching her phone between ear and shoulder. "Consider speeding up the elevator in the next remodel. Also, push the next remodel so that it will be finished by the following *Parata.*"

Tatiana clumsily jots the note (Make Elevator Faster) as the subtext of Irene making this request right this moment flies over her head and smacks against the back wall with a wet slap.

"Okay. Okay. Okay. And he—okay. Okay. And he's still asleep? Mm? So he is asleep but not because he's…

they didn't give him anything. He just went to sleep. Okay. Could you wake him up? Okay."

It only took six months, but the elevator pressures to a halt and opens up to the lobby. The Otterlake security escort has swept the path down to the front doors clean of any and all civilian foot traffic, demonstrating the Streisand Effect in cruel fashion. Were Irene and Tatiana to take this trip solo it's very likely they would board the yacht without interruption. Now that an armed and loaded billionaire protection agency has caused an irreparable scene, Irene and Tatiana can't help but feel every pair of eyes in Monaco train on the dinging elevator. A very pretty chime, this elevator. A genuine bell instead of the dreadfully common, digital facsimile. Irene finds herself reevaluating her request instead of dreading the next few moments, but Lucy Gideon made this so.

"Can you tell the nurse I don't give a shit about their wakeup policy? I wanna tell him where to find my Z-Paks."

"Was he well, when you spoke with him? Did he happen to mention where he was going?"

Damn it. This is all sounding more desperate than Lucy means. No doubt Olivia's reveal as the fastest hangerupper in the west has thrown the remarkably disciplined uberPA off her groove, so to say and so to make up some words. She delivers her questions while smiling. It's unclear who this smile is for.

"*I mean, like, he* sounded *fine,*" Olivia says, lifting off another 5 mental kilos. "*He's looked worse. Actually he was wearing the chain I got him, like, a year ago. Literally have* never *seen him wearing it until now.*"

It must be admitted Lucy has no idea whether this is significant. "He wasn't on a plane, was he?"

"*Sharapova?*"

"… That's the plane?"

"*Yeah. Yeah, he was in his big chair. I asked him where he was going because I thought he had the Italy thing and he—*"

"What Italy thing?"

"… *Like, the race. Or the car show. In Italy. I thought that was soon.*"

So, Olivia seems to think the Principality of Monaco is in Italy. Technically and literally Monaco is not *in* anything and if it were it would be France, but Olivia's hung up for less and Lucy knows better than to bring this up.

"Yes, the Italy—the Italy thing," Lucy resigns to agree. "Is that where he said he was? Did he say he was anywhere?"

*Cli—*

"Oh my fucking king and country—Magdalene, what's happening outside?"

"Uh…" Magdalene has to open up the window to check, "it looks like people are leaving the hotel?"

"Call Tina."

"Tatiana."

"Call her!"

The hotel spills to the sidewalks. Someone's made a consequential decision without running it by Lucy, and it's doubtful any yoga pose may relieve the pressure building in her blood. The back and forth juke she's started to dance across the penthouse floor suggests to Magdalene the chain of command is in danger of breaking. And while this creeping feeling bears no semblance to any personal assistant mantra hammered into her during her many weeks of shadowing, Magdalene begins to think she has a solution the exalted Lucy Gideon hasn't yet discovered.

Within the crush of bodies muscled out of the lobby doors (the five at a time falling out of the revolving door has a mesmerizing rhythm to it), Magdalene spots a putrid, argyle suit jacket. He's a stone in a river; the crowd parts and he will not follow them.

"That guy is gonna talk to Irene," she says only so whatever she does next will be understandable in the paperwork.

"Who is gonna talk to—"

*'FocusonOlivia,"* Magdalene spits, surprising herself with a snap of her own fingers. Nevertheless, Lucy does.

They have seconds to work with, and calling Tatiana would be a minute at least. Sooner than her mind can keep up Magdalene grips a champagne bottle upside-down at the neck. Frenchword Decadesago, crying down her arm and wetting her sleeve. What Irene Otterlake doesn't like must cease to exist.

The lobby is a frenzy of questions and comments and Irene is blood in the water and Tatiana has yet to tell her brother where to find the Z-Paks. One of these things is more important to her and it would be Sisyphean to tell her otherwise.

"Okay. Okay. Remember this: second floor bathroom—yeah? Okay. Bathroom. Second floor—"

"Miss Otterlake, good afternoon—"

"No questions! Yeah, second floor medicine cabinet, go behind the Adderall—"

Tatiana didn't think this sort of thing actually happened. There's not many billionaires she would recognize by face, even now that she works in close proximity to one. How this many people would be waiting to talk to or just see Irene astounds her. Let alone risk wrestling past security with rifles over their chests to wish her *good afternoon*. Unbelievable to do this right now.

"He woke up? Okay give him the phone."

The escort makes it all the way to the doors expecting a path to open outside that never does. The splinter cell working outside was supposed to disperse this crowd at least as far as the crosswalk. Seeing a rich person has overpowered the security being a rich person can afford, one that includes ex-Navy SEALs and their international equivalents. They find themselves pinned and it's either what Hunter S. Thompson called *The Fear* or there are indeed microphones within the crush. Tatiana's phone drifts from her ear as she mistakes similar words for Cameron and she seriously considers clapping both hands over

Irene's head.

Thankfully it doesn't come to that insanity. The outdoor crush has their attention momentarily diverted by the explosion of a champagne bottle on the tarmac.

The reporter checks his sports coat for stains as if slaughtering a pig could make that thing look any worse. He looks to the penthouse windows and curses, walking backwards at the same time and checking his ugly shoes for splash.

"I CAN'T SPEAK FOR MRS. OTTERLA—" is all Magdalene can get out before needing to switch to a "LOOK OUT," that arrives too late to save the reporter from the Datsun 240c speeding down the road.

The silver lining of dividing the personal assistant's orders so broadly is there's no telling whose fault this is. The *Parata* benefactor who donated the car in the first place? This is Jerry Seinfeld's fault.

Magdalene sucks her teeth so hard she feels an incisor wiggle loose. She creeks backward at Lucy who has somehow missed all of this in her brief pace to the other room. She's gotten Olivia back on the horn.

"*He said they were headed to Marshfield.*"

"Marshfield? Alright, but where the fuck is that?"

"*Uhh, lemme call him back and ask.*"

"You hung up?!"

*Click!*

Magdalene might be fired, and this may be why in her head, in this moment, she identifies as Maddie.

# (The) Caduceus

***Theo Arnold Magnussen, 16***

***Most recently employed at Amazon Retail Fulfillment Center—Marshfield (worked 42 minutes).***

***Average monthly income: $150.00***

***Income this month: $150.00***

***Marshfield, Wisconsin***

What a hustle.

Theo trained at the Amazon fulfillment center for a little less than one hour, pilfered one decommissioned computer monitor, corrected his supervisor on the spelling of Magnussen three times, and collected his sign-on bonus of one hundred and fifty smackeroonies in cash. Then he excused himself from the second round of collection drills with a pretend phone call, hopped on his street illegal dirt bike, and went home. His single regret is not taking the earbuds.

It's a regret he only feels because it was right there and, what, is Amazon gonna call the cops over 8 dollars' worth of company theft? He imagines the quarterly spreadsheets dedicate *bullshit our employees take home without asking* to a row all its own. Most everything in his bedroom could be justifiably identified as bullshit he just happened across—the Hermann Miller Aeron (Nygaard High School teacher's lounge [lock the windows next time]) tucked into his desk (dumpster out by the apartments five miles away) holding his battle station (Nygaard High School computer lab [accessories courtesy of the Nygaard High School library]). Maybe some of this wasn't found. Maybe none of this was found and a third party would sooner invoke the S word. To that Theo would say, first, stealing from Amazon is your duty as a member of the human race and, second, if you spent one thin minute in the halls of Nygaard High School you'd think to do something a whole lot worse than the S word. It's a professional courtesy that all Theo wants to take from the faculty is efficient lumbar support. His classmates must dream about taking more just running the mile.

Forget it, Jake, it's Marshfield.

Theo is so far correct in his assumption that his father will be home late tonight and likely have no need for today's warm water. Less than one hour of Amazoning has translated to twenty-five minutes of steaming hot water down Theo's bacne. He likes to think this extra hot water beats the fuck outta the oil but he's forgotten to look this up many showers previous and he will forget again before this shower is over. Until then, Theo squirts dish soap on an unfurling loofa. What's good enough for the oil spill ducklings is good enough for him.

Showered but undressed, Theo plops down at his computer in his not fresh underwear and an imprecise towel hat, ready to tell any hypothetical intruder this isn't what it looks like. He laughs a little. Wouldn't *that* be just the worst; an embarrassment the fastest motormouthed suggestions of computer viruses and feigned naivety couldn't sort out—getting caught watching his handwritten self-publishing flight logs.

Billy Joel landed in Berlin six hours ago. David Beckham is back in Ibiza when he was just there seventy-two hours ago—must've left his wallet. New York One, a commercial jet chartered for the highest-ranking WWE Superstars, requested a speed check eight hours away from its landing in Jeddah. If this were wholly determined by Theo's interests he wouldn't be tracking the stupid WWE plane at all, but next to Taylor Swift the wrestler headings are the most commonly requested updates. Apparently the autograph cretins find it useful so they know which airport to camp out at with all their unsigned memorabilia.

Jet Scramble, the cute name Theo's given his social media ring tracking the landings and departures of various private jets, is disorganized by design. While the same service can be found across Twitter, Tumblr, Cohost, Neocities, Mastodon, and probably a few others for which Theo forgets the login, one will not find any webring or modern internet equivalent connecting them all. All they have in common is Theo's very plain, extremely brief website directing affected parties to his crypto donation wallet, where they may pay him a negotiable sum to take their plane off the log. So far there have been no takers, only the empty threat that Kendall Jenner's legal team will pursue the renegade hacker collective making their very public flight records a tiny bit more public. Theo has received three federal government letters since launching the Jet

Scramble social media ring, but according to the anon who went to law school these are empty threats he'd be best served not responding to.

Theo posts via the Jet Scramble Twitter deck to confirm, yes, Drake's regular jet is being serviced and he is in the meantime using his backup, OVO-2 (if you're Drake and you name your jets OVO-1 and OVO-2 respectively you have no one to blame for this but yourself). When you have a backup private jet it's only fair the world knows where you're going, Theo believes. After doing this he runs upstairs to make a double serving bowl of SpaghettiOs. Grocery Outlet (Bargain Market) put out a few pallets yesterday and priced them two for one dollar, thus the second shelf of the Magnussen pantry has been rendered pure SpaghettiO.

His phone buzzes and Theo prays it's not that one guy who keeps asking him to put Kate Bush's jet on the log. He's told that asshole a billion times she doesn't have one. The second time that asshole messaged him Theo didn't know Kate Bush was still alive, and the first time he didn't know who Kate Bush was. The point is Kate Fucking Bush isn't getting up to any private jet activities and if he doesn't shut the fuck up he's getting blocked.

… Is what Theo fantasizes messaging that asshole, but it's just a text from his dad.

**>Running late tonight.**

No shit. Theo messages back,

**>No shit**

And he dumps the second SpaghettiO can into his

bowl. It's bulking season and it's a double up kinda night. An hour in the Amazon gulag has penetrated every stage of his bacterial ecosystem and cycling it out quick as possible is his best course of action. He counters the residual Amazon fulfillment center air particles by vaping.

In a past life, Oleg Magnussen fashioned himself a writer. To say he has a strong drinking metaphor kicking around in his head he's refrained from deploying in public for fear some leeching swindler would overhear and throw it in a generation-defining work of Knausgårdian autofiction before he could. For the enchantment of the private audience which fills Oleg's mind palace, a taster:

*The craving for stout at the end of a long day is not unlike the carnal urge for the dogs to bite down on a pillow, rocking violently a cloud of feathers.* –Oleg Magnussen

Pretty good? Nevermind. Say nothing. Oleg believes it was Robert Pirsig who said one becomes a writer the moment they conjure something they *know* to be good, and that no second opinion need be required. Pardon the egoism often demanded in the world of literature, but Oleg has detected parallels between himself and the late, great Pirsig. They both have sons who are probably autistic.

Following a boringly routine meeting with parole officer Mr. Langley (Wilson, to Oleg, but the former declined first names citing a need for impartiality which apparently extends to sharing a drink tonight), Oleg is feeling creative. It's in these brief sprints of opportunistic passion—glee for spending tonight somewhere other than a jail cell or this very car he pulls down the freeway with devilbaiting abandon, mixed with the craving for alcohol and hops described earlier—that Oleg expects to carve molten gold unto his Moleskine. What a great *introduction* this would be. Real Tom Wolfe shit going on:

*My parole office was always quick to remind me real freedom was yet to arrive. I was still at best a boarding school lad, made newly independent by my motorist license but expected in my bunk by eight, same as the children I was expected to raise as much as our faculty. But how golden ambrosia were those pockets of silence for it; my car cannot roll fast enough; her engine cannot growl loud enough to hear. My heart has lifted my body to the lower stratosphere.* – Oleg Magnussen

Hmm. What was it in there, pulling at Oleg the moment he'd committed the section—Theodore! Right. Don't keep him up worrying. At the first red light departing the exit, Oleg slaps out a text message, taking the liberty of the lonely nighttime Marshfield road to not immediately proceed at green.

**>Running late tonight.**

Forgive the lapse in authority, but the first time Oleg was called personally to the guidance counselor's office at Nygaard High School he was euphoric. So long as whatever Theo was doing had a glimmer of artistry he would walk out with something to be proud of. In reality Theodore had been sent out of English class for reading aloud a section in *Huckleberry Finn* with an odd enthusiasm. Oleg was a big supporter of banned books and chose to find something uncompromising in his son's delivery. No one would deny Theodore's attitude or, to be more precise, lack of patience for what he'd consider dishonesty or patronization. That seventh sense will serve him well. It will be on Oleg to mold that candor into something productive rather than destructive.

Oleg's phone vibrates on the dashboard.

**>No shit**

Exactly what he's talking about. Right there.

*Oftentimes I felt I could only observe my son through frosted glass or diffusive bathroom squares. In those moments he looked more like his mother. I grew up a shy, pensive child, and it seems more common today as I write this for our children to take on antonymic traits. How much we attribute Theodore's behavior to my suspicions of neurodivergence I won't venture to theorize. Know I am glad upon glad he has the pride and paramount self-confidence to tell adults no and, on occasion, to go screw themselves.* –Oleg Magnussen

The kitsch neons of the always reliable Bottom Dollar flood the car and Oleg feels with renewed conviction his dog and pillow metaphor is evocative and clever. Wait. Reverse it. *Dogpillow*. That's a title right there.

Theo's sitting comfy with his hot bowl of probably noodles and approximately tomato sauce, stirring around the rim so the festering sauce crust incorporates back into the pasta sludge, looking forward to several hours of nonsense YouTube videos about video games he's never gonna play, but that text from his dad is identical to the past three and this is starting to bother him. That classic line of his, about needing to meet with his parole officer before the building closes, made sense until he looked up where the building is and realized he's talking about a seven-minute car ride. Like, what, are they hanging out? Him and the parole officer hitting the town? There's no town to hit unless the Bottom Dollar is the vibe. Which it's certainly *not*, for the record. Painfully generic bar/grill most commonly signaling the end of a little league game or an ill-conceived swing at family bonding, in Theo's mind.

However, the devilish curse of word association has Theo hankering for a plate of the baked potato poppers. Whatever those ping pong ball sized potatoes are called, they bake them all at once in a fry basket and cover the plate in cheese shreds and sour cream and olives and chives and onions and bacon bits and jalapenos if you ask and suddenly the SpaghettiOs before him read like a peasant dish. Gruel. Theo's got a hundred and fifty big ones yet *this* is how he's eating. Jay-Z said in a quote he read online that you can't afford something unless you can buy it twice. Sagely, and the baked potato poppers are like ten bucks a plate. His stomach churns.

*BANG BABANG BANG BANG* goes the door upstairs and Theo grumbles about his dad once again *BANG BABANG BANG BANG* about his dad once again leaving his key inside or more likely forgotten inside his wallet like *BANG BABANG BANG BANG BANG BABANG*

"I'M COMING, FUCK."

Theo plants the spoon center in the bowl Excalibur-style, somersaulting into whatever clothes are already on the floor of his bedroom, and bounds upstairs two steps at a time. The carpet's matted to the route he normally takes and because of this he reverses the order. Couldn't tell you why. The fuller parts of the carpet may feel neglected.

At the entryway Theo begins to suspect this isn't his dad. Right now is where he would peek through the window right above the bench they're supposed to use for taking off their shoes but never do. Sometimes he'll even wave. But whoever's hiding behind the door and pounding, rhythmically like it's to the beat of a march Theo doesn't know, doesn't reveal themselves. And their door doesn't have a peephole—must be what the window is for. Theo takes a breath and prepares himself to send it. His mind scurries away to fantasies of home invasions that begin exactly like this, scrambling for a real-world scenario that isn't just that one part from *Last Action Hero*. In fact Theo worries himself enough to pop over to the living room quick as he can and grab the fireplace poker leaning against the brick chimney quicker than he can reckon with lancing someone.

He unlocks the door. How dorky must he look right now.

It's some boy. Too babyfaced to qualify for *some guy*, Theo thinks. Why is he sweating? Nothing he's wearing is what they sell in town. Don't ask how Theo knows but his pants just *look* expensive. And the necklaces? All three of them? Doesn't look like the real genuine 24-karat gold is gonna flake off after three weeks, so those from that one kiosk at the mall one town over. The Great Clips doesn't do tapers like that. Also, seriously, why is he sweating.

Cupped to his chest like a baby, nearly as tall as he is, the boy is holding a decapitated mess of plastic housing and thick rubber wires. Dusted black, hacked apart from wherever it's supposed to be. The complexity and specialization borders on military tech, the kind of gadgets Theo's too broke to afford and too chickenshit to try buying if he wasn't.

Theo goes, "Do you need me to call someone?"

To this, the boy lets himself inside, albeit timidly. His eyes outline the cramped entryway like he's desperate to be somewhere a little more open. When he peeks around the corner and sees the living room he stumbles down the step faster than Theo can tell him to watch for it, throwing himself over the back of the brown leather couch, rolling with his big, disconnected device. At rest, the boy throws the plastic wiry thing to the floor, which rattles the whole house with its black hole density. He makes an intense straining noise when he stretches his arms past his head.

"*Is…*"

Doesn't look like he's gonna finish that thought, not to Theo.

"Is what? Who are you?"

"*Is.. like is this the place?*"

"No."

"Oh. That's what I was told."

"I don't know who you are."

"Gotcha. Okay. Yea."

The boy rolls his ankle and redoes the laces on his shoes. Didn't look like there was anything wrong with them but his shoes apparently need retying. "Can I help you with something?" Theo asks. "Did your car break down? What is that thing?"

"I didn't *come here* in a *car*," the boy enunciates like Theo's being silly. "And actually I think you *know* how I got *here*."

"Yeah, no I don't. Sorry, but I don't recognize you."

"But the thing is you *do* know, I think."

"... Do you need some water?"

"FUCK! Yeah holy shit that sounds sick."

Theo's posture right now is like he just happened upon a reticulated python balled up in his living room. To say, he's concerned about what's going on but doesn't feel like his life is in danger. So, go get the landline and call Crocodile Dundee right quick, but still keep an eye on things.

Walking backwards to the kitchen, Theo uses one of the lesser cups in the cupboard to get the water and gets jumpscared when he shuts off the faucet, turns around, and finds the boy has moved from the living room to right behind his back.

"... Here you go, man."

The water is gone in two pelicanlike gulps and the boy smacks his lips quizzically. "Hey man did you put something in this, like a fizzy disk in this?"

"No I did not."

"Why does it taste weird like it's got something sweet or like a little tinny."

"Are you talking about fluoride? I think the government puts that in on purpose. It's good for you."

Too late now. He can't ungulp the water. Theo's never

left Wisconsin and can't speak for the taste of water in other parts of the world but *tastes weird* isn't something one says about the tap unless they actually don't know what tap water tastes like. He's a long way from wherever he's from.

"Do you…" the boy chooses his words carefully while sipping and savoring fluoride. Seems he's acclimated to the taste. "… Are you the one… who tells people… where my plane goes?"

Theo itches the back of his neck. "Huh?" he plays dumb.

"My plane. *Sharapova.* Someone checks where we've landed and posts online and I wanna know if that's you."

"Who's asking?"

The boy's face does whirlpools like this is a riddle. "Like you can't anymore I'm just here to tell you that you can't anymore and also I want you to stop if you still can."

Oh. Okay. "Is *that* what your brought in my house?" Theo points through walls and stairs to the hunk of machinery in the living room.

"I dunno."

"You don't know *what*?"

"So I had this dream last night where a guy told me to cut the thing off the top of my plane so yeah I went and did that."

*Jesus Christ*, Theo realizes, *that's the satellite antenna from a commercial jet.*

"... Without confirming or denying anything," Theo says, carefully, "the guy who you *think* is tracking your plane wouldn't use the satellite relay. He would just scrape air traffic data. Where the plane has taken off, where it's posted to land, et cetera."

"No fucking way you got the air traffic guys in on this? Like the guy's in the big tower thing?"

"Someone's gotta check on your plane, dude—it's not ideal for the most powerful nation in the world to have unregistered, unaccounted for airplanes buzzing around."

"I'm not even doing anything! Like—"

"Who are you, by the way?"

"Cam. Cameron Otterlake."

Well, then. The name does not instantly register with the peonic Theo, what with his triple digit net worth and Walmart pants. But if he has this right, Cameron here is richer than Richie. The sort of independent wealth accrued centuries ago and appreciated in ways that ought to be illegal. Truthfully, he has seen Cameron before. Online, thumbnailed in articles about a spoiled dumbass who rents out Disneyland for two weeks and forgets to go inside. A guy who, unannounced and uninvited, walks the red carpet at the Academy Awards because it looked cool, unaware of how much the celebrity-philanthropists despise him on sight, not only because he's terribly annoying and devoid of manners, but because that little twerp is unfortunately what real power looks like.

Yet in the most delightful of revelations, Cameron Otterlake is emotionally vulnerable.

"You didn't happen to come here with a lawyer, did you?"

"—Nah, I didn't like—y'know I didn't think it was gonna be like that I just want the Instagram to cut it out, man."

"All due respect, whoever you got beef with doesn't need to cut *anything* out because what that guy does is not illegal. Every bit of that is public info." Without a lawyer, Theo speaks in rope-a-dope, refraining from naming himself as the operator of Jet Scramble. Cameron's got no idea how bad he's fucked showing up here on his own. Already Theo's imagining the incoming Twitter thread: *today the Otterlakes threatened our administration team; please consider donating to our Bitcoin wallet in the event they pursue legal action.*

"No it's not it's where I'm going man why the fuck do people have to know where I'm going all the time?"

"... I think so long as our tax dollars—y'know, us regular people—are paying for the tarmac at the airport and the big traffic control towers and the wars to get the oil to fuel your *private fucking planes*—what a concept—then we at least get to know where on the whole fucking planet you people think you have to be. So with that out of the way, why do *you* think *you* need to be *here*?"

"Turn it off."

"How'd you find my house?"

"The Mortar."

"Well what the fuck is that? The Mortar?"

"Sorry but you can't know."

"Oh, what, because I'm *poor*?"

"Yes you fuckin' moron because you're poor why the fuck do you think?"

"Hey, hey, I got you tap water, dude. Can I get some respect in my own house?"

"Tap water? So it's not normal water you're saying?!"

What.

Theo acknowledges a beat and says "… How about this: you and I have had our own long days—by stark definitions. Let's go talk about this over carbs. Do you know what those are?"

"… Yeah," Cameron answers and it sounds like a lie.

"Duncan knows me."

"Well, Duncan can come get you."

Tough kitchen tonight. Oleg comes through the back all the time! Then again the Bottom Dollar has a notorious revolving door of summer job teenagers and food service vagrants. Anyone who can tie an apron behind their back is fit to serve on Duncan's crew, callous and unrecognizing of Duncan's good friend Oleg as they often prove.

Wait. There's something good in there.

*Ideally all employers are some flavor of Stonewall Duncan; hands spotted with fryer shrapnel, hearts of stone and years of service worn under their eyes and around the apoapsis of their mouths. Note the speed with which they can tie an apron—the white collar is rendered a child, clumsily somersaulting to fasten a shoe. These people I can talk to and know I'm broaching the jetsam. A human soul.* – Oleg Magnussen

And so Oleg waits on the waitress—watches the watchmen—to tell Duncan his good ex-con friend has arrived. Four times Oleg must step out from the window of the kitchen door, yielding to the bussers with trayfuls of beer, wishing he could jungle juice the whole flight. The collective backwash would be a pint on the house. Save the bussers the trouble and melancholy of dumping out perfectly good beer. Is this anything? Precluding some sweet somber bar poetry with regards to the unfinished glasses stacked

"—Magnum?" Duncan throws open the kitchen door and looks the wrong way.

"Oh. Right here."

"My fry guy called out and we just got a huge order. Mind working the baskets?"

"I'll take my paycheck in stout, good friend."

Duncan smiles returning through the flap. "There's a good lad. Watch out for the left basket!" Duncan stars to holler as he occupies a further spot in the kitchen. "It's been exploding all day!"

"Exploding how?"

"Oh, you know, bubbling over. Something might be wrong with the disposal valve. Or someone threw ice in it. We'll check when we're closed."

"Sure thing." He keeps it lowkey, but Oleg found a lot to admire in Chef Duncan, owner-operator of the Bottom

Dollar since inheriting the business from his father six years ago. What Oleg doesn't know is Duncan has a college degree in something that isn't however one earns restaurant qualifications (he's about to work the fry basket on the qualifications of his two functioning hands). Years ago when Duncan's hair was a different color and he pretended to read Friedrich Engels in the park to interest girls, Duncan had ambitions as a musician. In the nineties this would have put him firmly in Beck's sphere of influence—the demo tape he's never shown anyone reflect this. From earning his degree onward Duncan would tell himself working at the family restaurant was a means to his artistic ends, and when he had enough saved up he would move out of Marshfield and set up shop somewhere warmer. A constant fantasy of his in the first year was the day he'd throw his apron in the bin and never wear another one ever again.

"… Aprons are in the box by the walk-in," Duncan says.

Oleg gets right to work. This isn't his first time working the fry basket and this isn't his first busy night serving the good if philistine people of Marshfield. Credit to Duncan and his efficient *mise en place*, of course. Man should receive an engineering prize for this system. Waist high freezer to Oleg's left holds the frozen fry bags—slam one serving (typically a round handful) in the fry basket, give 'er a few minutes to get golden brown, into the basket, BAM with the seasonings organized right above the station. Beauty in the semi-organic machine.

*Blessed be what is in spirit the last of our Automats. To service a whole town in a day the line cooks we're rarely so considerate to meet with the eye have orchestrated a Renaissance of their own. I have seen neath stainless steel sheets naked ingenuity profound were its architects more than ants.* –Oleg Magnussen

Garlic fries call for a quick John Hancock of oil swiped back and forth and a drizzling of the in-house garlic seasoning. Close to a poutine by the time parley enters the mix—and they are close to the border all things considered.

"Order up, Sargant Major," Oleg slides the basket onto the server rack with a chummy raise of his brow. "When's my performance review?"

Duncan merely acknowledges that one order has been fulfilled. He tiptoes up to the serving counter, tilts the basket with one finger and says, "yeah, we're gonna need a few more of these."

"How many more?"

"Fill the vat."

"… Duncan, it was dead empty when I pulled in. Who's ordering these?"

"So where's *Sharapova* come from, hm? Is that a person?"

It's Theo's second time asking but Cameron's still trying to choke to death on garlic fries. And it's rare Theo repeats himself a third time without peppering in a Fuck or a Christ or an experimental fusion. Instead, he waits.

"*—Mm, Isnnntnnsplllll—*"

"Huh?"

Cameron shovels another fistful of garlic fries. At this rate the red plastic fry baskets are going to hit the ceiling and knock the hockey sticks loose. On his own side of the table, Theo nurses his single plate of baked potato poppers at a pace his dinner date's taking to the cleaners. Oh, and he'd hate to forget the pitcher of cherry Pepsi. One of the lesser cherry colas, but Cameron crushed two refills before the food arrived, which prompted Duncan, sous chef for the night, to bring out a pitcher. *I'll tell you when I had enough!*

"They don't sling garlic fries at the Ritz, do they?"

"*Mm,*" Cameron swallows dry and has to grip the table. "Dude this shit's crazy like there's so much going on in here."

"Yeah, there's probably more going on in that basket then the gastronomic foam you people eat. Salt, oil, some green shit like parsley or chives. Obviously a bit of garlic."

"What's garlic anyway man like I know it's a thing but I don't know what it *is* y'know."

"Like a root. Like an onion or a ginger."

"*Shhfkkcnnkzzmmm.*"

"I was just thinking that."

Slow night at the Bottom Dollar. The boys had arrived on Theo's daily commuter, a dirt bike lacking the apparats befitting a street legal motorbike—a fat ticket anywhere but Marshfield. Cameron wrapped his arms around Theo's waist so tight he nearly touched fingers on his own back and he laughed nervously the whole way down.

Apart from the freshly arrived young men there's a family wrapping up a boringly routine dinner and some men from the worksite a few blocks up watching the eleventh inning of a Twins game, surrounded by foam-stained glasses of beer with maybe a sip left in each. The sign outside says the bar will remain open until eleven on the weekdays and one in the morning on weekends but they will close sooner if the town collectively agrees to turn in early. Again, routine. The Bottom Dollar has operated thusly since opening in 1971, changing so little Theo's spotted the same wall decorations in a photo from his father's high school graduation dinner.

For the family bar/grill savvy there will be nothing outstanding nor offensive about the presentation and execution of the Bottom Dollar. Even so, Cameron eats like he's been freed from a prison camp, deep in the mountains of a country whose name Theo would only hear in Call of Duty. He's eaten enough potatoes to fund Boise State's ailing theater program the next six years and likewise enough garlic to seed wherever garlic comes from—Italy?

"Hey, where's garlic from? Do you know?"

Theo really expects nothing here but Cameron clears his tract with a gorge of cherry Pepsi and barks "China," without interrupting his meter.

"What, do the Otterlakes control the garlic farms?"

"Dude I've never had this shit before I mean like it bangs but nah we don't eat this stuff."

"Yeah, I noti—"

"Nigel has majority in a development firm did that rotating skyscraper in Shanghai you know about that?"

"It wasn't covered in Current Events, no."

"The fuck's that an IG?"

"… Did you ever go to school?"

"*Weeennbschool.*"

"Take your time."

Cameron swallows. "Boarding school."

"Your dad made you go to boarding school?" Note the shock coming from the humble Theodore Magnussen. He carries his net worth in his back pocket. Growing up he learned to associate boarding school with punishment, presented as it was in the context of moving away from all his friends and bunking next to twelve-year-olds with pomade in their hair. "I mean, I figured that's what you guys would do but… man, if I were you I wouldn't deal with fuckin' school period."

After a theatrical topping off of the pitcher, Cameron says "I didn't."

It occurs to Theo they've yet to negotiate Jet Scramble, and this time his putting off of the topic is conscious. "You didn't?"

"Oh I mean I went to the schools and I left some of my shit there but like nah I wasn't going to classes or anything not when I found out it doesn't matter like I'm gonna get passed either way."

"Because the Otterlakes are major benefactors."

"Was it you said something about China? I pay a guy in China to do the schoolwork. Still do man like he's my Harvard guy."

Cameron Otterlake. Harvard student.

"So… the plane you came here—"

"*Sharapova*? Yeah like the tennis player. So fuckin hot dude like Nigel is a big sponsor at Wimbledon so growing up like I always had to be there y'know and I was down bad like ten years old man."

"You named your plane when you were ten."

"Had to've been."

"You got a private plane when you were ten."

Taking his sweet time stacking the fourth basket on the increasingly unstable tower, Cameron says, matter of fact, "It's an old plane."

"Ah, I gotcha. Well, thanks for clearing that up." While Theo gives it a beat, Cameron does not pick up on the sarcasm. He adds, "I've never been on a plane."

"Is that why you keep tracking mine dude like you gotta focus on yourself. People tell me Nigel says you can't be comparing your chapter one to someone else's chapter ten."

"First of all, just to reiterate, I've admitted to nothing and I have nothing to admit to. Alright? Second, and please excuse me, but no Otterlake for the past bicentennial has had the right to tell *any* living soul they need to fucking *work harder.* Get what I'm saying? What's the last thing you worked for?"

"Took some work getting here man I had to get to the airstrip before Steve and I had to pay Rian to take off solo. Get me the fuck outta there. That's who flies the plane also it's Steve and Rian but they get mad when I call them that but I dunno why."

Forget it. Theo takes a breath. He helps himself to the second pitcher, which arrived mid-soliloquy and added an electricity to conversation, the maraca cha-cha of the ice rumbling against the plastic. "Would you pay to get it taken down?" Theo asks.

"I mean shit if that's how it's gotta be then that's how it's gotta be it's no problem over here." He giggles for some reason.

"You don't have a problem with paying."

"Zzzzzip."

"... Why don't you have a problem with paying?" Theo really doesn't mean to ask. Not with confirmation there was some money coming his way. It just slipped out because he was thinking about something else.

"I mean like I *can* have a problem if that's what you want."

"No, I just mean like... you've got billions. That's plural. What do we even measure in billions? Molecules and dollars. Neither of us have lived a billion *seconds* and you have several billion dollars to yourself. I guess my question is like, I dunno, if you got no problem paying to make this problem go away, what's the holdup eliminating other problems? Y'know? Some people in town haven't worn a fresh pair of socks in ten years. Half the guys who've been through here the past half hour are gonna retire with nothing. My cousins pick a day of the week to go without dinner. You ever thought about taking dad's money and doing what he never would?"

Mouth full, but getting the hang of talking through the mush, Cameron asks "what would Nigel never do?"

"Nevermind."

"He'd never what?"

*Success is when preparation meets opportunity, or so we tell ourselves so to believe the days toiled away with names pinned to our chests may have ulterior significance. Roots and grease are what scientists eons from now will find fossilized in the gut of Marshfield Man. These are the pockets of America too small to glimpse from the window of an Airbus, and these are the stories never bound and—is that Theodore?* –Oleg Magnussen

"You say something?" Duncan hollers.

"That's my son at the booth there," Oleg cracks a smile, peeking in the oily plastic window of a black kitchen door. "I don't know who he's sitting with but I thought he'd be in bed by now. Heard him in the kitchen at five this morning."

"Mmm," Duncan answers, uninterested, "they the garlic fry table?"

"Sure are." Oleg bunts the kitchen door with a foot but stops just shy. At the last second he's able to place himself in his teenage son's shoes. Would he want his dad to be waiting tables? In front of his new friend, no less? Certainly not. He aborts the delivery, finding a waitress stopped right behind his back doing what her job suggests by the most ignorant definition: waiting for him to get out of the way.

"Take these to that booth there," he says, sliding the twin fry baskets to her open hands and letting her by, peeking through the kitchen door's porthole to watch.

This would be a bad look, Oleg cannot deny. It's just that something about his son's new friend has caught his attention in a manner mnemonic, buried deep in his mind palace unmarked and unregistered. But he knows he's seen that boy somewhere. In any case seeing Theo talk to someone roughly his age—give or take a level of education—is a rare sight. Rarer still is Theo talking to someone and not having that one *look* on his face. The one that tells Oleg his son would rather be doing anything else, which includes lying down on the freeway.

A normal father would be happy to see this. Problem is a therapist some years ago inadvisably praised Oleg's qualities as an atypical father, citing how he allows his son to use swear words and allows his son to perform Blackhat -curious computer stuff in the basement.

Now there's where he and Theodore are most severely separated by time. If it were porn then at least Oleg would know when things were breaching normalcy.

Again the returning waitress asks Oleg to step out of

the way, but he returns to the window with increased hunger, this time pressing his nose to the filthy plastic. Very nearly there he felt the wires of his subconscious brush their exposed copper frays. Something to do with porn and the boy sitting there. But no, they couldn't be one in the same. That's not Oleg's part of vice city, typically, save for brief sightseeing. Something connects the two, but what? It frustrates him so terribly he misses the first time Duncan tells him the fry basket is bubbling over.

Midway through tossing out the burned rejects and filling up a new basket Oleg remembers @Liv_Abach on Instagram. Very impressive photos. Oleg's a longtime follower. And from there his thoughts spiral to Mykonos and yachts and teal g-strings and a boy trying and failing to cover his face in the accompanying reel.

Oleg whips back around to the door.

Yup. That's him.

Duncan hollers from the charbroiler, "I've got no use for freezers in my beloved corps, Private Magnum, let's see some foot traffic."

Oleg stamps a finger on the plastic window, seizing eye contact with the chef. "*That kid's a billionaire.*"

"Oh yeah? He's a YouTuber?"

"No I mean seriously that kid is heir to the biggest pool of gold coins in the hemisphere, Duncan. You know Nigel Otterlake?"

It takes some serious lip biting on Duncan's part but he does confirm, "The skyscraper guy?"

"Regular Augustus Caesar, Duncan, the Otterlakes have reshaped the skyline of every major city on Earth. Every generation in that family has doubled the fortune *except* for Nigel Otterlake—he *quadrupled* it. The number of buildings worldwide with the Otterlake named signed on the work order could fill two and a half Manhattans alone. And that kid, sitting in your booth right now, is set up to inherit *all of that.*"

Astonishingly, Duncan's not impressed. "Bet you he still won't tip."

"I'm being serious, here! The president walking in right now wouldn't be as big a deal; that greasy-fingered twerp won't ever, in his entire life, have to think about a penny he's spending."

"Mhmm," Duncan ruminates. "And he's friends with your son."

"… Yes. That seems to be the case."

"Unless the kid's got snipers trained on his head right the hell now, or he wants to buy the place, I don't see what you're getting at. And for your information, by the way, we *did* serve a president."

"What I'm saying—huh? Who?"

"Slick Willie. First term. We have the picture in the bar."

"Oh. I never noticed."

"*That's about the best burger I ever had, son,*" Duncan mimics, nobody, affecting a pretty decent Bill Clinton impression. "And y'know what," Duncan drops the impression, "bet you anything he went one town over and told some other joint the same shit."

Oleg's mind is on other things. The things Wilson (Mr. Langley) called intrusive thoughts best filed away and never acted upon. *Look where that gentleman bandit mindset has gotten you already, Oleg. Think about your son.*

He is thinking about his son.

*We were young when we had Theodore. At the insistence of her own and my own, we enrolled in parenting classes (second trimester if memory serves). I remember little from these weekly lectures, which I am afraid extends to the name of our instructor, but her closing manifesto delivered at our final class has informed my experience as a single father more than any successive book or internet video. She had said, in some form or another* "It is, I believe, your primary responsibility as parents, that your child never know the sacrifices you made." *When I exit stage left from this world Theodore will be left to categorize his father, my many errors, my verisimilar humanities. If he will call them sacrifices, I cannot say. –* Oleg Magnussen.

"—Which is crazy right because like I got a lot of good ideas."

"Hit me with one."

"Alright *ahahaha* okay so y'know what skateboards are?"

"I'm familiar."

"It's cool but like I hate how you gotta keep going like *mmm* when you want it to go so I was thinking like oh shit what if there was an engine on the back?"

"A Boosted Board, if you will."

"YEAH! Like it just fucking *goes* dude oh hey also do you know that guy there?"

"Who? Oh. Oh, no, he's just some guy. I think he's pissing in that bush. Y'know, right at the window, where we can see him."

"Ahahaha yeah flip him the bird there you go."

"You could be selling those in a month. Cameronboards."

"Oh I wasn't thinking about other people having them though."

"Right."

"But I could probably get you one I mean you're pretty good at naming stuff."

"With the money on your credit line, right now, you could have Cameronboards researched and developed in time to be the hottest Christmas gift."

"Ah but like sometimes Nigel empties my account if he's mad at me but he hasn't done it in a second. Probably gonna do it soon though."

"There's an ATM right there. It may behoove you to hit it up before it's too late."

"Do what to me now you said?"

"Behoove. Like, benefit you."

With a new word in tow, Cameron slaps the table and

makes for the glowing LED money screen past the billiards tables, fighting for the first time against a stomach more starch now than man. He's piled up some ninety dollars' worth of fries and probably fifteen's worth of the worst cherry soda on tap, by Theo's rough guesstimate. He hasn't even used the bathroom yet, which, good on him. Theo would put his Amazon fulfillment money down on the Bottom Dollar's stalls possessing the widest gaps of any comparable lavatory in the state, possibly the world. In a cruel Pavlovian twist Theo now feels the urge to pee but remains at the booth, worried that both of them leaving at once will summon the Bottom dollar's annoyingly eager bussers. He does, however, stand and stretch his legs, boosting his peripheral view of the restaurant floor just in time to see chef Duncan locking the doors.

Huh. Well, the next thirty seconds are going to be awkward. This has happened before at this very same restaurant and Theo felt then and begins to feel now it's his fault, even though by right it's not. Him and his guest (or the other way around; he'd led the night assuming Cameron would pay) are clearly still here, even if the remaining customers for the night have since exited. Why would any seasoned restauranteur start locking up for the night before "running a lap" or "sweeping a looksie" or whatever special jargon they developed for no reason—

"Hey, Duncan!"

The head chef does not turn and look at Theo before he finishes locking the front doors, floor latch and all. Only then does he acknowledge one of his remaining two customers. "Hey, don't worry about it kid, we're just bussing her down for the night. Take your time."

Oh, okay. The reassurance is nice, but… actually, no, Theo's now thinking, it's not okay. Who the fuck starts with latching the doors? Would a lock or a sign not be enough to keep incoming customers out? And why the windows, too?

The Bottom Dollar has jack shit worth stealing. Every prospective thief in town knows this at a glance. The cash from the ATM? At the pace Cameron's going, that'll be gone, too.

Duncan's teleported to the booth, disassembling the stack of fry baskets on the table and reassembling an unbalanced basket-pitcher conglomerate in his arms. "Clearing it up, now, don't mind me," he says again. "Who's your friend?"

"I'd really appreciate you keeping this to yourself," Theo says.

"Man, there's plenty me and your dad don't talk about. I don't ask about his time in the pen, he doesn't ask about his kid."

"He really doesn't?"

"Okay, I don't *tell* him nothing. Just that I never see you in here with anyone but ol' Magnum." Duncan pauses himself to examine Cameron. "I don't think I've seen that kid *ever*."

"… He's new in town."

A screeching *BEEPBEEP* from the ATM propels all three on the restaurant floor to a standoff.

First to shoot is Duncan "Do you need help—"

Proving the Gunslinger Effect true Cameron says "it won't let me take out anymore?"

"Well how much are you trying to take out? It'll give you five hundred at once."

"Yeah I know but it just stopped."

Cradled against his stomach is a bouquet of hundred-dollar bills. How many times in a row had he swiped his card, which Theo can practically feel in his hands from where he's standing. The authoritative clank it would make dropped on a counter precedes itself. A bright teal, a certain titanium, an unmarked unattainable sword.

Duncan's making for the kitchen. "I'll be right back."

"Yeah, he's fucking loaded," Duncan's saying as he dulls the kitchen door's sway to rest. "I got the doors locked but what exactly was your plan?"

Oleg's taken a stepladder like a throne, too late to notice his seat would be wet but in equal measure too late to go back on it. "If we took the money now I'm afraid this would splash back on you—thanks for locking the doors, by the by. If he's already used your machine then I'm afraid your restaurant is a crime scene. Do you have cameras?"

"Man, we don't even have fire extinguishers."

"What?"

"How am I implicated, exactly? If he's getting mugged that's got tangential shit to do with me, at best."

"I'm saying if he squeals you might have to talk to a cop. However, yes, in this instance, you will be a victim just as much as him. Your honest establishment the scene of grand larceny. I need you to stay back here until it's done. Maybe start cleaning the grill. That's your alibi."

A strong enough alibi Duncan neglects to notice Oleg's misuse of grand larceny. In reality this would be charged *extortion-threats to injure or accuse of crime*, a class H felony in the state of Wisconsin punishable by fines up to ten thousand dollars and/or six years in prison. Assuming the perpetrator has not already committed crimes against the state.

Apropos of nothing Oleg Magnussen is the next one to speak: "The rest is up to me."

"And Theo."

"Irregardless of what comes next you know I'd never involve Theodore unless what happens to me will be of immediate consequence to him. Now, that said, he won't be in high school much longer and he takes after me in concerning but currently advantageous ways. Namely befriending this… space cadet. What's his tab?"

"Over a hundred now that he's having beer."

"I'm sorry, he had how many orders of those garlic fries and now he's having *beer*?"

Duncan shrugs. "Play ball."

Indeed.

Ezekiel 18:20 – "The son shall not suffer for the iniquity of the father, nor the father suffer for the iniquity of the son." *I would not deny my anger as a leftist and a working-class citizen at the sight of Cameron Otterlake its synecdoche for his father. As far as I or anyone reading should be concerned, keep in mind we are talking about the same person. The rich clone themselves. Cameron Otterlake is Nigel Otterlake who is Quentin Otterlake who is another two hundred years of robber barons. Ezekiel never met a billionaire.* –Oleg Magnussen

Reliably Oleg has found forcing himself through the proverbial kitchen door to be all the confidence he needs, which he makes literal this very moment, letting his son's eyes fall on him for the first time tonight. Theodore is careful to hover around the bar area rather than sit down. Good. Catching himself in fantasy to ignore the look of objective disgust on his son's face, Oleg weighs the options regarding his Theodore's first drink: underage and among friends, or with his father on his first legal day. He supposes both will exist parallel in the superposition of truth. In any case he's glad it's not now. Theodore needs to be sharp, these next few critical minutes.

"Ahahahaha hey dude look at this video of a guy getting hit by a car."

But Theodore does not look at the video of a guy getting hit by a car. Shame because Oleg takes a glance and cannot deny the violent, kinetic beauty of the thing, punishment from the universe for the victim's ignorant taste in suit jackets.

Cameron Otterlake laughs throatily, as someone of his cut would. He's never been made to grapple with the permanence of injury or even death and from the mountain of microplastics and crude oil he sits atop he'd probably say anyone in such a haughty suit jacket deserves a life made pancake. Look at this kid and honestly tr

"Dad what the hell are you doing here?"

"Ah, Theodore, didn't see you there—"

"Is this what you're running late for?"

"Visiting a friend? Lay off your old man, would you? It's what all the Magnussen men are doing tonight." He's proud of the connecting thread there but broaching the question has gotten a little harder. It's too late before Oleg realizes he's been standing here silent. Does Theodore take after him or what? That's the same look Oleg served the late Tobin Magnussen as the old man thoroughly and decisively disapproved of his son's literary ambitions. And when the late Tobin Magnussen suggested giving Theo up for adoption, forgetting in his time men had *two* kids by nineteen instead of just one. It's good for a young man, not to lionize adults or take their advice uncritically. But It'd be great if Theo could put that shit on hold for a second.

"I actually do need to talk with you for just a second," Oleg snaps back. "If you'll excuse us," he adds for Cameron.

The rich boy finishes off the rest of his beer (sixty percent) before saying "they put oranges in this I think."

"Likely. It's a frequent character—Theodore, with me."

Theo groans internally. A rumbling in his spine. The

fuck does his dad want?

"You know I hate to pry into your personal life when I don't have to," his dad starts, stops, drags his son further away— "how do you *know* that kid?"

"What's it to you who I'm friends with?"

"Do you know who you're talking to?"

"My dad?"

"That kid sitting there is the closest thing to a trillionaire since Musa."

"Since who? –Dad, no one reads your oldass books—"

"Here me out, son, because there's money in this for you if you play your role."

There's a familiar polish to the ground his father saying this has guided them towards. If memory serves, the last couple times Theo's dad promised a share of nondescript, unaccounted money, it ended with friendly policeman peeking through the entryway window. How fortunate were they, those last couple times, that his father's semi-reliable silver tongue could spin those swindles a huge misunderstanding, personal taxing error, et cetera. But they've never had a bite this big and the risk has never been so high, and if Theo has correctly guessed what's coming next,

"*You wanna take his cash.*"

"Good on you to whisper."

"Dad, it's not gonna work. His whole security team is probably on their way right now, what are you gonna tell them?"

"We're gonna *tell them* their reliably cantankerous heir pissed away twenty grand on a drunken bender. Would we be lying?"

Theo's dad makes a gesture towards the bar, and Theo turns just in time to see Cameron doing the drunk cowboy sway. Right before proceedings turned theft-curious, Cameron had gotten interested in the jukebox over by the bathrooms. An advanced spin on the coin-op record players of old (for 2005), the Bottom Dollar's machine takes every card in the world but Cameron's. Alternatively it also accept cash, in either Washington or Lincoln, which Cameron had neither and has maybe never seen in his life. To get his music playing he traded Theo a hundred-dollar bill for a five, which makes no sense but Theo didn't press. He selected Madonna's *Like A Virgin* fifteen times in what was apparently not a mistake.

"*Been savin' it all for you cuz onl—HUGGHHGGNN—*"

Everyone who bet on Cameron wolfing down three pounds of garlic fries and thirty-two ounces of cherry Pepsi and beer and making it just over an hour without vomiting, blow the dice. A shade of yellow too rancid to be the work of God splashes on the wood floor and briefly takes the shape of water broken by a rock dropped from a bridge. Regretfully, Cameron's eagerness to swallow up the beautiful, humble food has resulted in some fries returning to open air unchewed. At the end of it all Cameron's gut makes a cocking noise like a shotgun.

His money fell from his hands when he lost control, and anyone who wants those hundreds now would have to be really desperate. In this case it's still everybody.

Bearing the stench on the restaurant floor eclipses cruel and unusual. Feigning a run for the mop and bucket, Oleg retreats to the kitchen and finds the reloading grease trap an upgrade.

Duncan, actually preparing the mop and bucket, asks, "you left your kid out there?"

"He wanted the first shift," Oleg pants. Hands on the sink, he's worried about going domino. But men who have been through jail come out with hog's hide—tougher stuff. A couple deep breaths and Oleg is ready to step aside while Duncan wheels out the mop.

It's not his weak stomach, what agreed to let Theo have the first swing. It's his pride as a father. Honest. Under unenviable circumstances, his flesh and blood agreed to the plan and persevered unperturbed in the face of chemical warfare. The terms? A thirty percent cut for successfully taking the money. Or that was Oleg's terms. Doing him proud again, in a way, was Theodore's insistence on an even fifty-fifty. Now they didn't shake hands on those terms, and Oleg does plan on explaining the seventy -thirty benefits at a later time, but right now his mind is on googling the best way to clean that money back to something spendable.

Somewhere in the middle of all this he's beaming. Six years running the majority of him and Theodore's bonding exercises have failed to launch. A therapist identified a lack of trust; when Oleg went to the pen, Theodore was alone.

Cattled off to grandparents and aunts. Pinballed from one quadrant of the loosely connected Magnussen clan to the next. In that time, the therapist believed, Theodore grew to resent the family tree down to the root. You can't hot potato a young boy like that. He needs a home.

Oleg likes to think all of this is giving him one.

A forum user suggests isopropyl alcohol, for cleaning vomit off United States Dollars, but another has counter-argued with the potential ink bleeding. Forum user number one has called him a chode in riposte.

*Something something vomit scented money. Rich people, guts, cash. There's something here.* –Oleg Magnussen

"I'll be quick about this—so, that guy who was just in here? The old guy?"

Cameron chokes on the water Theo's instructed him to sip slowly. "*M—mhmm* yeah?"

"He wants to steal all your money."

"Oh."

"Yeah. Oh. Tell you what, though: take all that cash there, hide it out—"

"It's all barfy though."

"… Yeah but it's still good. Take all that money, take my bike, get outta town, bury half out by the exit sign."

"Half though, like why half?"

"Because you're buying my bike and getting out of

here before that guy and all his goons can rob you naked. We don't have a lotta time, man. You need to run."

"Why are they gonna be naked when they rob me?"

"Nevermind. You ready to move?"

"You'll really sell me your bike? Dude…"

Too quick to dodge, Cameron brings Theo in for what is to him a very earnest hug. He'd return it but there's a membrane of vomit making this otherwise naively sweet moment gross as fuck.

"Alright, lemme uh…"

Cranking up the jukebox, the boys use their fingers like chopsticks to carefully peel the cash from the garlic fry slurry and deposit the bills to a plastic takeaway box.

"Wait but how am I gonna get my plane off the thing now?"

"I'll take care of it."

"For free?" Cameron's voice cracks.

"No, you're leaving half the money by the exit sign. Don't forget."

"Man I don't forget shit man."

He feels eyes on the back of his neck. It doesn't look like anyone's there now but Theo realizes now someone—probably his dad—has been using that plastic window in the kitchen door to keep tabs on the restaurant floor. Clocking this, Theo pulls the two of them to a window out of view, unlatching the lock and pulling the bottom half open to the cold, delightful outside. Both of them freeze and soak in fresh air for a moment.

"Here's the key," Theo deposits. "Just rip the handle for the gas. After that it's just riding a bike. You done that?"

"Ah hell yeah dude when I was a kid there was this country club up in Switzerland—"

"Okay, cool. Well, uh…" it's goodbye. "Better get moving, this is your only shot at bailing."

"Man what if like…" Cameron starts while clumsily hooking a leg outside and rolling outside using the frame against his crotch like a fulcrum. "Where do I go they can't find me?"

"Jet Scramble? I said I'd take care of it."

"I mean people like my parents or their security guys."

"Fuck them. You ripped the antenna, and nothing's out here, dude, no one will find you."

"No shit?"

"None whatsoever."

"You're like resourceful as shit dude like it's crazy man you got like small town swag or whatever like you keep shit down low to the ground. I dunno why the FUCK they keep looking for me when it's always boarding schools and shit like fuckin leave me alone if you don't want me."

"I'm telling you," Theo gives some urgency so Cameron splits faster, "forget about them, man, my mom didn't want me either. I'm doing fine."

"… Hey what do you mean like your mom and dad

didn't want you?"

"It's fine. I don't want her either. Get outta here and remember to leave the money."

Theo keeps his head slouched out the window, waiting to hear the rev of the engine and the dissipation down the road. It sounds for a second like Cameron can't get moving, but soon the bike is making its familiar gargle and screech out onto the road, to the left (wrong way) then the right (there you go).

Finally, the garnish on this deception al dente. Balling a fist, Theo takes some short breaths to psych himself up, then smashes his hand against his nose. He's gotten it right on the first try and blood streams from his nostrils down his chin.

"*Ugh*," he groans, slurping the instant saliva and phlegm, returning to the horrible vomit chamber. Just in time as the kitchen door is kicked open and he sees his dad rush inside.

"I heard your bike—" he begins, then stops. "Ah, shit."

"*Yeah*," Theo strains. "He's gone."

"He *attacked* you?"

"Sucker punched me. And he took my bike."

"Not your bike—" while Theo expected this it's still awkward to get a hug from his dad, a man who never learned how those are supposed to feel. If anything he only aggravates Theo's nosebleed.

This was supposed to end twelve seconds ago, this

hug, if muscle memory serves. "Dad?"

Is he crying?

"You weren't supposed to get hit, is all," his dad chokes. "Did… have you been in a fight before, son?"

"… A little bit, at school or whatever."

"Okay, I just didn't want—did you win?"

"Do you really win those?"

"Poetic—that's, that's *awesome.* Hey, I was going to tell you this tomorrow, but I—"

"Can you let me go, I'm still bleeding."

The Magnussens split apart and Theo looks up at the ceiling, feeling a coagulated snake of blood slither down his throat. "Tell me what?"

"I got a new job. Or, rather, I'm going to start training soon. It's not glamorous work, but it's the new Amazon fulfillment center outside of town. It's good money and the plan is I start working my way up the ladder. Hopefully we don't need to do this sort of dirty work anymore."

*What the fuck, dad.* –Theodore Magnussen

# (The) Gallivant ♃

***Arthur Leopold Fitzturner, 20***

***Heir-apparent to the Fitzturner family fortune***

***Gross Assets (personal): £84,240,779.00***

***Gross Pending Transactions: £3.00***

***London, England***

Three fucking quid for a Pepsi. Unreal.

Nevermind Arthur's family *owns* the building that very shop is so fortunate to nestle inside, with its green paint and its many unidentifiable smells and its three fucking note Pepsis. Why have they not fixed the prices, down there? Arthur may be *fresh to the world*, as his grandfather puts it, but he's wise enough to remember pound bottles. When his schoolwork was finished for the day the nannies would give him a coin and he would run across the street—

*Three!* Fucking robbery.

He'd gone for a swim this morning, in lieu of having a shower. For reasons he's yet to choreograph, the pool at the penthouse was unavailable. Or he imagines it would be; he didn't really check. Frankly Arthur couldn't be out of there fast enough—he was gone before the police arrived. Shame he were, really, because the evidence he wears on his person would by rights solve the case. Something pink and sticky paints his new dress shoes. A twentieth birthday gift from his grandfather and hardly twenty-four hours from gifting have already been ruined. The leather, apparently (he wasn't listening too hard) is some bovine subgenre too obscure to be subsidised in America or Italy. They shimmer gently in the light and collect the sun's glare in organic pockets when Arthur twists his heel.

Well, they *did*, anyway. Now they're pink in a disturbing, alopecian way. He did give the pink blotches a smell when he was preparing to swim. It's not vomit and it's not the spillover from some unknown, milky alcohol. He'd go back to the house to find more pink, ideally a donut-shaped puddle with a shoe-shaped impression matching his size, but the whole street is flooded with police.

"No crossing, son".

"But I live here".

"Is that right? What unit"?

"Every unit".

Forgetting his training, the policeman shows Arthur a definitive frustration. His mind casts back to Christmas, standing right about where he stands today, responding to what the men back at the station call a Hat Trick—three simultaneous noise complaints from the same block. Something about this did feel familiar, tapping him on the shoulder like. At the time he weren't so fortunate to meet the homeowner.

"I'm going inside", Arthur does declare.

"Be my guest, go talk to the"—

"It's my building, buckethead, the way I see this you're all my guests. "*Oh but we're on the road*—" my family *paved* the road"!

"Go talk to the inspector".

Unreal distribution of resources going on here. It's fucking morning and it's sure quiet *now*, officer. Go shut down an immigrant's snack cart. You'd like that. Or, better yet, go arrest someone for carrying a sneeze worth of hash and misplace the evidence on the way back to your *single* unit. Officer Dickhead.

But Arthur lets it go.

The biometric scan in the car park is a skip faster than the front door with the password. He sees the diligent and honorable Doorman Henrickson is there, still, standing resolute against this tax dollar bonfire. It's just that he can't hear too well and Arthur has to repeat himself enough times so everyone on Pall Mall knows the proper answer for *how does a Jacobin tie his shoes?*

No worry. Arthur takes to the sublevel parking and finds the second biometric scan for the elevator. His father had this installed last Spring and apparently never thought Arthur would be bringing up more than his own body at a time. Yesterday afternoon, when the party reached its populate capacity, there was a terribly long and disorganised queue for two—maybe three thinner people—to squeeze inside the otherwise luxurious personal lift. Yes, the sublevel car park became a party venue in itself, and Arthur's very nearly slipped on two gas cannisters from the pavement to here.

The lift is very fast, however. It pays to update these things.

Ding goes the bell at the penthouse foyer, as Arthur departs the lift and barely catches the last dozen party stragglers waking up and scurrying away. *No need*, he'd like to tell them, but no matter how briskly he endeavors to walk he doesn't see them again. One of the two nearly looked like Percy, from the back. That mad fucker's the type to throw off his shirt, at one hour of the night or another, and an astute party girl once compared his bacne to the constellation Ursa Major. Which is precisely why Arthur's not so sure that was Percy, just now, because theirs was more of an Ophiuchus.

Two entirely different London party vagabonds are cornered in the first sitting room (now rendered a standing room—some wunderkind thought it revolutionary to throw all the chairs off the balcony) by the inspectors Arthur had been warned about. He's not impressed. Barring their fashionable vests and twinkly shoulder stars the inspectors look identical to the police on the street. Impressive mustache on the tall one. Full marks for effort.

"Out"! Arthur claps, immediately taking a laborious sip of Pepsi so the lads know biblically the current depths of his aloofness.

"Were you here last night", tall one with the mustache says, not a request.

Arthur's still drinking. Well, pretending to drink more

than he is in reality. Three quid and all. Sip and savor.

"You are a guest, then"?

"—*Mm*—I *was* here last night, and the night before, and the one before that. Actually since last Christmas, if I'm doing my maths right".

"I see. You were the *last* Hat Trick", the other inspector realises. Unfortunately for him he's arrived with no distinctive features like a mustache or being tall, and he evaporates from Arthur's memory the instant he glances at the stairs and notices that one painting's been ripped from the wall. Huh. Rude. Well, the conservators can likely fix up the scratches on the frame and probably the massive hole punched through the canvas. They do good work.

Arthur says, "And you're standing in Fitzturner House, where your annual salary couldn't buy the floorboards".

"Yeah? You're talking about this scuffed up disgrace to your ancestors"? Mustache fingers the ground.

"I mean the two boards under your two feet. By themselves".

"We'll gladly get on our way and leave this to your *foundation*, sir. I just thought you'd like a quote on the damages to what is, I'm sure you already know, a listed structure".

"Tell me something I don't know".

The funny thing is Mustache just did. Now and then, Arthur's heard someone in the Fitzturner tree rant and gripe and spit a whole lot over how difficult it can be to remodel. On this rock, owning the fucking place isn't enough, and some board or unrelated foundation always has some complaint locked and loaded about painting over the specific and very rare shade applied in 1852. No Fitzturner from here to the Virgin Islands needs to be learned about their geriatric living spaces. Arthur's looking at a painting of a man in full military regalia hanging in the first dining room. They have the same ears.

Leaving Arthur with some acknowledgements to sign, or whatever the hell these papers damned for the bin would like him to do, the inspectors take leave of Fitzturner House. Not a scrap of evidence between the two. A sorry display for Scotland Yard, because Fitzturner House is so lousy with evidence at this moment they could reasonably arrest the entirety of King's College save the kids with any business studying there. Art vandalism (the Fitzturners, and presumably anyone with adjacent resources, are obligated to protect what they collect), smoking indoors, smoking illegal substances, smoking illegal substances indoors, smoking substances Arthur wasn't aware could produce smoke, public nudity (Fitzturner house opens to the public on select weekends so that may count), whatever tossing furniture out of a fifth floor window onto the public road would constitute, paying three pounds for a Pepsi which is a fucking crime if you ask Arthur, and—oh yeah—riding the grotesques on the roof for a cheeky photo op, which were installed around the same time as the Battle of Trafalgar.

For a more recent comparison, the last people to damage the roof of Fitzturner House were the Nazis. Last night it was Adam Clementine, who collaborated with a brick of hash and half a bottle of Cîroc on an impromptu

Assassin's Creed reenactment. Nine tiles broke under his feet, crashing onto Pall Mall in irreparable shards.

But you know, whatever. Arthur would fiend for an indoor smoke right now.

Seems Riley's stuck around. At some point last night he'd taken a pillow from the master bed and set up camp in the fourth-floor bath. Arthur happens upon him with legs in the air, a blanket struggling to stay inside the tub after a night of restless alcohol sweat, nursing a dart between chapped lips. When he notices Arthur, for a split second, he's angry. Seems he was also expecting the police.

"Morning, Riley".

Riley does not say morning back. Never fucking does. "Where are you keeping the Pepsi"?

"Went out and bought it".

"From where"?

"The shops they sell Pepsi, the fuck do you mean"?

Riley smokes. "Sounds good, is all".

"For three quid it better be".

"Fuck off. Three"?

"I said the same thing". Arthur takes a seat on the toilet, leaning back just enough to let the air from the (smashed) open window skate along his forehead. "Hey, let me bum one".

Ask, and the master of the house shall receive. Riley finds the beaten pack beneath the blanket and between his legs, searching a lot longer for his lighter while Arthur waits, bent cigarette armed between his teeth. The boys have to lean awkwardly and a bit painfully to make the magic happen, and the moment the smoke hits Arthur's lungs he coughs.

"The fuck are these"?

"Camel Crush. American. Good, huh"?

"It's fucking toothpaste", Arthur whines. Actually, he does acclimate to the taste fairly quick but he's already committed to insulting Riley's taste. He does make a note to import a box. Riley's always smoking something mildly exotic and also stupid. Seems impossible when his family owns and operates some of the oldest and most respected tobacco parlors in the United Kingdom. Well, the best what weren't opened by immigrants.

"Police are gone"? Riley asks.

"Fucked right off when I came back from my swim".

"You got a pool here, mate".

"Drained. Don't know who, don't care".

"Would you care if I told you who did it"?

"Bet it were Evan".

"Ah"! Riley sits up so he can laugh properly. "Inspectors left because you showed up. Cases closed. Whole squad".

"Evan still here"?

"I think most of us who matter already split when the police arrived. Went for a piss a minute ago and didn't recognise anybody. Just the *rats* who crawl in one way or another. Your home and all its secret passages".

"So you went for a piss somewhere else"?

"You piss in your bedroom"?

The boys laugh together now. Vintage Riley.

Riley blurts, "Oh yeah! Sabrina's still here. Was looking for you. She was wearing that jumper of yours last night but she doesn't want to leave without giving it back... personally".

"Fuck are you talking about"?

"Go and see. I'm told nothing and I've assumed that's on purpose".

In actuality Riley is told nothing because he's got the kind of loose lips that'd get him discharged if the Willoughbys had any honorable military legacy to start (three generations of deserters and counting).

By some definition maybe Arthur and Sabrina are sweet on each other. No disrespect to Sabrina or frankly any woman in the Bell family but Arthur hadn't interpreted the past four months as anything other than sportsman-like flirtation. He supposes, yes, they are more or less at the "girl wears the boy's clothes" stage. Though as he meditates on the overwhelming mintiness of Riley's gross yank darts he can't fathom what of his he could've left behind and Sabrina could be currently rubbing girl smells all over. He'd locked the doors to the bedroom he uses a week and a half ago. No one's been inside but him—not even Sabrina.

Now he's flat out curious and, sure, also wants to see

Sabrina. He slaps Riley's outstretched knee and sets off to explore the rest of the waking Fitzturner House.

The stairwell's been taken to hell and back. Chipped railing, scuffed up steps, dirtied paint and bashed in molding. The curtains on the windows between the second and third floor have been ripped off the housing and draped down the steps to the first floor Arthur doesn't bother to explore. Doorman Henrickson wouldn't let an unwanted flake of skin desecrate the historic foyer. But the stairs are not his department and no one could blame him for leaving the curtain be.

It's on the roof, actually, where Arthur finds the tightest remaining congress, comprising Sabrina Bell, her sister Toni Bell, Angelina Downs, whoever the fourth girl is, and the mad fucker himself—Adam Clementine, smoking away the fines he's about to choke down courtesy of the Fitzturner foundation. *Ya got something in common with* Nazis, *Adam. Think on it.*

Oh, lovely, they have the fire pit going. Reminds Arthur of the Fitzturner country retreat. Reminds him, also, that the roof does not have a fire pit. How did they—

"There you are"! Damn. Sabrina's too happy to see him and he's now lost what dismantled and currently burning cabinet that may be. "Where'd you run off"?

"Went for a swim".

"Oh but I thought"—

"Evan"?

Sabrina bites her lip. "I think he wanted to skateboard".

And here he comes now, the defiler. "I meant to ask", Adam starts, "about the… what's the word, the big marble in the library"—

"Column".

"The column! Two nights ago we were, you know, we were exploring a little, and we *noticed*—we didn't do anything to it, this is critical—we *noticed*, the column can turn a bit".

"Yeah, it opens the tunnel".

"Fuck off".

"I'm being serious. What, you all haven't seen them yet? When you were exploring a little"?

Having weathered two world wars and before then a half dozen messy consolidations of power within the family, Fitzturner House allows its occupants to, if they wish, never set foot on a public road. A network of tunnels, which Adam and the inconcrete We nearly stumbled upon two nights ago, connects the building to several others from City of London down into the harbor. It would be a tremendous conflict of interest were a few of these tunnels servicing the nearby government buildings, and precisely why Arthur's father had them walled off eleven years ago. As tunnels go they're rather comfortable. During the same remodel, LED lights were installed and the whole length was carpeted in red. Even *smells* nicer.

Arthur tacks on, "Riley said you had a jumper of mine".

Nodding, Sabrina rolls over to her pile of belongings. She's amassed a respectable collection of party souvenirs in the past week. Of course she's taking the empty liquor bottles which struck her interior design fancy. Ironic because she's heiress to the Old Promenade gin distillery. Can't imagine she's lacking for fun bottles within any context.

"Here… it… is… now…" Sabrina has to drag out dramatically since both sleeves have found themselves pulled inside out. "Ta-da".

She holds the jumper taut. A tremendous piece of craftsmanship: wholly cable knit and rendered in tight, unfrizzed wool, suggesting a breed who don't get sheared for just anything. In the morning's diffused, overcast sun, the platinum white threatens blinding. Behind the neck is a signature handwritten in gold; a custom work. Beautiful bit of stitching, here—worthy of laying on the floor of Fitzturner House and warming the back of a Bell daughter.

"It's not mine, though", Arthur has to admit. Shame it's not.

Her whole week's been thrown out of fact. Sabrina combs her mind for the steps between finding the jumper and sitting here now. "But I got it from the room I always find you".

"Where's that"?

"Snooker hall".

"I'm not *always* in the snooker hall; I don't know what you're talking about".

"I saw you," Sabrina gets offensive, "for the first time this week, sitting in the snooker hall with that… the"—

Arthur shakes the finger what solved the case, aggressively, so Sabrina stops talking. "I know whose this is".

"Is it… is it *Riley's*"? The thought of wearing something of his icks her out biblically.

"No, it's"—

Impeccably on cue, the roof access door explodes open. The crash wakes up the girls and momentarily has Arthur thinking the police are back. Maybe changed their mind about doing their job and are here to arrest someone. But no, it's only Evan.

"I thought you had gone", Arthur says for good morning.

"Yea, and people are thinking a lot of things about me 'cus Riley's talking out his narrow arse". Heaving, having clearly ran up the stairs like time is of some essence, Evan takes an MMA staredown with Arthur, breath still reeking of gin and hash. "I did not drain your pool".

"… Wouldn't bother me if you did, just so you know".

"Yea, but it bothers me! Fucking Riley"—

"Did Riley do it, then"?

"Nah, it was"—

Only because he just had the name on his mind two seconds ago, Arthur interrupts Evan one more time. "Was it Cameron"?

"Otterlake! Yes! Was just gonna say", Evan stammers,

"it was fucking Otterlake, who drained the fucking pool. But everyone's saying it were me just 'cus I was also skateboarding a little".

"... Who..." Sabrina peppers in. Her hands must be getting tired brandishing what is

"*Cameron Otterlake's* jumper, is what you got".

She's less disgusted to have been wearing something of his, it seems. "Where did *he* go"?

Now *that's* a mad cunt, there, Arthur believes seriously and Cameron's poor yank ears hate to hear. It's probably his energy alone what turned this Saturday get-together to the weeklong circus only winding down this *next* Saturday. That Arthur didn't immediately assume *Cameron* had drained the pool is entirely on him. He's done worse to Fitzturner house, and that's including when they were kids.

When a boy grows up like the Fitzturners or indeed like the Otterlakes, inevitably some of his first real friends are from some bloodline like the Fitzturners or the Otterlakes. A genuine slice of London's most luxurious flats are Otterlake-make, and to be on the hill people's good side, a lot of historic renovations are funded out of big man Nigel's pocket. In practice this meant the Otterlakes spent ages in London and needed something for little Cameron to do conveniently when the Fitzturner family needed the young Arthur busy. At a young age, Arthur's idea of fun was narrow and disgustingly wealthy—chess and sailing and cricket should they be at the country home. At hardly seven years old and Cameron eight, the latter introduced the former to the endless fun of filling a bucket with water and dunking it out the window while pedestrians on the sidewalk tried in vain to escape the downpour. Absolute gas.

Not a young soul still in or on top of this building will work a day in their lives, but Cameron Otterlake? He won't need to get out of bed. A strange feeling, at the time and even now. Growing up, Arthur was given superficial cause for envy at best. Little things, like a kid with their own yacht instead of a family yacht (Cameron), boys who knew intrinsically how to talk to girl without all those gab classes (Cameron), kids with parents who obviously love them (some immigrants on the road one time), and barring one instance which now escapes him, Arthur has to throw up a chuckle as he reckons, right now, that Cameron Otterlake has something to do with every interesting Arthur Fitzturner story. A fact which extends to the past week.

As he remembers, and one must exercise patience because he's been sweating alcohol for seventy-two hours, Cameron was one of the first twelve guests at Fitzturner House. No special occasion. Only the tremendous coincidence that so many of Arthur's good friends would be in town at roughly the same time. Riley's always around, same with Evan and Adam and the belt of mutuals between the four. And of course Cameron, making a brief stop in London before his engagement in… was it Greece? Somewhere mediterranean. An Otterlake affair. And while Arthur's never fashioned Cameron an eager family man, he'd arrived last Saturday afternoon looking uncharacteristically glum. As the two transitioned from boys to young men, Arthur had noted his American friend's increasingly drastic mood swings. But he also knew what fixed him right up, things already on the weekend's itinerary. The safe in the bedroom was stuffed with hash and Arthur had made an executive decision the previous night to have much of the rarest bottles in the Fitzturner house cellar permanently removed from public display and relocated to the stomachs of his good friends and the many stunning London girls he'd invited.

Cameron's disinterest in all Arthur's weekend plans was twofold. He was seeing a girl, for one. Olivia Achenbach. Third or fourth heiress to the Achenbach glamping dynasty and, if he may be frank, a fucking record catch. *Brings everything but the olive and pick*, as his grandfather says. She wouldn't be joining them that weekend, which is precisely why Cameron had no time for whom Arthur brought and considered England's finest (you too, Sabrina Bell). Impossible as it may seem he wasn't interested in the *hash*, either. Insanity. Cameron had introduced Arthur to hash, but he'd moved on to something else—and maybe that something had something to do with the utter mania the yank floated in on. Talking about mountains and zen and his plan to build a new house out in the wilderness of Canada or something.

Oh, he held court. Pipes were lit eons beyond schedule as Cameron talked for six hours about satellites with cameras watching him and how he'd show them all with the telescope in the observatory. That was day one.

Day two passed without an Otterlake in sight. It was only the last night of day three when Cameron reemerged in the foyer, tipping doorman Henrickson with the chain off his neck and leading a march of all the Piccadilly loiterers—only if Arthur were "cool with it", which in the moment he felt no option but to be. From that moment to day seven the population only exploded as Cameron's Pop Art party philosophy dominated the seminar. No committee on Earth could terminate his drastic renovation plans. For that matter neither could Arthur, who had been inhaling hash for days and admittedly heard nothing but capital ideas. *Yes, Cameron, the bathroom should be pink.*

Where in that rise of the bohemians did he lose his jumper, then? For that matter, when had Arthur seen him last? Seems impossible he'd already left. When Cameron leaves he makes sure to leave with a hug. A vice grip like he may march off and die.

"You know..." Arthur swaggers in and snatches the jumper from Sabrina's lap, "I think I may know where he went".

"You don't reckon he got the games running in Piccadilly"?

"I don't reckon he went and did what"?

"We were talking about it in the pool", Evan says. "Which he drained—putting it out there one more time. Anyway. He was telling me about when he was thirteen or fourteen and paid something like a quarter million dollars to commandeer one of the screens in Times Square so he could play video games. Said he wanted to do the same thing when we were out smoking in Piccadilly".

"When was this, then"?

"Tuesday"?

"Pardon me". Arthur excuses himself from the roof, stopping at the hatch and shaking the wool in his fist. "I'll get this back to him".

He hadn't lied, before. The library does contain a false column that, when turned, opens the underground tunnels. Enough people know that already it's a section in the Fitzturner House BBC special from 2004. What that special won't show you is where every chamber leads. Critically, the section lacking the red carpet and LED lights.

First is a horrifying plummet of black iron stairs. Really it's not so bad once one gets a rhythm for the steps, and some may say the total darkness beginning thirteen steps or so beyond the feet makes the trip feel shorter than its genuine one-hundred metres, but even as a man grown Arthur finds himself skipping steps to get this over with.

At the bottom is something more closely resembling the Paris catacombs than proper British rat middens (carpeted floors, don't forget). Dank by design, the correct sequence of chambers is left, left, right, right, left, right, right. If that's too hard, every incorrect path stops dead, so all one would have to do, really, is drag a hand along the wall until they inevitably find the door. Yes Arthur's had to do this.

*Closed awaiting refurbishment?* That's enough to dissuade the luckiest of tourists, but the main Fitzturner bloodline knows better. Guided by the torch on his phone, Arthur slips underneath the yellow chain and friendly sign, descending past the lovely, homely tunnels and into the dank origins of the word. His shoes will need some extra care now, stomping in the puddles. That on top of the pink stuff, which momentarily submerging in the deepest puddle does not sort out. This chimney terrified him when he was younger. If he recalls, his father had to pick him up and carry him through. Staying behind was not an option as much as he whined to make it so. He was heir to the family fortune, and as such, even when he was six going on seven, his audience with The Dukes was mandatory by something greater than flesh and consciousness.

Or something. Really The Dukes to him is another one of Dad's social clubs with unnecessary pageantry. Even now, as a man. Clean the fucking tunnels, you prudes.

The inconspicuous, bricked-off ending is false. As in, the fact that it is an ending at all is false. The bricks are genuine and, if Arthur recalls his family history, recycled from an abandoned fort erected haphazardly by working-class Englishmen during the famous Mortarboard Uprising of 1662. A superfluous detail? Hardly. To gain entry to The Dukes, one must know the origin of the brick they rap their knuckle upon. Only to the tune of the Mortarboard Army's classic four note mnemonic, a bastardization hummed by rebels atop the barricade, must a visitor knock. *BANG BABANG BANG BANG.* Keep in mind the knock is time signature sensitive.

Coming apart in the shape of a fabric swatch, with frayed edges and a cough of dust shaken loose, the wall recedes into itself, brick growling against brick and sliding true along an equally ancient track. Arthur understands historical structure but can't imagine the men who built The Dukes all those centuries ago would object to WD-40.

Standing perpendicular to and obstructed by his door, doorman Astoria (no relation to doorman Henrickson) scares Arthur to goose pimples with a fast attack, "*Quid est Deus homini*".

"Has Cameron Otterlake been through, David"?

"*Quid es Deus Homini…*"

Groaning, Arthur replies, "*Maximum creationis*".

"Welcome, young master", doorman Astoria bows.

"Did Cameron Otterlake visit"? Arthur has to ask again. Anything before the greeting of The Dukes basically didn't happen.

"I cannot tell you while the door remains open, I'm afraid. Though you're free to peruse the autograph book—*after* signing for *yourself*, naturally".

Quite *unnaturally*, though, for full-blooded Dukes of Arthur's generation. Signing in isn't his problem. His problem has a lot in common with every other problem down here—the bloody pageantry. Once he's made his way down the *Hall Closest To Heaven*—a cinema lobby tattooed wall to wall in some stupid old paintings regular people think the Nazis destroyed—oh, but only *after* bowing to doorman Astoria with the Dukes posture (left hand held out, palm facing up, right hand behind the back, right leg forward left leg back head tilted up to look your man in the eye *ugh*) Arthur has to pivot left and walk up a shallow set of stairs upholstered in ceremonial coats from old kings and enter an even older pulpit that smells that way only terribly asthmatic old wood smells and muscle open a book thicker than the first draft Bible and wider than his bed (why can't they leave it fucking open?! Christ) and paw through the King Jameses and Archduke Ferdinands and

Winston Churchills and Walt Disneys until he sees the next available page, where he's to print his name AND sign and write the fucking Duke's Greeting AGAIN. All of this just to go inside or, in this case, check for Cameron Otterlake's name which, thank fuck, is right there at the top of the opposite page.

To answer the obvious question, yes, somehow they know when a guest hasn't signed the book. Arthur's been disciplined for neglecting Dukes traditions thrice; a paddle to the arse, which the paddle-ee must then print their name upon and sign directly below.

To some relief, Arthur has now the skeleton of a timeline. Cameron Otterlake's signature was on yesterday's page. So while he hasn't personally seen Cameron since Wednesday, he knows Cameron was in London as recently as afternoon of the day previous. And who knows; The Dukes provides lodging for its guests. Personally Arthur would rather take the paddle than sleep a hundred metres below Guildhall but Cameron's famous for his ability to conk out as well as his shockingly un-Otterlake standards of living. That last day Arthur spoke with him? The adjacent heir hadn't switched his knickers for a week, citing his favorite pair.

Initiation into the Dukes has three exclusive determinations. The first is the easiest, both to do and guess: blood affiliation. The male descendent of a father already among the Dukes whitelist will be granted membership the moment he is born. Every Bar Mitzvah Arthur attended growing up happened in the Dukes Temple, as did every baptism including his own. He would compare the responsibilities to something like inheriting a timeshare. A load of redundant, humiliating rituals too many people expect from him to reasonably turn down. Oh, and paying fines he wasn't aware one could demand from their fellow man. He had to tip doorman Astoria with a gold coin, the one tradition he thinks the Dukes may agree is silly because there's a basket of gold coins just outside the bricks beyond doorman Astoria's sight.

The second initiation is by income/influence. Men of arbitrary but always eye-watering means may expect a bizarre invitation among his HMRC notices and divorce papers which, if they read Latin, means he's welcome to join the Dukes at their biannual dinner and begin his full initiation to the chapterhouse. A majority of new members will self-nominate by these means (less will be accepted) but one must imagine this type of man is whom the Dukes strive for. Self-made. No man is an island but he is entitled to one or two by commemoration of his grabbing the reigns of destiny. One may imagine the older members would carry some unspoken bias against new blood but Arthur has it on strong evidence they cannot get enough.

Influence is trickier but may compensate for lack of funds. There are fewer billionaire authors and poets and artists than there are billionaire chemical CEOs and hedge fund managers, but the latter aren't gonna pop portraits on the walls. Less common but with precedent are significant if not wealthy men who may be invited all the same. Less common still is those invitees turning it down. Those creative types love their access.

Finally, direct nomination. After ten years of membership (bit of an oversight because technically Arthur could have been making nominations as a boy) any current Duke may nominate their own candidate for consideration. Historically this is the rarest case for membership, foregoing both independent wealth and accomplishments. All the nominee would have to have done in their life is be friends with a current member, which in this upcoming generation could be anybody. A recent nominee, nineteen years of age, was immediately rejected for life after vlogging inside the chapterhouse. Before anyone goes making foundless accusations, no, he was not Arthur's nomination. Parallel with founded accusations, yes, he was Riley's.

Departing the *Hall Closest To Heaven* is the central chamber of the Dukes, packing its own unnecessary signature—*The Ark of Man.* Objectively The Dukes has a lot in common architecturally with the Guildhall it rests beneath, only buried deep underground and sniffing its own musk so severely even the Freemasons would tell them to let off. Not that anyone so fortunate to wear the Dukes ring would have any more use of those bingo halls.

Take Tobias Hubbard, here, wandering *The Ark of Man* like he likes to do, collecting freshly arrived members and showing off his impeccable Duke's Greeting. He's turned his ring inward so the open palm denotes membership where the stupid bow may not.

"*Quid es Deus Homini…*"

"*Maximum creationis*".

"Your bow could stand to be deeper, young master".

"Noted", Arthur pretends to note. "I noticed Cameron Otterlake's been through. Is he still down here"?

"Indeed".

"Where is he, then"?

"To say, indeed, he had recently blessed us with his audience. It is my understanding he has now taken leave".

*Enough with the taken leave shit*, Arthur would love to say. Tobias Hubbard's tongue is writing checks his man bun and trainers can't cash. Funny because Arthur seems to recall an uncanny Cameron Otterlake-type *called* Tobias Hubbard, downright prodigious in his ability to piss away the Hubbard's pharmaceutical investments. Then his family became Dukes and, presumably, all that youthful disregard was spanked out of him.

Exchanging the bow, Arthur can't help but feel a twinge of concern for the way he and his four-year senior mirror one another. If the day comes he's wearing his ring, let alone turning the fucking toy palmside, skip the paddle and just put a bullet in his head, thank you.

"He didn't say where he was off to, then"?

"Quite unfortunate is it, that he and I did not speak during his visit. That said it is my understanding his first cousin once removed is still present, though I cannot say where precisely".

Fuck him dead, this guy. What was that, *quite unfortunate is it?* As Arthur recalls, Tobias Hubbard was deported from the Bahamas for trying to smuggle in enough smack to personally reseed the opium trade, what, one year ago? Christ, what did they do to you, lad? Almost sad.

"I'll go speak with him. What's his name"?

"Eugene Otterlake, first cousin to patriarch Nigel Otterlake. You best hurry because I believe he also arrived looking for Nigel's only son".

Something to the way he enunciates *Nigel's Only Son.* Gives Arthur the jitters. He ties Cameron's jumper about his waist and hurries past Tobias Hubbard, between the many tapestries and portraits handing about the walls of *The Ark of Man*, making sure (though under protest) to rub the foot on Old Anthropologie's bronze likeness. Another tradition and another paddling should that foot go unrubbed. Nearly bone white by this stage.

A much-needed respite from the empty freakshows preceding, *The Jolly Tenement* is populated and electric. A banquet hall catered by some of the finest and most retired chefs from all over western Europe and one bloke from Japan also, *The Jolly Tenement* feeds for free and in total fairness bangs. Top shelf wine and spirits, as well—some of them so old they exceed Arthur's estimates of when whisky had been invented. No wonder the overwhelming majority prefer to do the chinwag here instead of *The Gumption Zone* or *The Gash Penthouse.*

His nerves are soothed by the rumble of human speech. Tablesful of old men with older money, dressed nice because they haven't got anything poor, arriving from one of a half dozen other means of Dukes entry—the elevator in Guildhall, the other elevator in Westminster, 10 Downing Street (in theory), Tower Bridge. Apparently the next passage will be beneath The Shard and, lads, Arthur thinks all these hundred-meter dives are getting absurd.

You'll soon disturb the load-bearing dirt beneath one of the four tourist traps.

Buckingham Palace was not omitted from this brief list of entry points. The Dukes do not permit nor count royalty among their ranks, for every man is a king. However that goes in Latin.

"*Is that Chester's boy*"?

*You really, seriously don't have to ask me, Gordon*, Arthur thinks really hard for hope Gordon somehow hears it. *I'm his only son and you're addressing me anyway.* "Fuck's sake". That one slips out.

"Ah", Sir Gordon Lightfoot of Leeds smiles warmly, genuinely, rising and waddling over from his table but refusing to leave his glass. An old Sherry, a smell who invites itself in without asking. "You young men, your uncompromising youth. Where's that terrible father of yours wot dragged you down here again"?

"Came here in my own, actually".

"Ah! I hear they're carving a new Oar for what you did to Fitzturner House", Sir Gordon Lightfoot laughs and slaps Arthur's back. Oar is what the old people call the paddle. "I'm only joking you, lad—let boys make their mistakes".

"I am looking for someone, actually", Arthur says.

"I could have sworn your father had visited ou"—

"Eugene Otterlake".

His face falls. Obviously anyone who wants to speak with an Otterlake better have some business. But Arthur didn't think it was as big a deal as it now seems to be. He's only the brother, for Christ's sake. In an unbecoming lock and preceded by a mouthwatering of Sherry, Sir Gordon Lightfoot pulls him in close, asking, and it really sounds rhetorical, "do you think just any man worthy of being up *here* can venture down *there*"?

"What are you talking about"?

"I am telling you, lad, that the Otterlake men are at present *unavailable*".

"Uh-huh. And where is he off being unavailable"?

His uncompromising youth isn't cute anymore. All said the Fitzturners outrank the Lightfoots (Lightfeet?), and Arthur gets the suspicion this does in fact bother Gordon here. Knighthood hasn't changed the pecking order. "All due respect to the Fitzturners, but might I ask why you of all your generation need to speak"—

"Cameron left this jumper here at my place".

"Password, good man".

"There ain't one".

Doorman Caine nods in a painful looking shock and spins from an old (what isn't, down here) single speakeasy door which must be muscled forward and pulled aside. Years ago Arthur's father showed him all over this proud social club, up to and including rituals a very young Arthur was probably not yet qualified to know or remember years down the line. There are no passwords at The Dukes, because independently wealthy and/or influential men from the enterprising to the tenured have no secrets. Least of which with one another. Or something. Maybe someone a hundred years ago couldn't be fucked to remember the names of boring operas.

Before he's allowed to move on, doorman Caine produces a matte white domino mask from his suit jacket and takes the liberty of snapping it over Arthur's head. Whatever.

The door opens to a thin hall, critically uncluttered by paintings or decorative curtains. His only light is what wanders inside from the ricocheting marble stairs he'd descended from the library (*His Memory's Grand Keeper*, is what they insist on calling the fucking library for fuck's sake). On his left, midway down, is a wide redwood desk on thin legs, glowing with varnish and adorned with only another autograph book. Rather than be wrong and take another paddle, Arthur throws the book open to his first best guess where the empty page may be, finding he needs to flip to a more recent section. Flip, flip, flip, two pages, nineteen pages, floppy chunk over floppy chunk, until he gives up and checks the very first page. In spite of a copyright page dated 1778, the autograph book is empty.

He hasn't got a pen anyway.

Here's another bit of formative savvy from those father-son tours: a Duke opens double doors with both hands, neither asking permission nor announcing his presence at any time before its apex. He invites himself as he does for all life's necessities and pleasures. Again, and Arthur cannot stress this enough, *or something.*

The mask is already agitating the foundations of a pimple somewhere under his cheekbone. Worst of all is he doesn't believe there will be time for adjustment any time soon. He's just happened upon those annals of The Dukes his father had very intentionally left out of the grandiose spiels.

A ballroom. Three layers, a large open floor, a currently unused and curtained off stage, and two wrapping mezzanines painted in dark varnish, carved with flowers and swords and filled to the shallow ceilings with masked men. An earthy, botanical smoke stretches through the negative space, around the lighting rig and speaker system suspended from the marble roof. Dress varies, in a narrow sense, from man to man. Suits of earthtone and blackwork, shirts buttoned up to the neck, sometimes beneath stranglingly tight vests. Only when Arthur arrives at the crush does he notice their shoes have been removed, placed in wood cubbies along the south wall. Remaining consistent among every man is the white domino mask, though some carry quite explicitly a personal mileage Arthur's does not.

Without shoes, most of them still stand over Arthur's head, and he cannot see to the center of the ballroom to whatever has their incognito attention. To say their *attempt* at incognito, because Arthur peeks to the second mezzanine and almost instantly clocks John Patrick Rainow, first runner up for Prime Minster at the last election. His chin has been the subject of figureless online ridicule. Next time spring for the full mask, hm?

Politicians interest Arthur less than his family would like. He'd already shook that man's hand, John Patrick Rainow, at a charity gala last year. Not as a supporter; in truth he's never been fired up to vote even when the right illuded him. Also, and this is critical: Arthur's not so hot on where that hand he'd shaken appears to be now.

*Fuck this*, he thinks, muscling his way through the sea of black shoulders. *I have the mask, I have the surname, I have just as much a right to see the hot ticket as any wound-up bloke brushing off his lost-election frustrations.* In doing this he steps on more than one toe, postponing his seizure of life's necessities and pleasures to go remove his shoes. *The ones with the pink, yes, thank you.*

Back to cutting through the jungle. Packed in like sardines down here. Unideal if it's alright to just have yourself a wank, as it seems frightfully alright to be. This better be good.

Maybe a waltz' worth of space has been surrendered to a thin purple rug circling the square of the ballroom's floor. At its center stands two cloaked sticks whom, going off the brushed ring they've made with their feet, have been dancing the dullest dance in vintage Hawaiian time. It'd be something cousin to frightening had he not seen a failed Prime Minister a moment ago, and had he not noticed the current vice president of Tesco standing under the first mezzanine. Truly how could either man hold horrible secrets any worse than…

At the click of an unseen church organ, the cloaks hit the floor in weak circles. Here was, to Arthur at least, the most uncommon sight in any nauseatingly pretentious room in The Dukes—women. Nude, but, not impressively so, all due respect. Why all the walking, why the swinging thurible, why the masks, why do the women also have masks, why the organ stings. In fact, consolidate this all down to why everything and leave *why are the women snogging* hanging off the end.

So this is the appeal. The darkness merely a perverted hand-me-down from the Dukes who began this bonding ritual centuries ago, standing in this very ballroom, passing their shoes to those very cubbies along the south wall. These are the dank corners of the club protected by oral barricades. Where the indulgences of man break through the membrane of public decency and splash down to the unlit gutters of sin. All the while, audience to locked lips and glimmering, skating flesh, the next generation of Dukes finds himself without words, senses clogged by cigarillo smoke and incense, naught but the seed of introspection budding in his mind.

"Is that really it, then"?

Sir Malcolm Edwards Swinburne II—another knighted Duke if it can be believed or even parsed—is the only circumference of a face Arthur recognises since departing the ballroom and exploring the bowels of what he now knows to be called the *Devil's Tenement Hall.* Licensious. Someone call the police.

"Just you wait until proceedings move to the…" Sir Malcolm Edwards Swinburne II leans in while hunting for the most devilish adjective. "*Intimate* spaces, good man".

Oh, yes, and he's acting as if him and Arthur hadn't been introduced to one another three months ago at the Fitzturner invitational feast. What Arthur would *give* to forget some of these mickies, believe him. If not for eighteen straight years of boarding school and portrait sessions and tagging along with his family to all these handshake parties (not literally this of course) has instilled in him an impeccable yet personally undesired memory of faces and names. Were everything his way, instead of only most everything, he'd like to live like Cameron Otterlake. Speaking of,

"I'm here looking for Cameron Otterlake. Have you seen him"?

"Oh, *pssh*, good sir", Sir Malcolm Edwards Swinburne II feigns a lot of shock and offence, "I'm certain you don't need reminding of the discretion policy, where it concerns the *Devil's Tenement Hall*. Even if I did know who you were talking about—" (he does) "—or if I knew who you were—" (he does) "—it would be a gross violation of this venue's trust to disclose that knowledge here. *Even* among friends".

Whatever. "Whatever. I'll look for myself".

Beyond the epicenter of "action" is a mirrored length of short half-length halls broken up by sitting rooms. Fun-sized approximations of the ballroom in themselves, the day's itinerary slowly shifts to small pockets of entertainment for limited audiences. In fairness this does seem the sort of attraction Cameron would call "*wild*," or "*sick*," or "*holy shit like wow man like they're really going at like that damn.*" As in, if he turned up anywhere and neglected to leave, it's here.

If he has this right, the Devil's Tenement Hall is working on a no-touch policy. That, or the Dukes are decisively *not* seizing all life's necessities and pleasures. Clammy fucks. At this first stop, scanning the room for a recognizable jawline in the circle, trying to be gentlemanly and not watch the girls on the table kiss (with tongue; oh stop this before someone *dies*) he doesn't see Cameron. Rats. Just the Oplyxocon Chemicals guy and probably Jeff Bezos.

Two rooms down he asks Dennis Rodman if he's seen Cameron anywhere, since those two party sometimes, but he hadn't. Both of them forgot the anonymity thing while talking and only remember when the interaction is long concluded. Pete Davidson hadn't seen him either.

After four failed scans Arthur's found himself at the corner, where rather than continue straight through, the hall to the next lady kissing room is to his immediate left. He's the first to arrive, and the female entertainment duo hasn't bothered to get started until more people showed up. Evidently one still isn't enough.

"Is that Judy"? Arthur blurts.

But he's correct. Judy, just as surprised to see a familiar face as he, rolls over on the table and lifts her mask. "Is that Fitzturner"?

They laugh extra hard to dilute the atmosphere of all this. She's pretty naked there which, granted, isn't new in the presence of Arthur. The problem is only the circumstance, but otherwise they get to talking. Her dance partner lying beside scrolls her phone, her venetian mask pulled up on her forehead.

"Haven't seen you since Thursday," Judy says. "What've you been up to"?

"Me? When the fuck did you get down here"?

"Thursday. I just said".

"Why? Like, how? Is this your job, then"?

"I dunno, *what's your job*"? she returns, pithy and sarcastic.

"… Can I ask what this pays"?

"Less than being Chester Fitzturner's son, more than holding the door at Burberry".

Right. That's how they know one another. "I just… didn't know women were allowed in The Dukes. Even like this".

"And what the fuck do you nonces get up to if we aren't"?

"Judy, I'm not certain what we're getting up to now that you are. Is this like…" sputtering out, Arthur gives up and drops the question. "Has Cameron Otterlake been through"?

"Your mate with the jewelry"?

"Him, yes".

"Hmm…" Judy drops her head on the table and looks at the ceiling. "I thought maybe I did. It's why I figured you were down sooner—you'd be with him. But *narr*, I think he might've come through on his own".

"So you've seen him"?

"I'll cautiously say I spotted him for a moment. Strolled through. Looked like his mind were on other things. I didn't call for him—*we aren't supposed to speak*".

Her friend hover her phone over Judy's face, laughing from the back of her throat. "Man's getting smashed by a car, lookit this".

They have a laugh. They play it again.

"Did he go this way"? Arthur points, crossing the room to the leftmost chamber.

"With another *man*", Judy's friend pipes up, sounding neither like the son of Chester Otterlake nor one who holds the door at Burberry. Sounds more like a Beatle. "I seen him too. Talked about popping down to *The Mortar*".

"*The Mortar*"?

"Just figured you'd know what it is. Fuck if I do. But that's what they said".

"Folks coming", Judy pulls down her mask over her eyes. "Get moving or you'll take the paddle, Fitzturner. Down here *we're* the ones handing 'em out".

"I'm headed down to The Mortar", Arthur does declare to the doorman of unconfirmed identity.

"Return your mask", he beckons with two hands, placed together palms up. Another goodie-goodie who turns his ring inward. Can't believe no one's called Arthur out on forgetting his.

Context clues acknowledged, Arthur removed his mask with two hands and makes the transfer with the same two. The doorman begins, "A Duke uses both hands"—

"Take life's cashes and gashes, yes. I'm in a hurry, please".

Did that just work? How did that just work?

This single door opens to hardly a broom closet's worth of door-sized hallway. At the end (to be nice and say it's long enough for an end) is a set of brass elevator doors. In place of buttons is an ancient-looking switched polished white by centuries of use. If elevators are that old. Scratch that, actually; the dirty plaque nailed above dubs thee *His Dumbwaiter Servicing Gracious Perdition*. Christ.

An elevator car lit by four candles in respective corners and exposed to the unpolished rock by grated walls, operated only from the outside by that same doorman, cracks shut and slowly, slowly, slowly, snails down its pitch-black chamber. Atmospheric were Arthur not fed up with all this horseshit two hidden chambers ago. He rocks back and forth on his heels realizing he forgot to grab his shoes, discovering a level of impatience heretofore uncharted.

*What is eating Cameron Otterlake*, he has the isolation to wonder. Genuinely. A strange case, but that's his mate. In all honesty sometimes he worries. All Cameron's ranting over the constant monitoring from his family and obligations he'd rather set on fire. This isn't the first time he arrived in mania and vanished in the whirl of something stronger, orchestrated by his unfortunate paranoias. When they were kids, Arthur remembers, Cameron refused eating with a fork. Not since jamming a piece of veal in his mouth and lacing out a labouring baby tooth. Then on he'd take pasta with a spoon before developing the hand dexterity for chopsticks. Only in the company of adults, then again. In their privacy, Cameron ate with his hands.

Cameron's neuroses developed alongside them. To this day he refuses to drive European roads. He won't fly on a plane with more than seven bodies including crew. He hates when people yawn and those who know him best know to duck into their laps should biology call. He hasn't worn a pair of socks more than once since he was ten. And how much of this has to do with the unnatural means by which he was brought up in this world, how much of this is a freak mutation of post trauma considering what happened with his birth mother, how much of this is what makes Cameron his own star in the sky, Arthur won't say. He's hoping, as the lift tenses to a stop, he can ask the man himself.

He's reminded of the Fitzturner family tomb. The shallow brick arches laid by men whose great-great-great-great-great grandchildren are dead. Somehow this far down cobwebs neglect to materialise. Lit by candle still, Arthur pounds the only pavement available to him, undoing Cameron's jumper from around his waist and holding it aloft in his hand.

Down at the very end, past what reads to his feet as a kilometer of the same repeating chunk of stone brick and candlesticks, is a constellation of TV screens. Analog, boxy, old in proportion with this deepest chimney of The Dukes they service. Thirteen tall and twenty-six wide, the screens each occupy themselves with their own security camera footage—shaky, diffused approximations of their point of capture. For many, nothing is going on. Some shift perspectives for every twist of the subject's foot. Two men take the two leather armchairs in front, neither sharing Cameron's hair colour. Fuck. Just some more Dukes blokes.

"*essfffaaahhhsssshett*", one of them is saying and Arthur can't put words to from where he's standing. Should he announce himself? The lift rang no bell heralding his arrival. The stone bricks deny his feet a characteristic tap-tap coming down the way. For the present moment, he thinks, he'll observe.

"*... asked about you, by the way.*"

"Uh-huh? What for?"

"A professional congratulations, that's all. On the Joshua Tree project."

"Ah. Well, can I thank him in person, or..."

"Nigel's busy. You know that. Have you two never met?"

"I spoke with someone on the phone before the, uh, the Tahoe project. He was in the room with the person I was talking to, I mean. I wanted to call him, actually, when I heard that nasty rumor. Y'know what I mean."

"He's not dead, Nigel Otterlake is just a private man who would rather not be disturbed."

"Oh, oh, I know. I'm aware. Never believed it, y'know, it's just. Tabloid shit. Forget it. Just at the time I figured I'd call and confirm—"

"We would call you."

Something to that assertiveness. Otterlakes talk like that. Not all of them, but only them. Eugene Otterlake, on the right. Cousin to the Patriarch, first officer, et cetera.

"Of course," the non-Otterlake says. "I'm gonna check on Agatha."

He's a yank, this stuttery non-Otterlake. Where it concerns poise and dignity this is where the commonalities between the two men stop. The number of times he's shifted in his seat *alone*. He tells someone out of Arthur's sight to switch a screen, or maybe no one in particular, to direct some of *The Mortar*'s attention to Agatha Louise Achenbach. No one in particular does him one better and gives him six screens: a bedroom, a kitchen, the dashboard of a car, a washroom, the exterior of a New England townhouse as captured from the road, and a top-down satellite. Agatha is in the kitchen, on the phone.

Good use of the terrifying incorporeal surveillance grid, lads. Well done.

This is *The Mortar*, though its particulars are unknown to Arthur. His hunch is right on, however. In centuries past *The Mortar* made clumsy use of verbal telephone, in days predating even the telegram or global post. Even in these days of antique inefficiency, The Mortar could win wars. That is if The Dukes believed in doing so. There is policy—more of a Gentleman's Agreement—on using *The Mortar* for interfering or eavesdropping on sovereign nations. Their Latin greeting puts men above god but does not grant them the same false power. Well, that, and the fact warbucks got many of its proudest members the ring and the bow—frankly it would be in their better interest to *start* issues.

Its popular function is for monitoring the often-cantankerous families orbiting its members significant worth. In this instance the lesser yank looks to be just trying it out. Agatha Louise Achenbach isn't doing anything. At worst, at the highest peak of pedantic criticism, she's shoveling a lot of dip on her chips. Too much. Gluttenous amounts of dip. Hardly worth the spy camera treatment.

The yank seems to agree. "That's enough, thank you," he tells no one. The monitors switch to unrelated, live footage.

"You're worried about her?" Eugene Otterlake makes conversation in that tense, testing sort of way Cameron's adult family does.

"… It's her second marriage, that's all. Next week. She ate herself sick before the first."

"Does Olivia have the same problem?"

"You tell me."

"Funny."

"No, I meant it, actually."

No one in particular takes the initiative. Five screens flicker to, in order, a car park, a shimmering white staircase, a different staircase of the same make and polish, a bedroom, and a living room the size of a car park in itself, where a girl sits crisscrossed on the couch and swipes a finger across the tablet in her lap. The Achenbach daughters don't get up to a whole lot in their lonely.

"... You don't..." he makes a face, nauseous at how quickly these cameras find his daughters. "You don't look at these all the time, do you?"

"Most Dukes are only concerned with their own families," Eugene answers.

"Most?"

"In some cases, other Dukes' families *become* our concern. Yours, for instance."

"I never got to thank Nigel for this, either."

"You never could."

The yank lets it dissolve. He says, "the Raiders game," maybe just to try, and twelve monitors unite their power to show him the Raiders miss a field goal so severely the kicker must be trying to take a fan's head off. "Wish I didn't ask," he laughs off.

Eugene sits up in his chair, elbows on knees. His suit jacket's folded up on his shoulders. "Arthur Leopold Fitzturner."

Arthur's blood goes cold as the same twelve monitors scurry to separate rooms of Fitzturner house: the first floor foyer with reliable doorman Henrickson standing at attention, the stairwell with the ripped-down curtain draped over the steps, the second floor gym, the billiards hall, the drained pool, the newly christened standing room, further up the stairwell with the punched-in portrait, the scuffed up third floor hall, the washroom with a sleeping Riley inside the dry tub, Arthur's locked-up bedroom, the roof, and the deepest chamber of The Dukes, the short tomb right before The Mortar, the back of Arthur's head.

Eugene Otterlake and his yank friends turn around in their seats, staring back at him.

"... I got Cameron's jumper, here", Arthur says.

"Don't be a stranger," Eugene Otterlake demands, returning back to the sensory overload. "You're a Fitzturner. You're a Duke."

Arthur moves ahead to *The Mortar* proper. There's no third chair for him, only what turns out to be even more monitors against the pockets of wall he couldn't see. Snapshots of Westminster, gilded age mansions off central park, rooftop palaces on Riyadh and tennis courts in Mumbai. And a few others Arthur can't recognise but, for completionism's sake, include Sao Paolo and the church of Scientology and the Chinese embassy of Toronto and Steven Seagal's house.

He hovers the suffocating perimeter made by Eugene Otterlake and, impedingly beknownst to him, the very lucky Joseph Achenbach. Success is when preparation meets opportunity or, as it happened with Joseph, when managing a small jet ski rental depot on Lake Tahoe meets a multibillion-dollar heir who thinks your third daughter is hot. One of life's comic intersections. What irony, their children growing sweet on each other weeks before Nigel Otterlake himself put money down on Godel founding WaterNife, invested a couple ten million in the dealerships, and sold the latter a number of lakefront properties for a very flippable steal. Salient questions were asked by the resulting Forbes cover story on meek to millionaire Joseph Achenbach—how did he do it?

"Cameron left two days ago," Eugene says plainly, unprompted. Arthur had still been focused on all the screens and could've sworn one, which he's lost, was rebounding the live feed inside the White House.

"Left London"?

"Left the hemisphere."

"Oh. He didn't say where he was going, di"—

"Look around you and tell me if it would make a difference whether he said." This is not the first time Cameron Otterlake made himself scarce to his inner circle and all orbiting bodies therein. It's just that before at least one other surname of his showed some semblance or worry. "We've checked his progress. And if only due to the facts you're a Fitzturner and valuable as his close friend, you're entitled to knowing."

"… Alright"? He was waiting, but Eugene stopped dead.

"I won't ask a Fitzturner if he would *like* to know because he and anyone else who deserves to be here would tell me."

"Tell me where he's been, then", Arthur says. *Fucking hell, cunt*, he leaves in his head.

"Cameron Otterlake's presence was requested at The Dukes early Wednesday morning, the invitation relayed by your doorman. We mean no offense to patriarch Achenbach but we felt it necessary to introduce Cameron to a more obviously worthy suitor. Rather than leave the option untested. That's all."

Eugene waits for Joseph Achenbach to speak his mind regarding this, who throws up a perplexed five fingers and shakes his head, finally settling on "*none taken*?"

"It was a mistake to let the two alone in The Dukes, in hindsight. Cameron, and a suiter who will go unnamed so we can avoid the knock-on issue of Daughter Envy, found their way to *The Mortar*, here, and it can be surmised exposure to the surveillance grid triggered another one of Cameron's meltdowns.

"At approximately ten forty-six pm, Wednesday, Cameron made three calls to Olivia Achenbach—two returned, one to a United Kingdom volunteer-based crisis hotline—returned, and one to his father—unreturned. His personal jet was scheduled to take off, with him, for Monaco to rendezvous with his current mother and be photographed, in person, at the Otterlake-sponsored *Parata.* Scheduled takeoff was anticipated to be late considering his phone calls and rescheduled in preparation. Cameron boarded at 12:14am, Thursday. Late but within flight estimations. Every flight itinerary issued to his crew is scheduled for takeoff two hours earlier than otherwise to accommodate for Cameron's mood swings, which I hope won't be news to you.

"Thirty-three minutes after takeoff, before his jet had reached cruising altitude, Cameron entered the cockpit, unauthorized, and demanded the pilot and copilot instead divert course to America under threat of termination. It's been convenient in the past for Cameron to believe he has the power to do this. The pilots radio the Dukes European flight tower, who relay the situation to The Dukes, which I received under the callsign Merchant. We approves the diversion and Cameron is left to believe he's defied orders. Which is true to a negligible fraction.

"A skip across the pond and a refueling in Boston later, Cameron's jet lands at the Otterlake family airstrip outside of Malibu, California. *Harriot, Otterlake residence:*"

The Mortar complies, dealing five camera feeds of a bizarre, glitched piece of southern California architecture. A patio swimming pool just beyond a large set of windows and a busted open door mummified in police tape, a stairwell, a pink iron spiral staircase, a comically gigantic couch, a kitchen with rotten fruit on the island, and a top floor bedroom adorned with a massive pizza-shaped skylight, slices and all. Lest the infestation of chinchillas go ignored, they occupy every frame.

"He arrived Thursday afternoon where, with it being an Otterlake residence, he could be more easily monitored rather than rely on the three sometimes unreliable cameras within his jet. Text messages exchanged between Olivia Achenbach and him suggest an unannounced plan to take her with him as he attempted to run away from familial responsibilities. She's been at the Achenbach compound in Aspen for seventeen days and her behavior in that time suggested no plan to join him—I mention this for Joseph Achenbach's sake."

"Thanks."

"Early Friday morning, Harriot suffered a break-in. The perpetrator stole money from a planted safe filled with marked foreign currency. Useless to him long enough to locate and alert authorities. But the important moment here is his motivation that Cameron attempt his most ambitious skating of Otterlake duties. The Otterlake satellite hedge fund with interests in housing acquisitions will invertedly discipline the perpetrator by acquiring the apartment block where he currently lives and increase his rent. But I digress.

"His first stop was to our primary deferred scapegoat. A sixteen-year-old boy operating out of Marshfield, Wisconsin, rebels via the insignificant means of monitoring some Dukes private jet routes. He poses a nonexistent threat to our security and makes for an easy target in the event Cameron's neuroses about constant monitoring needed to be 'eliminated,' as far as he knew. Sometime after he had deboarded, satellite reception to his jet was lost, though this was reported as a system failure rather than tampering. It's unlikely Cameron would know how to disable the antenna even if he wanted to. The Otterlake family's security splinter cell was dispatched to Marshfield, to wait until he returned so he may be forced back to a more manageable location to wait out his most recent episode. Another mistake. *Marshfield, Wisconsin, ten pm last night*."

In a chorus of hums, a four-square of monitors elaborates with the exterior of an unimpressive suburban home, a bottom-level bedroom lit by the three workstation computer monitors, the exterior of an unimpressive greasy spoon roadhouse, and shaky footage of an unimpressive teenage boy sitting across from a gorging Cameron Otterlake. The boy, somehow, clocks this camera and nudges his head to the feed's direction. Cameron looks.

"How he knew about our field cameras we're still working out," Eugene says. "Regardless, Cameron takes this kid's motorcycle to the interstate. Last sighting was two hours ago. *Interstate 90, Cameron Otterlake*."

A TikTok, presented vertically on a screen with naught the resolution to express the caption. An (American) passenger side passenger records the grassy length alongside the unending road, shouting to an unwashed, unhelmeted, unrested Cameron pulling unsafe speeds on unsafe ground. On the second shout, Cameron looks over and pumps his fist.

"The Otterlake development bureau is poised for what would otherwise be an unpopular corporate merger. Cameron's public adventure, as you can see documented here, makes for a convenient distraction from his family's business deals that would otherwise face public scrutiny were their attention not diverted to him. He's been useful in same way countless times before now."

Arthur can recognise the end of the story on his own. "… So he's not really running away. Is he".

"We talked about this in private. Other Otterlakes and I responsible for his well-being and poised ascent to patriarch. We think it's best to observe rather than compound pressure. Interstate 90 will end at Seattle, Washington, where a security detail is already waiting to escort him to a more manageable position."

"Aspen," Joseph smooshes in with a raised finger.

"Colorado"? Arthur asks.

"My suggestion. Visiting with Olivia might be good for him."

So that's why this donut's here. There's two mysteries solved.

Arthur remembers the first time Cameron ran away, as far as either boy knew. They were sixteen and seventeen, operating out of the Otterlake family's second Tokyo penthouse. It's illegal to drink underage or on public roads over there and not even of the Gentleman's Agreement persuasion they'd tandem grown to know. Both boys, and whoever else were with them at the time, were very nearly arrested had senior Duke Tojo Tomoari not stepped out of that adjacent nightclub at the same time and vouched for their dismissal. The Duke's Bow looks different over there and Arthur's never bothered to learn it.

What transpired next may have been Arthur's fault. Infuriated that a policeman in a different country could have the authority to touch him, Cameron demanded the vacation be moved somewhere more remote. His good chum Arthur Fitzturner, going back many years, knew better than to offer his agreement then and there. He only meant to entertain the notion from a consensual distance. A fun fact incame; a paragraph just large enough to take his mind off the indignity. Rather than hop on that plane of his, named for a Russian tennis player who hugged him for an impromptu Wimbledon photo op and made the grave error of resting her boob on a ten-year-old's head, might he consider taking the S9 line. Japan's newly fashioned and fastest bullet train (funded largely in part by the Tomoari family; neither here nor there) would get him to the wildspace of Hokkaido (that's the big nub at the top, Cameron) faster than the Sharapova could clear for departure. This in hindsight was the most obviously wrong thing to tell Cameron Otterlake.

He was on that train in an hour. He was wandering the forest of southern Hokkaido in three. He passed out from exposure in seven and was on a crate back to the Otterlake family's third San Fransisco penthouse in nine.

At this present moment Arthur reevaluates what had happened to the two of them that night. How much of Tojo Tomoari's surprise rescue was either word. How psychotic would Arthur be to surmise Tojo's dispatch from the nightclub was to bring to mind that fun fact he'd gotten from a security escort some hours previous. In an unbiased vacuum, how much of that attempted vanishing from Cameron was his choice. How much has anything been his choice.

"Thank you for the update", Arthur says.

"Naturally," Eugene turns his head only enough to get his violently cyan eyes on Arthur. "We may need you for Cameron's recovery. Try and be available."

"Yeah".

Arthur departs *His Dumbwaiter Servicing Gracious Perdition* with the suffocating sense that he needs to get to sea level and stay there until he dies. He's spent too long a hundred metres underground and is losing ground to the sick end of his brain that prays for the ceiling to collapse.

*The Devil's Tenement Hall* lit the palatial fireplace in his absence. A few masked men sit or stand nearby, entranced, wondering where the smoke escapes, how high the chimney must stretch, fighting their own sick brainends to not squirm inside and crawl up. Arthur, still gripping Cameron's jumper, stops. He steps on the brick threshold and tosses the wool to the fire. The two embrace passionately. A fraction of Cameron goes where he can't be followed. It's the least Arthur could do for an old friend.

"*That's getting rid of old shit,*" a tall yank cackles under his tongue.

"Oh", Arthur says, eyes on the fire. "Morning, Matt. Or afternoon".

"*Doesn't matter much down here, does it?*"

"Sorry I can't stay and chat. I need to get out of here".

"*Yeah, I think I'm about to follow you out,*" Matthew McConaughey concurs, finishing his lowball in a gulp. "*Thought this place'd be cooler.*"

# (The) Archaeologian

***Conrad C. Tomas, 39***

***Vice President of the Western Amateur Treasure Hunter Society/Motorcycle Appreciation Club***

***Net Worth: $22,789***

***Alimony Payments (monthly): $565***

***Vancouver, Washington***

He brought into the meek border town of Vancouver nothing but his able body, his well-traveled motorbike, and the gruff residue from a few thousand miles of open road. The enviable man in all his grime. It was just after nine and it would be another hour or two before most of the town would wake to greet him; his favorite part of the day, and if not, second to when dawn crawls over the trees and cooks through the stiff fingers locked to the handlebars. When the cold sweat on his back comes to a stinging boil and sparks through his hair. He thought about coffee the whole way up and, while parking his TR65 just outside the once-gas-station-now-café, knew he would ride ten hours, twenty-four hours, a week, if he knew this feeling still waited at the end.

Before heading inside, he wipes down the bike. Currently named Dassin but in all honesty he's changed the name several times since buying her. The first two were women, a decision that in hindsight might be objectifying. That, and the second name turned out to be someone he knew from college. That's a level of intimacy necessitating permission he never had. As much as he'd've liked to, at the time.

*di-ding, di-ding,* goes the bell when he pressures the door open. He smiles to the clerk, nods to his fellow morning people in arms, and takes his seat at a stool upholstered long ago enough for the seams to begin failing. His shoulders roll, his hand goes through his hair. His elbows are on the counter.

"Morning," the woman says. She must be a longtime coffee jerker. Wife of the owner? Is she the owner herself, and he stills has biases to reconsider? He likes to think she's an inch taller than it seems, factoring in the Looney Tunes style hole she's paced behind the counter in her years of service.

"And a good morning to you," he smiles and removes his sunglasses.

"What can I get going for you?"

"Black coffee, please. Grits with butter and some of the hash browns that man over there's got," he fingers down his left.

The man smiles beneath his cup and laughs a "*get your own!*"

"Good idea."

"Did you just arrive?" The woman behind the counter continues (her nametag has one fastening and flops in and out of legibility, but on concentration reads Abagail).

"Hardly a minute ago."

"Going north?"

"… East, actually," he hesitates. An undue worry. He expects no competition. "Seeing the Washougal river."

"*Oh,*" Abagail swoons. "Perfect day for it. Here's that black, I'll have your food out in a minute." As she sets down and slides over the stock white mug, Abagail glances out the window, considering a scowl she aborts for more important things. He doesn't turn and look.

"Thank you."

"Beautiful bike you got there," the man to his left says, a man with no reservations turning around. "That's '83, yeah?"

"Well, '81, but she doesn't like talking about her age."

Diner humor with no contemporaries. The joke kills. "My brother had one of those," the man remembers.

"A better bike was never made," he agrees.

"Say it again so the Lord hears it." A respectful moment of silence for coffee is observed, then the man adds, "and I needed to see a good-looking bike. Isn't that right, Abbie?"

Abagail, working with her back turned, hums her concur. "A sight for sore eyes. And I don't love bikes like you two."

He laughs from the throat, if only to taste the coffee again. He has a yet to be disproven theory that coffee brews on an incorporeal bell curve. The more care offered to its creation, the better it turns out, and his mind goes to those cafes from the Paris study abroad. Conversely, the more matter-of-fact one goes about its creation, the better still it tastes, the faster still the heart peeks over the counter to get a whiff.

"Kawasakis come through or something?" He means as a joke, though it may be true where the west coast is concerned.

The man turns and sort of leans in. "Did you see—can I have your name?"

"Conrad," Conrad says.

"Did you see that hideous dirt bike parked out by the pumps? Did you see the owner?"

Conrad pulls up his brow, pulls in his lips. "No, I didn't notice."

"He came in here maybe ten minu—Abagail, you look like you wanna tell it."

Abagail does wanna tell it. "That… *space cadet*, out there. Came in here same time as Mark. Did *not* hold the door open—"

Mark concurs: "Did *not* hold the door open."

"Did *not* hold the door open. He comes in wearing that ugly… *dirty* ski mask. I say 'sir, you'll need to remove that if you're coming in here.' *Be nice once*, I say, *but only once*, I also say. He says no, I say it again, and he tells me he doesn't have to. In my own *damn* business—excuse me—but my own business."

"And the way this kid talks," Mark butts in to add. "Just the lousiest motormouthed idiot you've ever heard. Goes on and on and on, and on, you get nothing in edgewise, can't convince him."

"No respect," Abagail says. "He wants everything *but* what we make, then he wants coffee, I tell him he already knows the rules, he tells me he'll drink it outside and..." Abagail finally turns and checks, and Conrad thinks now would be an appropriate time to do the same.

They weren't lying. Not about the ski mask, or the dirty clothes, about the dirt bike nor the operative word working overtime. The boy has his back turned to the café, a saucer in one hand and an identical coffee mug in the other. He watches the horizon with stiff intensity. The mountain's out.

"Still hasn't paid," Abagail huffs.

"Bet you he won't," Mark says. "Bet you something else: kid's from Los Angeles. Son of a movie producer or a real estate shark. Those guys have more money than they could ever spend, and they don't spend a lick of time with their own kids. So they grow up to be just the biggest stuck-up idiots. Couldn't tie their own fucking shoes—sorry, Abbie."

"No, please, that's exactly right."

The three watch in silence as the saucer slips from the boy's fingers and shatters on the asphalt. He spooks himself doing it.

"... I'm calling the cops," Abagail says.

Mark slaps the table. "Feed him to Sonny." Conrad imagines Sonny is a cop whom residents of Vancouver would be familiar with by name.

"I don't want him on the *road,*" Abagail adds. "He's on *pot.*"

Conrad, merely taking this all in, always the reliable shoulder to rant on, sits up to collect the wallet from his front pocket. "I'll cover the kid's drink," he says, slapping cash down. "And the saucer."

"Honey, you don't have to do that," Abagail insists on waving hands.

"Please," Conrad insists harder. "You shouldn't have to deal with this. It's early. I'll get him out of your hair."

Did he forget his food?

Things to circle back to later. Abagail did ask him to swing by on his way back from the river, if he's going back the way he came. Should he successfully deal with this, what did she call him—*space cadet*—then his next coffee would be on the house. Very nice of her, but Conrad believes he would do this regardless of reward. Always the man to offer solutions. Sometimes the man to execute on them.

Admittedly, Conrad has never been a dirt bike guy. In all honesty he's never been enough of a country man to know for sure dirt bike guys exist. The motorbike connoisseur in him wants to put a name to the filthy thing kick-standing before him. A manufacturer, at least. But either this young man or the previous owner took the puzzling time to sand away the accoutrements, leaving only the obnoxious orange shell chipped by misuse rather than hard love. Comparing this thing to his TR65 is like comparing himself, an adult man who can recognize the interstate like one recognizes the driveway, to this untraveled, untested boy. Him and the bike deserve each other, a notion going both ways.

Still, this is a rider. Maybe even an easy one. Uncouth, but sentiment in the mod community as of recent may vouch for his terminal lack of swagger. Riders of old were not supermodels; they were not riding carefully and taking only the cleanest roads as if they were riding to pose in a Ralph Lauren catalog. Riders were liaisons; two wheels and a national highway network needed to get to know each other. If this kid just needed to ride—get away from that movie producer father, then hell. Maybe Conrad has someone to talk to. It's been a few thousand miles.

Sunglasses are back on. "How you doing, man?" Conrad begins.

"*Mm!*" the boy sputters on coffee, a sip not ready to be disturbed. Conrad's not the stealthiest man in the world. Sometimes this has been a problem but this time he wasn't trying to be. His riding boots have a way of winding back and slapping the pavement. Can't forget the leathers. With all the squeaking, his jacket and his satchel defy being forgotten. All to say this boy having any shock that Conrad is here—standing just within his periphery, even—lends some credence to Abagail's fear he's on something.

"You just get into town?" Conrad wafts some congratulatory air towards his bike. "Well-traveled number, there."

He says nothing, going back to his coffee like Conrad isn't here and never was here. The saucer splayed on the ground in three tectonic chunks goes unremarked. That Abagail even trusted this kid with a saucer is proof of her undeserved kindness and also maybe a lack of forethought.

Conrad strategizes, saying, "must have put some serious miles on this thing, to get all the way up here." He pats his breast pocket, feeling a crushed pack of cigarettes he was supposed to throw out. He quit three months ago. "Welcome to Washington."

"It's *cold*."

A little short, but it's something to work with. "Sure, but it's not a bad cold. Now, *me*, I love the bite up north. Did you catch the sun this morning?"

"Man like I'd be warm if PEOPLE WOULD LET ME INSIDE," the boy shouts.

"… Yeah, they were a little short with me, too," Conrad agrees. To keep it a crisp buck, yes, he's lying. A rude removal of his interaction with good Abagail and okay Mark. In situations cousin to this Conrad has found benefit in playing both sides. Risky, but this is the first time the boy has looked at him. His head is hugged tight by a thick-weave, olive green balaclava. In a split second undetectable on his face, Conrad weighs the possibility he's talking to an AWOL. Problem is the boy's blue, bordering on vibrant teal eyes, the only strip of face his mouthless cover permits, shimmer without that iconic inhumanity observed in most deserters and very successful United States Marines. A dark, drippy smile paints a picture—he's been drinking coffee double-filtered through the wool.

"*They kicked you out*?!" the boy whispers.

"They sure did."

"*And like you don't even have a mask or anything*?"

Conrad shakes the bandana wrapped loosely around his neck. A simple wind parameter on dustier roads. Some months ago the screen on his very vintage and, forgive the brag, very cool bubble visor cracked while riding next to a truck on Interstate 40. Scary stuff, necessitating the switch to his reserve, equally vintage helmet, sans-bubble visor. As if his forefathers needed anything but a tough pair of goggles and a paisley cut pulled over the mouth. Objectively the current loadout is less road safe but if this kid can cover similar ground in the IRA special Conrad can file his personal risk away.

"*What the fuck is their deal?!*"

"Thought very much the same," Conrad turns and stands parallel. "Name's Conrad."

The boy says nothing.

"You got a name?"

"… It's like uh…"

Yes, the time he's taken to find his name crossed into the unnatural three seconds ago. But Conrad's never been one to judge. One constant with him is respect for the classic and embrace of the new. If this kid wants to experiment with being a new man, well, where better than the open road?

"… *Did I say it yet?*"

"Nope."

"Cameron."

Could be true to the day he was born, could be true as of right now. Either works.

Conrad lets Cameron finish off his coffee, which he sets on the ground, on the three saucer chunks he slides together like nothing had happened.

"Headed anywhere in particular?"

Cameron tries shaking his neck broken. Looks closer to a no than a yes.

"Didn't think so. How about following me, then? Day trip. I'm going to the river."

"… Uh… ahahaha like I dunno man like I dunno what's over there."

"Plenty," Conrad starts and already knows he won't stop. "Couple of waterfalls, snakes, fresh air. If that's not enough… how does two hundred thousand dollars in cash sound?"

He says nothing.

"Really?"

Cameron stands still, gripping the handlebars on his bike. "Sorry is that like a lot up here?"

"It's a lot everywhere," Conrad finds himself laughing. In defense, he would admit. "Especially if you know where it came from."

"Oh. Well I don't, so…"

Slapping his back, circling around the orange dirt bike, turning and walking backwards for adventurous effect, accidentally kicking the coffee mug and sending it shattering against a decommissioned gas pump, Conrad says, "I'll explain on the way."

"Picture this, kid," Conrad feels good to project, glad to see Cameron is okay with riding in formation and, more important for enjoying the weather, taking things slow. It's twenty-five minutes to the Washougal at the pace they're going. Just enough to tell the story and wet the appetite. "November 24th, 1971. Unassuming middle-aged man in a dark coat boards a Northwest Airlines flight from Portland to Seattle. One-way ticket. Minutes into departure, he tells—"

"*From where to where*?!" Cameron shouts.

"Portland. To Seattle. Former's just across the bridge due south, latter's north on I-5. Where are you from, exactly?"

"*Is this about you*?!"

"No, it's not about me. Can I guy tell a story? Anyway,

"Minutes after takeoff he slips the flight attendant a note. Says he has twelve sticks of dynamite in his briefcase and he wants to have a chat. Poor lady sits down, she asks him what he wants. Under unnegotiable terms, the man wants two—"

"*He took dynamite on a plane*?!"

"—Yes, in his briefcase. And he wanted—"

"*Don't you guys like need to get your luggage checked or something*?!"

"What do you mean *you guys*?"

"*How did he get dynamite on a plane*?!"

"Listen, man! He tells the flight attendant he wants two hundred thousand dollars in hardcore Escobar, and he wants it as soon as they land in Se—"

"*He wants hardcore what*?!"

"Money! Money and a set of parachutes, or he blows the plane."

"*Where was she gonna get that kinda money like I thought flight attendants didn't have money*!"

"No, no, Seattle First National Bank picks up the tab while the plane draws circles south of SeaTac. They land, passengers disembark, but Cooper keeps the flight attendant by his side, finger on the trigger. He wants the money and parachutes loaded onto the plane—"

"*Who is Cooper*?!"

"... That's on me. Whoopsies. The man's plane ticket identified him as one Dan Cooper. And at this point in the hijacking, he wanted the plane to refuel and take off for Mexico City. The pilot renegotiates to a refueling stop in Reno. When they take off, Cooper sends the fl—"

"My girlfriend has a house in Reno!"

"What was that?"

"Okay well like I dunno about girlfriend or all that but we do shit together know what I mean."

"That's great, man. Where was I? Takeoff. Now at this point flight 305 carries only the crew and Cooper, along with his money and parachutes. Quite inexplicably, Cooper is familiar with the procedures of military-grade parachuting, refusing help from the pilots. It's here where, obviously in hindsight, Cooper's choice in aircraft makes perfect sense. The Boeing—"

"*I didn't know you guys could like pick what kinda plane you wanna fly on*!"

"*We* can't. Typically. Suspicion is nonetheless Cooper did. The Boeing 727 was fixed with a ventral stairwell at her aft. Unorthodox for a commercial jet, unheard of to-day. But it makes a whole lot more sense knowing the 727-51 flew covert military operations in the Vietnam War. When the unfor—"

"*Wait why does that make more sense*?!"

"*When the plane landed in Reno*, the flight deck unlocked to find the aft stairwell extended. Cooper, the money, and two of four parachutes were missing. He had jumped, somewhere over southern Washington State."

The pair ride in silence while Cameron takes it all in. Or however much he's prepared to.

Then, Cameron waves for Conrad's attention, leaning over the handlebars. "*Did he die*?!"

"No one knows. What we do know is the money was never found. Nor was it ever spent. Take this left:"

The pair take this left.

"See, kid, major banking units, like our friends in Seattle, carry what's called a *ransom package*. These are cataloged bills reserved specifically for circumstances like Cooper. Ever notice that green string of numbers on your cash? That's how the mint keeps track of le—"

"*No*!"

"No what?"

"*Like I mean I haven't noticed a buncha green numbers nah*!"

"… If he spent one dollar from that ransom, the FBI would know about it. Thing is, he never did. Not one bill was ever recovered—That is for a select few. I'll tell you the rest when we're on foot."

And Conrad thought his nephews were bad listeners. They are, but Cameron seems to possess no care nor regard for the verbal intentions of anyone but himself. Absolutely childlike without the excuse. It'd almost be cute were that fear of Cameron's wobbly balance going nuclear at any moment not nagging at the back of Conrad's mind. A fatherlike tendency of his. Not that he's a father. He had just prepared to be for so long.

Conrad and the son he never had break off from Washougal's best attempt at a main road, proceeding to the Washougal river trail's best attempt at parking. On their way out from the café Conrad had heard a terrible metal cracking sound he can now blame on Cameron's kickstand coming loose. The boy has laid the bike on her side with something close to but not quite tenderness, occupying a whole parking space on her own. On a busier day someone might be upset. In truth, it's subrural Washington State and someone might be upset regardless. If Mark and Abagail are a reliable sample pool, these people take umbrage on principle.

Conrad wants to tell Cameron to move his bike somewhere else but, alas, he really wants to keep dropping this DB Cooper payload. "Have you figured out why the money would be here?" he asks before he can remember who he's talking to.

Cameron says nothing.

"Riddle me this, then: the Columbia river, just south. Parting Oregon and Washington. We're a skip and a hop from the west coast. Ipso facto, the water from this river must be flowing to…"

Again.

"The river water flows west. This is interesting because the only portion of Cooper Cash ever recovered was found along the Columbia. So it fell in the Columbia, right? Wrong. Where Cooper landed does not support this. Flight 305 was taking what's called a Victor airway—straight down through Portland. Recreations of the hijacking supported, initially, that Cooper had jumped somewhere along this line. Without some critical details one could surmise he landed close to the Columbia and, I don't know, lost the money along the bank. I disagree. They were close, but I propose Cooper landed further East.

"You see, Cameron, the Columbia stash," and Conrad starts using his hands because he's excited, not because it illustrates anything, "was *south* of Cooper's projected landing zone. Were the money dropped, it could not have fallen in a river flowing northwest and washed up south. Get what I'm saying? So he needed to have jumped somewhere that the money would fall in an adjoining river and eventually finds its way flowing west, then north, on momma river—"

This time Conrad lets Cameron interrupt him. He waves his hands much the same way Conrad had been doing a second earlier, and it really looks like the boy has a question. Finally. He's got him. "Yes, Cameron?"

"Who's Victor?"

"—What?"

"Is he like a famous pilot."

"What are you talking about… oh, Victor 23. It doesn't matter."

"You said that motherfuckers in the FBI were tracking the money though so I dunno how you think you know where it is when they don't."

"It's not microchipped like a baby. It's the serial numbers, what they have. The only way anyone would know where the money is going is if it ever *went* anywhere."

"Where would they put the microchip though because like when—"

"—They didn't *put* a microchip *anywhere*—"

"—my family put one in me they did it in the back of

my foot at like the meaty part so I'm saying like yeah I don't think it's got one of those and besides they'd gotta like put one in every dollar y'know."

Conrad lets it go. "Let's stop real quick. I wanna have a smoke."

"So what's your story, man?"

A rampage of nicotine through the blood had dulled Conrad's teacher-like annoyance. In this state, Cameron's unending disrespect for other's people attention isn't nearly as grating. It's almost cute.

Conrad would've liked to teach, he thinks, but only in specific contexts he would admit skew cinematic more than realistic. *O captain, my captain.* It would be a job he fell into, rather than doggedly pursued. Just another gig as he rode through this crazy ride called life. And those kids, minds poisoned by Common Core and Instagrams, would have never known a teacher like Mr. Tomas (but they would call him Conrad). He'd sit against the front of his desk and regale stories of the open road, imparting on these unpolished gemstones valuable perspective with Pirsig-like subtlety. He'd tell those few troubled kids of the greatness he sees in them, probably while splitting a cigarette with them (marijuana? An overstep, probably. He strikes this out of the fantasy). And they would grow into responsible, ambitious adults, never forgetting what Mr. Tomas told them.

By then they would call him Mr. Tomas out of respect, by the way.

Cameron's bogarting the cigarette. Maybe he didn't catch the significant bond innate to a smoke split between men. Conrad lights his own.

At least he's not smoking through the mask. He's removed it entirely, leaving the ratty wool thing laid over his propped-up knee. A dirty racoon mask leaves an impression about his eyeline, telling a story without words. Not a great story, mind—just that he's been on the road and hasn't removed that thing in several days. His oily, gold flake hair flares off his head like the instable corona of the sun. A good-looking kid, in theory. The kind that's obvious in every state of distress and cleanliness. Boys like that have no clue how good they've got it. That more-or-less girlfriend of his makes all the sense in the world, now. Conrad's not so old he cannot see the appeal in an attractive, stupid guy. Like owning a dog.

"Wait what did you say?" Cameron barks.

"I asked where you came from."

"Oh like I'm all over the place honesty but I think I was born in New York."

"A New Yorker," Conrad peppers. "You strike me a Staten Islander. Did I get it right?"

"Where?"

"… So you're really all over the place, then. Pardon my guesswork but you wouldn't be an army brat, would you?"

"HM?"

"Has your family served in the military?"

"Oh no never like Clark told them he had glaucoma whatever that is and my Quentin said he had a bum leg but he didn't really and my Nigel wasn't forced to do it for anything so he just didn't and then I didn't either. Why."

"… You're tough to figure out, you know that" Conrad declares and smokes. They use a rubberiron picnic table like a bench, watching the tough waters of the Washougal work millennial magic on the expanding riverbank. Conrad's got a good feeling about today. It's just not about to end the way Cameron may be thinking—whatever he's thinking. Ever.

"Where you headed on that bike of yours?"

"I dunno man I thought maybe like I'd go to Seattle."

"Beautiful city—"

"I don't even know why though I just was thinking about it on the way over and people kept mentioning it to me at the gas stations which by the way why the fuck do they make me do it?"

"Make you do what?"

"Gas!"

Cameron twists around and flips off the evergreens rather than hear the history and adoption of self-service American pump stations. He's been doing that ever since the duo rode into the thick of the surrounding Washougal forests. Add it to the list of ticks, right below chewing the filter on his cigarette and neglecting to inhale. Woven between the boy's neuroticisms, Conrad gives him the itinerary: years of research and triangulations and one occasion where he and a Cessna-owning uncle recreated the jump and accrued an unauthorized skydiving fine ($700) has led him to a personal, trapezoid-shaped best estimate of where the money fell. A conclusion removed from the most popular square of interest just north of Battle Ground, Conrad's drop zone takes into consideration Cooper's inability to steer his military grade chute as well as a strong, divisively considered draft from the west. This combined with that small chunk of cash from the Columbia beach led him to the Washougal theory years ago, but Conrad's highly condensed search area is motivated not by Cooper's likely death atop the density of Washington's forest, but the arguable likelihood that his visibility while falling through the black of night. All the most popular recounts and theories, whether that be the FBI file or the many books or even manier YouTube videos (of which Connor has seen every single one), have one thing in common—they're crafted by normal people who, in their infinite naivety, can only understand the hijacking through a video game-like optimization. Only someone who themselves share a not dissimilar grudge to Cooper could hope to occupy his mind, his intentions, and ultimately his decisions.

For years, for a powerful chunk of his life, one which has unfortunately led to the dissolution of many jobs and friendships and matrimonies, Conrad had imagined himself one day taking seat 18-E and asking the flight attendant for a chat. He has a grudge, and it's with Cooper, a man who has in many ways continued his life of crime in a ghostly form, terrorizing curious but good men, mutating them to obsessive wrecks.

An ignorant travel partner nonetheless more inclined to ask strong questions may ask Conrad why he's here if that version of himself is largely gone. First off, Conrad would recommend his darling of a therapist but, moreover, explain that he's really here to bury rather than unearth. He knows his trapezoid is strong. Maybe stronger than any projected drop zone ever before put to compass. That's why, for the sake of Conrad C. Tomas, he needs to not find anything. D.B. Cooper plummeted from a 727-51 directly to Hell and left nothing but madness for the scavengers and clerks.

Hope he hasn't gotten Cameron's hopes up. "Ready to rock and roll?"

"Man I was just thinking that someone needs to like invent a Segway that can do sixty."

Bless Cameron. Honestly. He'll never have to carry this.

The Washougal river is mercifully narrow. With Conrad on the north side and Cameron on the south, they can cover the search area in half the time. Cooper would have gone to the water. In virtually all cases of emergency jumps, survivors are drawn to the sound of running water. A man who works as quickly and diligently as Cooper would lose the money as soon as he could, returning only when the smoke had cleared.

"Is the money in the water or something?!"

"What was that?!"

"I said like is the money in water because I dunno where you want me to be looking!"

"Draw a triangle with your eyes!" and Conrad points to his own, "from the water to the bank, ten feet out. In a fanning motion like this!"

Conrad rocks his sightline back and forth theatrically, playing to the cheap seats. Cameron does a puppylike nod but it's unlikely he understood if he already can't fathom the geological means by which something in water might end up on shore and vice versa. But it's no problem. In a way, this boy is the perfect partner for killing the theory. A more obsessive mind like Conrad's would *never* leave good enough alone. Not until every pebble was turned over twice and every garter snake was stopped for comment. At his worst Conrad would sleep ninety minutes a night, waking up on compulsion to phone libraries hundreds of miles away to see about their 1971 newspaper archives. He would obsess over inactionable steps for months, talking what is laughable nonsense today with therapists who really should have been cutting him off. To that end, yes, Cameron, stare at the water so long you trip over a fallen long. The team needs that factor of non-attention.

Apart from his partner's semi-periodic hollering of stupid questions (no, the money will not be in a safe), Conrad feels now a quantum of peace greater than he had been prepared for. Talk about missing the forest for the trees, back when his only trips to Washington State were to look at the ground the whole time (he'd disqualified Cooper getting his chute stuck on a tree years ago). Today he looks up more than a younger Conrad would advise, admiring the peppering of sunlight through the leaves, how it splats organically on the Earth below his boots. He listens for birds. He stops completely to watch a squirrel on the tree to his right make a perilous jump between branches. More than once he thought about living here and maybe he should.

Between the cool waft against his face and the trickle of water to his right, Conrad feels himself washed in a minor but considerate way. A surprise party he already knows is happening, but it's fun to play along. He looks ahead to the future of three hours, sees a cup of coffee blowing steam on his chin as Abagail asks about what he saw. And he'll say, *oh, nothing much.*

Yet still he has to discipline himself. He's always been a man who could lock in when required, but what is he or Cameron or any comparative man if not made of clay. Of course his eyes are still drawn to places where he would hide money if he needed to. Under that log, for instance. The overhanging chip of rock right by this banking, where the river goes from a rushing bluewhite to a near-stagnant gradient of green and rust. Just a bit further, past this gargle of rocks which must have been a powerful waterfall eons ago, they'll find a forest giving way to residential homes and commercialized swimming holes. Where the trapezoid ends.

For a few blissful minutes Conrad forgot to check on Cameron's work. Where he ought to be walking there is nothing, and perpendicular to where he ought to be walking there is a comical splashing of water. Conrad feels entitled to a laugh. Where they are the water won't be deep enough that he'd be pulled under. Hell, the kid could probably stand right up. "You doing alright?!" Conrad hollers just to be safe.

On cue, Cameron stands up, a boy remarkably comfortable in his soaked clothes. "Dude it's so fucking green in this spot," he waxes.

"Plankton."

"I dunno if you seen the water up in Greece but it's blue as fuck."

"Lack of plankton."

"Ya'll got waterfalls here!"

What Cameron enthusiastically but incorrect refers to is a clumping of rocks, roughly as tall as he is, which churns but ultimately fails to make water fall in any meaningful sense. While Conrad tries to play Captain Semantics, fruitlessly, his words are drowned out by Cameron's sloshy bounding upstream. Feeling like he's watching the kids play, Conrad lights another cigarette. Fellow river appreciators have been sparse, today, and he's sure the teens of Washougal come down here to do a whole lot worse.

"It's slippery, careful!" Conrad mumbles through tensed lips, struggling to get a light. From the day he heard the superstition onward, Conrad has only used white Bic lighters. Thus far the only stroke of bad luck had been their cantankerous jump to light. He'd investigate the white Bic superstition himself, as a personal project, but his very good therapist advised him to hold off on personal projects until he, for sure, has a firm hold on perspective. Standing where he does now, he sighs, having not seen a single odd pebble or disturbed reed that would interest a weaker-willed state of himself. Maybe it's the riverside homes he can make out behind the dissipating, morning fog. But the end of the road looks nice.

Now might be a good time to tell Cameron the bad news. He's not about to have his share of two hundred thousand dollars, nor the glory of finding such. But, hey, chin up kid. Your twenties are for being broke. It builds character.

"When you're done with that, come over on my side," Conrad hollers to Cameron's back. "We have to talk about something!"

Cameron says nothing.

The waterslick rock climbing is not going well. He lost a foothold and went stomach first on the egg-shaped foundational boulder before stopping and just holding himself there while he figured out some move that won't end up with dropping to the water below. That move doesn't work, and down he goes, and just as quicky he kips to his feet and tries again. An arm-sized chasm catches his attention and he slides an arm inside all the way to the shoulder.

"Careful!" Conrad barks again, nearly losing his smoke. "Snakes make nests in cracks just like that."

"Aw dude fuck yeah man snakes are dope!"

"The garters are harmless, but I wouldn't go shoving my fist in their homes. Word to the wise."

"I got one! I got one I got one I got one I got one—"

"Let go!"

"I got—aw hold up ahaha nevermind actually I think I got the skin tube shit they leave behind."

"The shed?"

"My cousin's got Black Mambas dude it's crazy like he used—aw nah I think this is a bag or something."

"Don't touch trash," Conrad says, "teenagers and homeless people come up here to shoot smack, you don't wanna grab blind *and touch a needle*

His gruff parental advice peters out in the midst of a headrush. Odd. He did unquit smoking fifteen minutes ago but he figured his tolerance would be higher than this. Actually, now that he takes personal inventory, his vision's fuzzing up kinda bad. The kinda bad which reverberates in the eardrum. His very nice doctor told him to watch out for these sorts of sensations, especially after physical exertion of any kind—including hikes. He's no doctor, and he has all the respect in the world for medical professionals, but a lack of chest pain is telling him this a head thing, not in fact the fatal heart attack like he must admit to fearing for a few seconds. As if the corporeal form would only last as long as the legend it chased for so many years. Do all dead dreams feel like this? Conrad was feeling pretty good just then. Now he falls to the bumpy rock below his feet and crunches out a spike of stomach pain as he sees Cameron yank out from the rock some ratty piece of tarp.

Conrad occupies his fuzzy brain with thoughts of primordial viruses, frozen in glaciers and threatening to infect the squishy, unequipped sapiens of today. That's what this is reminding him of. Conrad's feeling sick and palpitated because Cameron, who represents climate change in this comparison, has "thawed out" the narrow rocky overhang. Naturally the virus is the ratty tarp actually no it's a canvas bag and Cameron's holding both straps of the canvas bag and looking inside the canvas bag it's a canvas bag wait why is this bothering him so bad and why does he knows it's the canvas bag precisely what makes his stomach do somersaults Cameron found the fucking bag twenty-one pounds does it weigh twenty-one pounds Cameron no wait does it weight nineteen-point-eight pounds Cameron bring it over here stop fucking touching it with your wet hands bring that the fuck over here

"I didn't make them all ripped up like that by the way like they were like that when I found them. One of them broke up on its own when I held it though so like it *behooves* you to be gentle with them."

They've moved deeper into the trees, far out of the way of fellow hikers, to a Cha Cha Slide of clearing with a sturdy log for sitting and gathering oneself. Both history makes have since sanitized and dried their hands. To leave nothing for the fatty oils on his fingers, Conrad handles a dissolving wad of cash, selected at random, with a handkerchief normally reserved for wiping his sunglasses. What infuriates him now, placing second or third on the list, is he bought supplies for handling the money years ago and regularly replenished the perishable items every few months. He didn't expect to need them. He threw it all out when he moved apartments, on the recommendation of his shrink.

As carefully as he can, Conrad turns the handkerchief and looks at the cash. All twenties, just like Cooper requested, wrapped with disintegrated rubber bands in companies of ten thousand. The bills are rounded at the corners, eroded, very nearly fraying like wool. Some, not all, of the serial numbers are those he has committed to memory. One of them is tattooed on his left forearm.

"This is it," Conrad squeaks. Just so it's been said.

He was eighteen years old when he and D.B. Cooper first got acquainted. Mr. Allin told the story, off the cuff, on a drowsy sunny morning at the top of English class. In his memory he calls him Mr. Allin, out of respect, but at the time he preferred Geoff. Got along like a house on fire, the two of them. Mr. Allin must have seen something in the troubled Conrad. Never an A+ student, but a bright young man nonetheless who had "got it up here," as Mr. Allin would say, rapping his temple. All he needed was a point of study he could sink his teeth into. Luckily Mr. Allin had been around the block more than one. He had seen a lot on that Harley he rode to school, revving the engine as he rode in convoy with the school bus. God, it took them forever to get around to the rubric, between Mr. Allin's stories of backpacking through Europe and leading the first motorcycle showcase in the Monaco *Parata.* At the time it felt like he and Conrad were alone in that classroom, like he wouldn't make eye contact with just any other student. Mr. Allin had a class to teach, but he had *things* to tell Conrad in specific. So, Conrad listened, like he hadn't before. Really like he hasn't since.

It wasn't only the raw story, compelling as myth on its own. But Mr. Allin had gone looking himself. At the incorrect landing zone, of course, but so did everybody at the time. Turns out what Conrad needed to be told, more than there's this incorporeal spark of greatness within him, was that a quarter million dollars were out in the woods and all he needed was a bike and an open schedule to be made pure unleaded history. So, at his miraculous approval to graduate, following a congratulatory swig from Mr. Allin's flask under the bleachers, Conrad told him he was going to continue the search—no, he was going to be the one to finish the job. They embraced on it, and Mr. Allin told him he'd be at the newsstands the day of. For certain.

Of course, Conrad knows today Mr. Allin will not be at the newsstands. Two years after graduating, Conrad caught wind of a scandal resulting in that great man's termination. Never again to wax New Journalism for dazzled young dreamers, never again to inspire like most if not all teachers only dream. All because he slept with a student who was eighteen anyway and could make her own choices as far as Conrad was concerned. Also he ran a red light in front of a freight truck and exploded against the grill. Declared dead on the four-way. And newsstands aren't really a thing anymore.

We did it, Mr. Allin.

"Yeah cool sick so like there was nothing else back there by the way like I checked all over the plane just so you know. But yeah how much do I get?"

Is this kid serious? "You understand none of this is spendable. That's not the point."

"Oh nah I don't care about the money because like it's not a whole or anything I just thought since I saw where it was I'd be getting—"

"Who are you exactly?" Conrad is far from conspiratorial, despite what the shrink might say. He thinks in absolutes; he does not *guess*. Every move he makes is backed by data, and the data tells him, in absolutes, that there's more to this "Cameron" than he's let on.

Cameron says nothing but he makes an inquisitive noise from the throat.

"Because you've been scatterbrained to an… unorthodox extent. You're from New York but don't know what Staten Island is, you don't care about a quarter mil or the glory, and yet you just… reach your hand *exactly* where it needs to be. Without being told."

"I know right ahaha like how fucking crazy is that."

"Uh-huh. Hey, if we're good enough chums, *ahaha*, you mind telling me who sent you?"

The throat noise comes back.

"Who sent you to find me? How did they know what I was doing? Don't fuck with me right now, kid."

"OH, that."

"What do you mean *that?!*"

"It's all good I just didn't think anybody else knew about the cameras is all."

"Cameras, you said?" Conrad repeats, a vibrato from his heartbeat.

"Yeah like they just got em everywhere and I guess they're always looking at what I do or something. And I dunno what for dude it's crazy LEAVE ME ALONE!" Cameron gives the birds in the trees the bird.

"... Just so I have this right, and please attempt a complete sentence with me... there are cameras watching us. You and me. Right now."

He takes a terribly long time to answer: "... What's a *complete* sentence what do you mean by that."

"Forget it. How about... Cameron, I've changed my mind. Y'know, given the significance of this discovery, it's altogether *orderly* that you get your own cut. And just so you know you're getting your due fifty-fifty—that's right, half the cash—I think you should get it out yourself. Please use my handkerchief."

Conrad stands and momentarily fears his flushed legs won't support him. Transferring the hankie and switching spots with Cameron, he takes a knee and unlaces his boot. Even the birds have stopped chirping so they can watch.

The highly suspicious and highly stupid boy quickly loses his moxie, now that he's been giving partial liberty to handle the treasure. Hardly the wicked, human delight, handling this variety of fragile and actively crumbling paper. One imagines themselves Tony Montana, not... and

Conrad loses the comparison. Robert Langdon? Doesn't matter. Cameron handles his share, placing corroded stacks directly on the dirt against the bag. As his pile grows he seems to want less. Were his mind not currently on other things Conrad would tell the kid to exercise some perspective. *That's more money than you'll ever see again*. But he holsters the thought now that he clutches his boot in his right hand.

"Hey like by the way I shoulda mentioned how I don't really have any way to carry all this stuff. Like I know you said something about how I can't spend it but it's still money but how am I gonna be putting this stu—"

A swift crack, as merciful as gas blasting a cow between the eyes, Conrad throws with his shoulders and conks his boot, steel-toe first, off the side of his treasure hunting partner's head, and Cameron goes down. Just the crack is enough to get birds stumbling away into the air. With with Ichirolike follow-through Conrad is already hopping over Cameron's writhing body and tossing the money back in the ratty canvas bag. A subtle juke of his feet illustrates the internal debate between putting his boot back on or making distance right now. Pounding the dirt mercilessly, bag clutched in one hand, boot in the other, cigarette falling to the forest floor in the print of the sock dragging twigs and moisture along for the ride, Conrad picks the latter. For the first time since discovery, he smiles. He laughs.

On his Hail Mary sprint back to this backwoods towns miserable excuse for parking, Conrad plows through a child, inspiring little guilt and a euphoric sense of liberation. The doormat of thirty minutes ago might have apologized, the Conrad C. Tomas (C.C. Tomas?) whose name inhabited only drivers licenses and divorce filings rather than the golden slates of history. While the poor (in both senses) parents shriek, Conrad rolls, collects himself, does not apologize, does not look back, and keeps running.

At the parking lot, Conrad allows a seconds hesitation to check on his lead. The greatest drivers of all time still check their mirrors—y'know, probably. No sign of Cameron. Good. Clocked him real nice, it seems. Conrad pulls up the seat on his TR65 and jams the cash down in the cubby space, swapping for the rain shell already there and throwing it over the bag. With that situated, Conrad will waste no more time getting the fuck out of Washington. South on I-5 sounds wise.

As he retraces the Vancouver road he used this morning, he honks the horn at the café. Sorry, Abbie, but he hasn't the time to stop inside and redeem that free coffee. But know this: the boy's been sorted out. It's all coming up justice. One day, by rights one coming soon, news vans will descend on this town so quiet you know the cops by name. *Why, yes, you did serve a Conrad that morning. What is this about—singlehandedly solved the greatest American crime mystery of the 20th century, you say? Hmm. He had that look about him…*

Interstate 5 is as empty as he'd left it. Empty enough he doesn't feel bad taking his TR65 up to seventy, eighty, the only music being the Viking percussion of blood pumping in his ears. Oh, fuck, he'd gotten out of there so quick he never pulled the goggles over his eyes or the wrap over his mouth. So there's where the blindness is coming from. Some sensations are not spurred by spiritual ecstasy, and this clever allusion snaps him to reality somewhat. Just over the Oregon-Washington bridge which, by the way, he may have just set another world-first crossing at near-ninety, Conrad comes to a stop and allows his soul to return to its shell.

Fuck it, he thinks. He's calling her.

"Morning! Hey, hey, bet you know who it is! You never blocked my number so forgive me for thinking you'd been waiting on one of these! How you been? –Oh, wait, I don't care. Because if I got anything from those shrink sessions your *wasp* of an attorney got me doing, it was a six-pack of Mike's Hard Perspective. Just wanted you to be the first to know—and please pass this on to your *philistine* parents—I found it. You know what I mean. I just got back from the river. HA-HA. HA. HA-HA-HA. Okay I'm done. Nevermind FUCK YOU no I'm not. Can you… fathom, what comes next? I'll give you a second. Time's up. Couple of late-night interviews, half a dozen books, my *own* book—and let's not forget the money that, might I repeat, you will no longer be entitled to ending *this year*. Oh yeah, and you don't wanna get me started about the movie. How um… uncharitable, we'll say, Shailene Woodley is going to be.

"Know what I just remembered? When you threw out my progress on the Castle Rock Triangle. Juuuust before I had the third side. Now, that ended up being the wrong drop zone, I'll concede, because unlike you I am not so stuffed with pride my eyes are popping out. But *imagine* you did the same to my trapezoid theory. Now go ahead and keep imagining because that's all you can do now. And every night you get in bed next to *Tom* keep in mind that I really wanted you to be here with me. A version of you. So I guess now, between gloating to everyone in line behind you, I need to go look for her. Should be easy. Greatest treasure hunter of our time and all. Ciao!"

He bites his lip, snuffs out a laugh, and puts his phone back in his jacket, zipping up his inside pocket at the exact moment he sees the Tesla roll up, nose to nose with his bike. An interesting seal squeezes the numbers on the license plate closer together.

It's fine, Conrad supposes, but he didn't think the media would be on him this fast.

The passenger door floats open. Out comes a decent looking man, if Conrad may say, in a decent looking suit, which Conrad will say definitively because he used to visit the same haberdasher as Frank Sinatra Jr.

"Sir," the man says.

"Decent looking suit you got there."

"Thank you. Congratulations on your discovery."

"… Is that Cameron kid with you?"

"We're here to ask you the same thing." At that point, the driver's door pops open and another decent looking man in a slightly better suit joins the obstruction.

"I have discoverer's rights. Who are you two?"

"Entirely concerned with Cameron and not at all with you or your discovery. Did he follow you?"

No, but Conrad does look back at the ugly green hunk of scrap these quirky folk call a bridge. "No."

"Can you vouch for his safety at your last point of contact?"

"Why. What would happen if he got hurt?"

"Some very powerful men, whose extensive connections and resources grant personal liberty above government jurisdiction, would not be happy with the one responsible."

"… He's an awkward kid. Would trip and bang himself up something fierce if I weren't watching. Which I'm not anymore. Capisce?"

"All we wanted to know. Thank you," decent suit bows(?). "Given your recent self-orchestrated exploits, we may be in touch. Check your mail."

… Okay? "Okay."

The Tesla reloads and hums off.

He took through the unpleasant border town of Portland nothing but his clammy body, his nineteen-point-eight-pound heaver motorbike, and blood of an unbearably stupid enigma's head peppered on his neck. The deplorable man in all his wasted progress. It was just after noon and it would be another hour or two before his attorney called. One count of aggravated assault, and worse, government property he would be obligated to surrender for no compensation. The cold sweat on his back comes to a stinging boil and sparks through his hair. Today will end when it's actually tomorrow. He will think about money the whole way down and, when parking his bike just outside his room at the Motel 6, will break his sobriety under celebratory guise and further undo all personal contentment in lieu of wife-changing money and legacy, confident he would kill another relationship, the next ten, every person so unwise to box with God, if he knew this feeling still waited at the end.

# (The) Dragooned

***Scott Holden, 24***

***Talent Manager, Defyance Esports***

***Annual salary: $92,000***

***Dogs: 1***

***Boyfriends: 1***

***Projected dogs and boyfriends following Alaska trip: 0***

***Nome, Alaska***

"Where did you put the vape?"

"Good morning to you."

"Mornin'. Is it under the pillow?"

"Real easy way to find out."

"*God*, you're funny."

"It's in the shower."

"Why?"

"Because I was hitting it in the shower, inspector."

"Cool. I'mma go grab it."

"Might I suggest *taking* a shower, while you're there."

"Can you drive while someone's using it?"

"Like is it physically possible? Because yes, I do believe it is."

"I mean is it safe. For the van."

"The guy who peed on the van two night ago is asking me this."

"I peed next to the van."

"You peed directly on the van."

"Didn't you fuckin'… put the new fuckin'… whatever it is. On the paint."

"The clear coat?"

"Yeah, before we left."

"I did get it detailed. Wasn't so you could pee on it."

"*For my next trick, I will… piss in the shower.*"

"Knock yourself out."

Scott will soon wish he hadn't said that. Blake never uses the fan, so his showering and his peeing in the shower concocts and wafts about the cabin a rancid urine steam alleviated only slightly by Mango Guava Ice countermeasures. Cross-chemical warfare. He rolls down his window and the passenger side window as Amsterdam struggles to climb to the parallel seat. It wasn't very long ago that he would bound up so quickly and stealthily Scott wouldn't notice he was there begging for pets until a tongue was lapping the hand which idles on the gear shift. Now he boulders on shaking legs and stops moving the moment he's in the seat. Scott leans over and scratches his head.

Looks like they'll make town before the guys'll be ready for breakfast. More for Scott and more for Amsterdam. It's altogether fair, Scott thinks, glancing down at his best friend. Their day began at five o'clock Alaska time. Amsterdam did his business (away from the van which is apparently too much to ask of some passengers), Scott didn't pick it up because it's the sticks and who cares, he got a little reading done, and the gang was off. That said, Scott is currently on a mountaineering memoir kick, and every one of those guys agrees that climbing down is multitudes worse than climbing up. He's trying not to think about how, after today, he will need to drive back. Another week and change with Blake and the other two.

Breaking up with Blake now might be a lateral move, he thinks. His hand grazes the cup holder and he laments to remember where he left the vape. Dammit. Godammit.

Hands clap the back of the passenger seat and give Amsterdam a little spook. Parker's up, his body up and moving sooner than his mind.

He sniffs the cabin. "*Is that Blake?*"

"The piss? Yeah."

"*Mm.*"

He leans over the seat, clocks Amsterdam sitting there, and gives the back another rap with his knuckles before retreating to the sink opposite the roaring shower, which he also gives a knock before helping himself to the coffee pot. Vintage Parker right there.

For a second there Scott was worried they might have another situation on their hands. Way back during day two of the trip, north of Vancouver BC, Parker tried ordering Amsterdam out of the passenger seat. Was it Scott's fault for not including that in the Van Rules? He agreed it was, partly, if only to deescalate things. Point is, Amsterdam sits where Amsterdam wants to sit. *Nobody*, least of which the boyfriend of Blake's friend, has the authority to move him. Certainly not with the tone Parker elected to take. Telling Parker to go fuck shit was an overreaction, *fine*, but this trip is not about Parker or Roy or Blake or even Scott, really. The short notice additions only here by the unearned kindness of Scott's heart should exercise *extra* consideration for the *intended* passengers. That's what Scott thinks. He also still thinks Parker should go fuck shit. He hasn't changed his mind.

Oh. Parker's naked, too. It's fine. Just that Scott didn't notice.

Roy's officially the last out of bed. Always the last to do everything, that Roy. *Never change, Roy.* Or change a little if it's not too much to ask. You can start small. Like changing your fucking socks, for instance. Make sure you bury the old ones half a mile underground beneath five tons of lead and leave a slate for future species, warning in thirty languages of the inglorious horrors the human race is so irredeemable to have produced.

"Mornin', Scott."

"Roy." Okay he actually doesn't smell that bad today.

Ix-nay on the solo breakfast idea, then. Shame. Scott had started looking forward to it. Moments to himself haven't been frequent this past week. The hiking excursion down in Tatogga was nice. First time since embarking that Amsterdam moved like his old self. Anchorage was a much-needed refresher, too, and it had to be because that was where this odyssey officially began. Four days deep.

Not long after, when roads ceased to be roads and all they saw from the windshield were mountains they were apparently going to cross, Parker and Roy's enthusiasm for the road trip plummeted to a place it has not yet reemerged. In fairness the next four days were brutal. Nome is not connected to the Alaskan highway system and is broadly considered inaccessible by anything but airplanes and the dog sleds it's most closely associated with. Quora's power-users underestimate how much Scott loves Amsterdam, however. His camper van would make the eleven-hundred miles, albeit with a diversion or two. Private municipal roads, unpaved and poorly maintained clearings for getting to and from the reservations, a pasta bowl of interlocking rivers hardly half a tire deep. These are the roads that send Apple Maps into cardiac arrest. But they worked. How confused are the good people of Nome about to be?

The showerhead squeaks to a drought and Blake turns off his music. The trio of Scott, Parker, and Roy find themselves bonding for the first time in the past week, roasting him for how bad he's made the van smell. He, honestly very rightly, tells them the van has smelled like piss since they left Seattle.

1049 miles, the sign says. END OF IDITAROD SLED DOG RACE, it says more prominently. Scott imagined the sign he saw on Google Maps would arch over a main road they'd drive under like they were now entering Walt Disney World. Alas, no, in fact the van would be too tall to fit anyway. The woodcarver (Scott imagines is dead) didn't make that tiny, ceremonial end marker for vans. It sits unearthed on a sidewalk while Scott, running loops around the same sidewalk, argues with Apple Maps over where their hotel actually is.

Frankly none of Nome looks designed for cars. Residents walking their non-sled dogs, opening the banks, the restaurants, watch a muddy van take the town from the East and stop dead so they can piece together the trip these boys must have taken. *Yeah, that's right*, Scott thinks. *We roughed that motherfucker out. Alexander wept, for there were no more lands to conquer.*

Amsterdam wept, for the bathroom break this morning wasn't enough.

Every warm body in the van piles out once Scott flips the bitch back around to the sign. How did the photo op not occur to him on the first pass? He needs the vape back, so he ventures to the end of the van and finds his machine sprinkled with water and slick with soap. Whatever. He carefully removes himself and Amsterdam through the open side door and wipes the thing off on his shirt.

Holy shit it's cold.

Amsterdam is an old dog. He hasn't needed a leash since the last time he could run. For Scott that was two boyfriends ago. So Amsterdam slowly and shakily sniffs the ground, getting a pat on the ass from his owner, who stretches so hard something really ought to pop.

The dog sees the man & Shiba Inu combo rolling up the sidewalk before Scott does. Encountering other dogs is a spot of worry, these days. They have a latent energy Amsterdam simply does not. But dogs are smarter than the guys Scott dates seem to think. The Shiba Inu clocks the age of this new dog quickly and resigns itself to only the orthodox canid traditions. No jumping. Though it looks like it would really want to.

Like any fellow dog owner can be reasonably expected to do, the unshaven, Carhartt-wrapped owner says hello to Amsterdam before extending that salutation to Scott. The old dog sniffs his hand and seems to only swipe his tail out of respectful courtesy.

"Never seen a Husky so unenthused to be here," the man makes himself laugh.

"He's a mix," Scott says. "Part Lab."

"Old man, too." He kneels to massage Amsterdam's head. "*How ya doin…*"

Returning from the van with his jacket, Scott greets the Shiba Inu (nametag says Daisy) and asks about the White

North hotel.

"Down the way you were going," the man points, still kneeling, "two rights," he twists his hand, "and a left, same side."

"Thanks," Scott says. "Uh… I'm Scott, and that's Amsterdam."

"Clark," Clarks returns. "There's Daisy, there. Sweet lady but she's my daughter's. Visiting for a few weeks.

"Speaking of visiting," Clark sounds like he's wanted to ask since he and Daisy rounded the corner, "am I right to think you boys came in from the East?"

"Yup."

"You took the trail, huh?"

"Me and my Husky. Yeah."

Clark laughs again, pats Amsterdam. "Hell of a sled you got there."

"It was a little rough but, y'know, we made it."

"Is Amsterdam a sled dog? Or *was* he, once upon a time?"

"No, never, it was just a…" Scott feels a story overtaking him. "When I got him, as a puppy, we had just read this book for school called *Woodsong*? About the Iditarod? I wanted a Husky then and, yeah, next birthday we got Amsterdam. For years I joked with my parents about doing the race with him. Just as a joke, y'know. And of course now, not to bring the mood down, but… obviously

Amsterdam doesn't have a lot of time left. Nothing bad going on with him. He's just getting up there. He might have Arthritis? I give him pills for something. But the vets told me a month back we might wanna consider… y'know. Before he's in too much pain."

"I hear ya."

"So I thought, y'know, I got the van and all. Him and me should go see the trail. I would carry *him*, know what I mean?"

Clark smiles, scratches Amsterdam's head. "It's real sweet of you to do this with him. Congratulations on a finished race."

"Yeah. Thanks."

Then Clark stands, a bit suddenly, that warm scratchy face of his eroding to annoyance. Somehow Scott doesn't have to be told whose fault this could be.

Obstructed by the corner of a short wood building making one side of the end sign's alley, the other three boys have been taking photos. Freedom from the van and quick access to food and shelter has lit a fire under them, apparently. Roy's getting his picture taken with Parker, Blake operating as cameraman, This guy is handing from the middle of the fucking sign by his fingers. By those fingernails he doesn't clean.

"… Oh," Scott says. "Those are my boyfriend's friends. They should not be doing that."

"Alright. Could you get them off the sign before I have to."

"Yes, my apologies," Scott awkwardly shuffles away, snapping his fingers for Amsterdam to follow. "*Roy!*"

Roy's too occupied with keeping a grip to try and look at Scott. "What?"

"Fuck do you mean what? Get off the fucking sign!"

"Blake's getting the picture! Leave me a second!"

"Now, shitlips!"

Reluctantly, probably because he planned on doing so and definitely not because Scott said, Roy's feet hit the platform below. Still Scott feels the eyes of Clark stinging the hair on his neck. "That's a landmark, you know," he adds. "They only have the one."

"It's not fragile, man, it was holding me just fine."

"Doesn't matter? Hands off the old shit."

It's then Roy sees Clark standing back there, further down the sidewalk, and apologies in a pointedly ingenuine way. So that's just great. Ten minutes in town and relations with the locals are already tenuous. Scott wants to believe that Clark's mood was so obviously soured by disrespect to the local landmarks alone. That said, with respect to the Nomeites yet unmet, Clark's learning one of them was Scott's boyfriend doesn't seem to have helped. If that's the case, whatever, fuck them, but Scott would prefer if things could stay cool enough that he can get his picture with Amsterdam, under the sign, and under calmer conditions. That time doesn't seem to be now, and he instead corrals the party back into the van. Coffee from something other than the pot no one's seriously cleaned out in over a week will smooth things over. No pressure, but it has to.

"Cool, but I just don't see why you gotta take sides with people we don't know."

"Blake, I hardly know Parker and Roy as it is. Trust I would've told him to get off the fucking thing if it were just us."

"Coffee tastes weird."

"It's instant."

"*Instant*?"

"Pretty sure. It's got that bite."

"We pay money to sit down and be served and what we get served is instant."

"Everything here has to be flown in. Or brought on a boat. Maybe instant is more… shelf stable. Maybe it's cheaper. They can't exactly Amazon Prime shit up here."

"Of all people, you're fine with instant. In a café context."

"I know receipts make you anxious but, just so you know, I didn't pay for much better than instant. If *you* would like to, be my guest."

"The fuck was that guy's problem, anyway?"

"Who, Clark?"

"You're on first names with him. Little networker, you."

"He didn't like you guys climbing on the sign. That was all. He was nice to me when we spoke."

"Roy was the one climbing the sign and, also, he does rock climbing. So I think he knew what he was doing."

"Look, I thought about it too, but he doesn't seem like that kind of guy."

"You didn't see the way he was looking at me. Did you tell him we were together?"

"I wasn't aware that had to be a secret."

"In Bumfuck Alaska, I'd say shit's different."

"He didn't have a problem with *us*; he had a problem with how we were *behaving*."

"Scott," Blake sips his instant. "That's what they all say."

*Fuck it*, Scott thinks, willing himself to pay a little extra so Parker and Roy got their own room at the White North.

"Aaaaaaaaaaand," the front desk woman stretches out longer than maybe she wanted to (slow computer). "Oh. I think we might've just hit capacity before you arrived."

"You hit capacity?"

"I thought the same thing," she says, then chuckles. "We only ever sell out for the race season. Sorry about that. If you'd like, I can phone the oht—"

"What's going on now?"

The front desk woman is as lost as he is. "Well, I thought you would know."

"No one's said?"

"When it's race season or a potluck, well, we all know the occasion. Three thousand folks live here, less so permanently. Travel destination we are not."

"If I find out what's going on, I'll come and say. Don't worry about us, we'll find something."

Looks to be another night in the van. Fuck Scott dead.

The wandering population *has* been younger than Scott would've assumed. Wearing nicer coats, too, if Carhartt Jones back there is a safe Mendoza Line. What they're here to do, Scott didn't ask, and they being non-Nomeians Scott wasn't aware. In the time it took to check in, he felt three or four groups waft through the lobby doors, dressed to the Alaskan nines, and disappear to wherever one disappears in Nome. So anywhere past the airport and the Subway. One wonders why the town of Nome bothers to confine their dead to a cemetery. Guys, you aren't lacking for space.

A text buzzes in Scott's pocket as he exits the White North lobby. Remarkable service, up here. He's hungry and Amsterdam's probably hungry, so that's two errands to run while otherwise taking in the sights—oh, and getting the picture, if he runs into Blake somewhere near and sometime soon.

He buys a thing of wet dog food from the corner store and lets Amsterdam dig inside right outside the doors, taking a knee and holding the open can in his hand so the dog doesn't knock it all over the sidewalk. For the past two months he's sought out the most expensive cans. Amsterdam gets only the best from now until his time is up. Today's special is Sheperd's Pie with added vitamins. Dig in, bud. Careful of the rim.

With Amsterdam fed (the vet recommends letting him lie for fifteen to twenty minutes so he can digest) it was time for Scott. He wanders down roads with names like Tobuk Alley and Bruce (just Bruce) and only realizes at the end of Bruce that he's crossed the whole town. And the entrance sign has the nerve to call this place a city.

Walking all that way and unintentionally making Amsterdam walk more than he'd like has put Scott in a sour mood. Though maybe a consolidating Tupperware of gripes whose marinara stains telling the story of this past week finally catches up as he crosses the road closest to the shore and takes a seat on a rock, looking to an opaque horizon that may or may not be Russia.

Gary Paulsen said he finished last. In the book. Then he said a whole lot more about where the mind goes when options crush down to survival and death, and something about ghosts, probably, and something else about accomplishments in spite of losing. Maybe Scott should've read the book again before setting off.

Several partners in camper vandom, constrained to the internet, told Scott driving the Iditarod trails would be impossible, regardless of route, even with the new tires and the new suspension. But the weather has been perfect going back five months to the point where even the mud pools he'd been warned about were a non-issue. Alaska's great untamedness seemed to unfurl for him. This isn't to say every step of the journey was peachy, it's just that all his biggest challenges have called from inside the house.

Things have only started to feel right at this moment. Just him and Amsterdam, resting. Rather than him and Amsterdam, stalling, making the most of their brief hiking excursions or piss breaks before they have to return to the frankly unwanted party. He should've known Blake would invite himself just like he invites himself to fucking everything. But, y'know, him being there wouldn't ruin anything. He and Amsterdam get along fine. By rights this trip should have smoothed over tensions as resulting from the seven-month itch. A bonding exercise punctuated by an emotional denouement concerning a treasured member of Scott's family. The best friend he ever had. The first breathing creature to know Scott was gay (he'd practiced telling his parents on Amsterdam).

This just should've been better.

And the morning before taking off, Blake asked if Roy could come along. Or maybe an agent acting on behalf of the Seattle Chamber of Commerce planted the idea in his head so Roy's rancid smell could then be Alaska's problem. He'd met Roy only once before, which was enough to know he smelled like shit but also that he wasn't a bother. To pepper in some guilt, Blake mentioned how Roy's childhood dog had *also* recently passed. Fine. Better he comes along than Blake act all pissy. On the morning they were set to depart Scott offered his condolences to Roy. Y'know, on the recent passing of his dog. It's then he learned Roy's dog had died three years ago. Blake's reasons for bringing Roy, then, remain unknown. Just because he could.

Parker is Roy's current boyfriend. That's why he joined as the fourth. That's it. At a rest stop Blake said something about how Parker's experiencing a spot of tension with his roommates (oh, you don't say). This didn't change Scott's mind. As he experienced it, Parker hopped out of the passenger seat of Roy's car, five minutes to departure, and Scott wasn't comfortable with him coming but equal parts uncomfortable telling him to get back in his car and fuck off.

Blake said, on day three, he should've said something if he wasn't happy with the extra guests—including himself, which he did not at the time but Scott will right now. Should he have to say something, though? This is a hell of a trip to feel entitled to and it's not like Roy or Parker have had a *great* time. Survivormen they are not. Much of *their* seven-day trans-Alaskan escapade was spent inside the van, cuddled up in one of two cots, placated by weed and, on one night while they were fortunate enough to catch the faint nebula weaving among the stars, acid. The blotter paper was branded to Neon Gensis Evangelion.

*Try to enjoy this*, Scott tells himself, pulling Amsterdam closer and realizing, then, that the need to order this from himself invalidates almost everything. Still, he tries. For the faintest puff of neurons he does, watching as a Cessna flies low across the harbor and gurgles to a stop.

He's gotten an idea and postpones enjoying the moment until he can sell Blake and the other two on it. His boyfriend found a pizza place that serves real coffee. That's what the text was about.

"I saw some rich looking kids at the hotel, but I didn't hear anything about a music festival."

"Me neither, but it's happening."

"Did Roy know?"

"I don't think so? He'd say something if he did. Him and Parker are gonna go check it out tonight. Apparently Steve Aoki is here."

"Where is this happening? In town?"

"Out in the middle of nowhere. Rave-type shit."

"A rave."

"Guess so."

"In Nome, Alaska, a town not even connected to the Alaskan highway system."

"You think I'm lying? You've been around town. Look at those four over there. Bet you those are the only four black guys in Alaska."

"I didn't say you were lying; I'm saying the idea of this happening is like… weird, y'know? Am I crazy?"

"People throw raves in strange places. Out in the desert and jungles and shit."

"It's just remote, is all."

"Great place to drop the heavy shit."

"Roy told me they didn't bring anything tougher than acid."

"Did you try some of that, by the way?"

"No. I'm the driver."

"No shit. Anyway, it wasn't great. Super fuckin' diluted. But I took one of the Shinji tabs so maybe that's on me."

"You said Roy and Parker are going to that thing?"

"Pretty sure. It's their scene."

"… I just, apropos the hotel, I wanted to offer them a faster w—"

"There was this guy in here. About fifteen minutes ago. And, dude, he was fuckin' like… gone. Fuckin' raver supreme. Rave-*ist*."

"Did he break that light, there?"

"Huh? —Oh, I don't think so, I think it was already like that. No, like, so I walk in, right, and there's this waitress talking to this guy. Young guy. *Filthy*. Head to toe, just mud and pine needles and water and deer shit. A mess. Waitress is asking him something and she, like, she brushes his hair? Like a consolation thing? Guy starts *crying*. Just loses the plot. Yeah, apparently he'd been sitting under the awning all night. Took something fuckin' *nasty*, I'm thinking."

"Hm. A drifter?"

"It'd be a long way to drift, you said it yourself."

"True… what was I about to say? Before you said your thing."

"Don't know. Did you get your picture with your dog yet?"

"Oh? No. Not yet."

"Could do that when I'm all done here."

"When were you think that'll be?"

"I just said when I'm done here; didn't say I was rushing out the door. My mozzies just got here, dude, and you got a salad to worry about."

"Couple dry chunks of lettuce and half a bottle of ranch I didn't ask for is a hell of a lunch."

"This coming from the 'instant is okay' guy."

"Is instant not okay?"

Blake doesn't answer.

After brunch (his, not Blake's), Scott calls his parents. An awkward conversation no matter how necessary. A little of his father complaining about Canada's shit highway system, his mother misunderstanding how big Alaska actually is, reaffirming that he does make good money from his job, actually, fielding questions about forest animals he didn't see, and a promise to drive home safe. Oh, and his mother wanted him to put Amsterdam on the phone even though Amsterdam has barked three times in his life. Amsterdam says hi.

Next he saw about availability at the other two hotels. Both of them were booked out for the weekend. Same story for the handful of Airbnb's. Forgive him for thinking vacancy wouldn't be an issue and not booking in advance, but why the fuck should anyone book in advance for Nome Goddamn Alaska and why would vacancy *ever*—forget it.

Whatever. Another night or two in the van appetizing several more unbroken nights in the van. *Wheee!*

Having time to spare (forty-eight hours) and wanting Amsterdam to have a little break, Scott cleans the van he's relocated to the outskirts of town. It wasn't a long drive. Neither is sorting Parker and Roy's dirty clothes from him and Blake's since it's a matter of what is on the floor and what is in the hamper. Also a matter of which socks are and are not unpleasantly rigid to the touch. Those get trashed, along with every bit of Roy's clothes for which no washer on Earth could recover.

With musical guest Jim Croce, stalwart companion Amsterdam having a little snooze in the cot, a bracing Alaskan wind inviting itself in through the open side door, and the ontological satisfaction that comes with cleaning, Scott, dare he admit it and risk soiling the fragile thing, starts to enjoy himself. An unidentified tensity in his shoulders loosens. His breaths are deeper. At every reclaimed square inch of vinyl flooring, his mood rises. The final sweep is nothing short of divine. Half a can of pine tree scented Febreze later (tough job), it feels like a new van. Amsterdam wags his tail at the sight of so much extra space and his owner grins in kind.

Scott remembers that idea he had before meeting up with Blake. He tells Amsterdam to wait in the van, rolls the passenger side window just a smidge, and rolls the heavy side door shut. *Be right back*, he knocks on the iron.

"Hey, hi. Um… are any of those planes outside going to Seattle by chance?"

"We don't service Seattle direct, no."

"Oh. Alright. Thank you—"

"*But* the nonstop to Anchorage tomorrow *morning* is eligible for a transfer when it lands at Ted Stevens. If that wouldn't be an issue."

"How much is that?"

"Purchasing right now? An extra four hundred dollars per person."

"I'll book three."

"Three?"

"Anywhere there's an open seat."

"Alright then. Give me just a second… to check… availability."

"Hey, do you know what's happening tonight?"

"A music festival, no?"

"That's what we figured. Just didn't know that was happening."

"You and I both. We got a call early this morning from the Department of Recreation. Sudden, but, whoever's sponsoring has enough money for the town to sign off on the short notice affair and, well, you saw the tarmac. Effectively fly in all the guests."

Billy McFarland type shit. Sounds like it'll go about as well.

"Oooookay. Flight 304, 5:35 tomorrow morning. Looks like there are two seats left in coach, and one in first."

"That's first class?"

"Yes."

This better numb things for Blake. "I'll take them."

The rest of the kind Alaska Airlines representative's spiel fizzles out as dreams of open, isolated road with Amsterdam take over. Ironic he feels this way about coming back. Or proper that he does. This was the right thing to do.

"You're all set for 5:35am tomorrow. Thank you for flying Alaska."

You're welcome for flying Alaska.

Cute litter river just up north. Good place for pictures if Amsterdam is feeling up to it. When he was younger he loved dropping in a river and floating with the current. He was strong, back then. Knocked over Scott's cousins like bowling pins one Thanksgiving. After that Scott had to lock him up whenever they'd visit.

*Aw fuck*, he thinks, exiting the corner and locking eyes to headlights with his van. The door is open. Sure, whatever, it's *fine*, but he's never been hot on anyone but him or his parents watching Amsterdam. Yeah, it's not like he's gonna go sprinting off at his age, but still. What if his sinus thing starts up again? What, is Parker equipped to deal with that? No, he's not, but he's what's sitting on the floor of the van, side door flung open, smoking a joint with his feet planted on the road.

"*Van looks good*," he says.

"Could I get you to smoke somewhere other than one hundred feet from a police station?"

"*Legal state, brother. Mobile property rights.*"

"Fair. Hand it over a sec."

A wrinkled eggwhite thing dotted in chartreuse oil, whose effect is as immediate as the damp filter touching Scott's intolerant lips. It's been a minute since he smoked flower, more often partial to the immediacy and incognita of his pen. Washington State growers have not been sitting on their hands. If this came from the glass bottle Parker keeps on the sink, Scott may be in for a sneaky uppercut.

T-minus six minutes.

T-minus five minutes. Not a word's been spoken. This has to be the friendliest Scott and Parker have been with one another thus far. Drugs, and this may be the strongest argument for federal decriminalization, are a lot easier than talking or being remotely vulnerable.

"Hey, Blake said you and Roy were gonna check out that festival thing," Scott barfs.

"Yuuyaraq."

"If that's what it's called."

"That is what I just said, yes."

Parker's just so easy to talk to, wow, so friendly. "Hey, question:"

Parker has stopped smoking. This might be him listening.

"So I don't know how hot you and Roy are on taking the trip back. Far be it from me to trap you guys somewhere you don't wanna be. What if I said, at no additional charge, the three of you—including Blake—could be on a plane back to Seattle?"

Just putting words to the circumstance gets Parker's sweatpants legs folded. "When? Tonight? We have the thing tonight."

"5:30 tomorrow morning—5:35."

"I just said we have the thing tonight."

"… Tonight isn't tomorrow, what are you talking

about."

"I mean, like, when we get back we're not gonna in shape to hop out of bed at five."

"Could you, though? For a plane back home?"

"I'm just saying… before you buy the tickets…" Parker takes an unnecessary number of pauses, but it's an excuse for Scott to peek inside the van. "Let me and the other guys talk about it. We made plans, is all. Oh, right—your dog went looking for you."

Three minutes. "What?"

"When I opened the door he hopped out and went that way. The way you came."

"… And you let him do that."

"Did he not find you?"

"No, he didn't find me, because he wasn't getting out to find me, he was just getting out why did you let him out."

"You're the one who told me not to bother him."

"Fucking hell—" Scott does a shuffle on his feet between running off to find Amsterdam and slapping the contacts off Parker's eyes. The weight eases back on his ribs with a wet compression. "There's wolves out here!"

"Okay, he's a fucking dog?"

"…" Scott blanks. Good lord.

"The dog'll come back. They got better noses than us."

"… I don't know what's going on between you and your roommates. But it's probably your fault. My guess. If I don't see Roy before you, tell him the two of you are getting on that plane or staying here forever, because the two of you aren't coming with me."

He kicks up gravel with the pivot of his feet and rides the assisted kick of adrenaline back to town, eyes darting from road to road so fast they risk unhinging themselves from their stalks and spinning free in their sockets.

"*What did Roy do?!*" that jackass hollers over Scott's shoulder.

"*He smells bad!*" Two minutes.

In his old age, still, Amsterdam is not incapable of a sprint. His owner runs a forward pass down the vertical slice of Nome, stopping with ready hands at this proverbial forty-yard line (the ocean) and turning around to find nothing but the matchstick width sidewalks packed off the curb with migrating festival attendees. He takes off again, parallel against the current, watching the legs for a thinning wash of brown fur or set of blue eyes. For good measure he ducks and checks under parked cars, remembering when Amsterdam was younger and hid under Dad's car if he were spooked by a snake or heard the garbage truck roaring down the hill, which prompts yet more memories of crawling under there with him and waiting out the terrors in lock. Amsterdam was never the bravest Husky. Must be that Lab in him.

Scott retraces all the way back to the ill-greeted END OF IDITAROD TRAIL sign. Festival goers straggle all the way back here though a studied analysis of this road, one Scott is not calm enough to make, will reveal the small café currently overrun with bored attendees waiting for sundown. Their sardine tendencies block Scott's view into the alley. He knifes through the crush, two hands together, to find a platform occupied only by that same Yuuyaraq attendee profile, photographing themselves with and on top of the sign in a similar display to his own party. Maybe the wood really is that tough.

Scott blurts, "*Is there a dog here?!*" sooner than he knows he's gonna say something. Somewhere in his jog down to the water, Parker's joint activated, whose immediate symptoms include Scott no longer feeling his shoes on his feet and an itching around the crust of his eyelids bordering on unpleasant. Guess motormouthing should be cautiously marked as number three.

A young guy (cute to be honest) standing on the platform with a hand around a girl's hip (nevermind, overrated) starts barking. Scholarly listeners will identify this as a decent impression of a DMX adlib, but Scott's not a fan and interprets this as mockery. "*Please I'm looking for my dog,*" he blurts again, bracing himself for someone to start doing *Who Let The Dogs Out* or do the Muttley laugh.

"Is he brown?" A shrill voice asks, like, right in his ear.

"Mm? Yes, yes, he's a brown and white Husky—"

"Is he old?"

"Yes! He's old! Is he here."

"Couple of minutes ago. But he left. Went that way," they point, too thoroughly swaddled in brushed metal Arc'teryx to put any facial features to the voice. But god it's annoying. "He's friendly. What's his name?"

"Did you see which way—"

"What's his name?"

"—Amsterdam. He went this way, you said?" he matches the pose, back the way he just came, towards the airfield.

"I saw him run up to a different guy."

Blake. Amsterdam does like seeing Blake even if Blake doesn't *love* seeing him. This goes all the way back to when they first hooked up. Nearly cost him the night. But the pressure on Scott's chest gives slack. "Thanks. Were they headed to the festival?"

"Who isn't? There's nothing to *do* here."

Half a mile adjacent to the Nome Airfield and the fleet of unmarked Airbuses its five-thousand attendees rode in on, by golly, there is a festival—many tents and one nuclei stage assembled and ready with Amish-like efficiency. Branded, too. Sponsored by, give Scott a sec—Prime Energy. Huh.

He should be colder, but a combined rush to find his dog before thing get truly wild tonight compounds with his quickly incoming inebriation. That paranoic dragon whispering freak nothings from around his heavy skull. Dead shrubbery looks for a second like Amsterdam. Thin wisps of cloud are simply moving too fast. Is that an atomic bomb detonating over the horizon or an evacuating sun, yoinking with it the last rations of natural light. Amsterdam doesn't like the cold. Amsterdam is scared of the dark. Amsterdam doesn't like large crowds. Amsterdam is thinner than he used to be and can't hold body heat like he used to. Amsterdam has to go to bed by sundown so he wakes up sooner than he can soil his bed. Amsterdam needs to eat before he goes to bed also because hunger pangs sometimes wake him up at night and he has a hard time going back to bed after that.

He calls Blake's phone but he doesn't pick up. Amsterdam can't sleep unless Scott is there. He picks up the pace and finds the quickly forming wind chill inviting. Determination fills his unstretched legs at the apex of the short plateau of dead grass and frozen weeds which Yuuyaraq has commandeered as its own. Amsterdam doesn't like large crowds. God this crowd is large.

Excuse him Red Bull truck have you seen his dog Amsterdam he's a Husky and he's got the blue Husky eyes he's brown oh okay nevermind.

Hey sorry hey you just look like people Amsterdam would wander up to have you seen him by the way his dog Amsterdam ran off he's a Husky he's brown he's this tall alright cool thanks keep an eye out.

My dog Amsterdam got out of the van have you seen

him around yeah he's a brown and white Husky with ears that stick out like this no okay sorry to bug you.

No that's a chihuahua but thanks for trying.

Have any of you seen his boyfriend Blake around he comes up to about here he's wearing this old Noah hoodie oh no okay nevermind.

—Actually have you sorry to bug you again but have any of you maybe seen his dog Amsterdam he's not on a leash and got out of the van oh okay.

Oh sorry no yeah no he saw the sign he just thought maybe his dog Amsterdam got back here y'know he got out of the van and he thinks maybe he wandered back here okay yeah he'll go but like if you see him can you just let him know somehow like bring him out and ask for him he'll be around looking for him alright yeah he's leaving guy Jesus.

HEY ALL YALL HERE HAVE YOU OH WAIT OH SHIT DOES THIS GO TO EVERY SPEAKER AW FUCK HIS BAD HE THOUGHT IT WAS JUST THE ONES RIGHT HERE BUT UH YEAH HAVE ANY OF YOU SEEN HIS DOG AMSTERDAM HE'S BRO—

Hey has anyone in here seen his dog Amsterdam it's warm in here so I thought maybe he'd come in here he really doesn't like the cold y'know oh yeah hey did you see him somewhere BLAKE!

"Were you just on the mic a second ago?"

"Someone told me Amsterdam was with you."

"Who said that?"

"I don't know just somebody is he here?"

"No. He's not. I haven't seen him."

"But someone told me he was with you."

"Well maybe you need better sources than 'someone.' I literally don't know who you're talking about right now. Are you stoned?"

"I had a little with Parker before I knew Amsterdam was gone and when I went down to the s—"

"Speaking of, dude, Parker told me what you told him. He texted me. You're putting them on a plane?"

"Hello? Scott?"

"Sorry I was just thinking maybe someone dressed like you is around and maybe Amsterdam found them—"

"Wanna answer me? What did you buy plane tickets for? And why would you do that without talking to us?"

"I don't fucking know *Blake* why would you invite yourself and two assholes I don't know on this trip that was supposed to be about me and Amsterdam?"

"Did it stop being about you and your dog somewhere? We're in Nowhere, Alaska. We're a skip and a hop from fuckin' Russia. I wasn't dreaming of this place; I came because I wanted to be with you. Is that crazy? To wanna spend time with you? Get out of the city for a bit?"

Scott's too zooted for this. A very salient comeback floats around the top of his brain but he can't reach quite high enough. What he does know, and what the sober yet currently unavailable Scott Holden has been aching to say, is that he does not like Blake very much at all, and maybe the past seven months following an unwise declaration of love to a college freshman beneath dirty bedsheets at said college freshman's parents house has in fact been a relationship closer to buyer's remorse than what Scott Holden, sober or otherwise, needs at this stage in his life. If Blake were to ask, right now, *does Scott love Amsterdam more than he loves him*, he would be actively stupid to think the answer was anything other than *yessss* with the S's drawn out like a cartoon snake. No fucking shit he loves his childhood dog and best friend ever more than he loves, who is and nothing else, his current boyfriend. Why even ask.

In an unfortunate social faux pas, brought on by the intense cannabis strain known colloquially as Dirty Magician, Scott has been saying all of this out loud.

"I got you a ticket also by the way," Scott adds. "It's in first class."

Blake left wordlessly. *Good*, Scott thought in the moment and still thinks now as he muscles through the dense jungle of Yuuyaraq attending bodies and will likely keep thinking as he peeks out the window of his van and sees Alaska Airlines flight 306 take to the harsh Bering wind.

Like he'd be any help finding Amsterdam anyway. He never liked Amsterdam. Well, the feeling is isosceles. Like it's two ways, zeroing in on an inferior third way, which is Blake. Yeah? Nevermind. Whatever.

An hour into the search, Scott finds his lungs operate on diminishing capacity. In those pockets of personal space he feels sundowned Alaskan wind stab the thin skin of his fingers, his ears, the bridge of his nose, and his clouded mind seizes cognizance to visualize Amsterdam's shivering legs. Visibility worsens with the second, made infinitely worse when the lights shut off and the music kicks up, inverse concert with the final vanishing of sunlight. Stars aren't bright enough despite their abundance. Tonight may ruin stars for him.

Five thousand more eager and somehow more collected people use ten thousand shoulders to force Scott from general admission, right on his ass in the flashfrozen dirt. Oh god, that *is* Steve Aoki. The live music industry has conspired to rip man and beast apart, before his search of the impromptu festival grounds could approach what he felt was thorough. Amsterdam may be frozen to the ground already, as dead as the weeds Scott digs his heels into while he thugs back tears. Maybe he can slip the pilots a twenty and redirect flight 304 to somewhere in the Pacific ocean.

Eventually, when frustration lands a nasty right on self-discipline, Scott takes his tired legs and half dozen tears to the police station. Yes, his dog is missing. Yes, he's high. This does not change the situation. Yes, he's gay. You didn't ask but, y'know, just in case you guys wanted to shoot him. However you get things done around Nome.

"Oh uh hey guys."

"Ahahaha yeah right on."

"Nah I just got here I didn't know this was going on. Steve! What's up dude?"

"No nah no I didn't come here on the plane I actually took this bike I got from this kid over—"

"My plane is here?"

"Who brought it?"

"Oh. Alright. Right on. Cool."

"I uh… yeah I found this dog or like he ran up to me but he's real friendly."

"No I think he's a wild dog or whatever they're called."

"A stray? Do they got strays up here?"

"I thought about naming him maybe like Ricky?"

"Cuz look at him dude's just a *Ricky* look at him."

"Huh?"

"I didn't know someone was asking about a dog like I said I just got here."

"They'll let me hold the mic?"

"Okay but can I like sing something real quick?"

"You know about Madonna?"

"Then clear it like what's the problem."

"Alright cool so it's just this way?"

"*Heyyyy heyhey wassup ahaha wow there's a lot of you out here for this.*"

"*Yeah alright so like I found this dog.*"

"*Is this anyone's dog?*"

"*I'm naming him Ricky if he's no one's dog.*"

"*Dude, where the fuck are you?*"

"Looking for Amsterdam don't talk to me right now."

"*Are you at the stage?*"

"I said don't bother me dude get some rest you guys have a flight to catch."

"*I know. We're getting on it.*"

"Capital. I'm hanging up."

"*There's a guy on stage right now and he has your dog.*"

"Fuck you."

"*Deadass! I'm looking at him right now.*"

"If you have something to tell me do it now."

*"He's gonna name him Ricky!"*

"Hanging up in five."

*"I promise I'll be out of your life in just a few, Scott. Okay? You'll be free to hike and manage E-athletes on your own. Go find whatever the fuck you want. But that dog you love so much? More than me? He's here, and he's freezing, and the guy holding his collar is a fuckin'* space cadet. *If I can do anything for you on the way out, I just wanna let you know."*

*"Did he seriously fuckin' hang up?"*

"I'm on my way."

Eyewitness reports attest, yeah, there was a guy up on stage a second ago. He did have a dog with him. But no one made a claim so he retreated backstage. Goddamn. And Scott pounded some serious pavement to get here. Set a trans-Nomeian record, sprinting from the outskirts of the police station (Amsterdam likes to sniff around shrubbery) down the straightaway at what felt like Olympic speeds. Evidently Olympic speed doesn't cut it up north.

Scott plows through the general admission floor, mercilessly, throwing elbows in divine refusal to excuse or pardon himself, overpowering anodyne efforts to stop him like the tug on his jacket or the grip on his shoulder. Children. Diminutive, all of them. Scott has synapses flaming out in hemispheres where most of them don't have hemispheres. At the barricade he takes a hard left, slicing through hands gripping rail until he realizes it's faster to hop the cage and outrun a security guard he'd long clocked too cold and bored to chase him down. A skip over sound equipment, a trip over ungaffed wires, a selfish glance back at Steve Aoki (when's the next time gonna be) and Scott faces a familiar backstage fence. So delectably climbable even with how unbearably frosty the chain is on his exposed hands. Still, he forces himself over the top, plopping over to the wet ground on the other side, skittering to his feet and taking off.

Scott shouts "*Someone's got my dog!*" at first contact with light, garnering stares from the frigid backstage crew but nothing more. Theirs are minds more ardently occupied with the space heater. As far as potential Amsterdam hiding spots go, the backstage area is overstimulating. All manner of tables and tablecloths and open trunks and structural underbellies. In the time it would take to check it all Scott would experience three hours in Dirty Magician time, convince himself Amsterdam is dead twice, and cry once. Inefficient use of his time given the stakes. Like… *Ricky?*

The flashing red and green of a taxied plane at the top of the hill catches his eye.

Attuned feet carry him across the backstage and over another fence while his eyes struggle to discern the idle blinking from active motion. Scott's own actions surprise him, at this stage of combined euphoria, dysphoria, and hypothermia. How fast he runs, how loud he screams. If this pearly black private plane, engines growling, tattooed in a seal he's too poor to recognize and lettering on the aft wing it's too dark to read, is about to take off with his dog, then Scott has half a mind to jump right in the closest turbo and ruin everybody's night.

A speaker from somewhere amorphously in or around the plane coughs to activity: "*Get away from the aircraft.*"

"Where's my fucking dog?!"

"*We're only asking once. Turn around.*"

"Suck my ass!"

Whoever took the comms doesn't hang up quick enough to muffle their sigh. "*Stay right there.*"

"Do I stay here or go away huh which one gets me my fucking dog?!"

If Scott made any error in the past few seconds, it indisputably would have been antagonizing the twin suited and jacketed men who now disembark the jet with rifles strapped around their collars. The bewitching burn of Dirty Magician momentarily disperses so Scott's resurrected ego can slap him on the back of the head. As best he can, Scott fixes his posture and puffs out his chest, trying his best to look unafraid, unflappable, as armed men triangulate upon him.

"You're the original owner?" One says, hand lazily clawing the butt of his gun.

"I'm the only owner actually."

The man doesn't riposte this. He opens his shoulder to the man standing beside him and signs something so quick it evades Scott's sixth grade sign language elective. One hand touches four fingers to one thumb and slaps on the opposing palm twice. The other one nods a reception and says, plain as fact, "ten thousand for the dog. Right now."

"No."

"Twelve."

"I'm not selling him he's my fucking dog! And he's old, what's he to you?"

"You would be wise to accept."

"Or what you mean you'll shoot me?"

"Under Alaskan law, the perimeter of a private aircraft constitutes private property."

"Literally what the fuck do you guys want an old dog…"

It's hard to tell with the sunglasses, but the men have indeed taken their attention off of Scott, looking instead to the depression he'd just cleared. Their posture fixes robotically and they march past Scott, knocking him on either side and sending him back first to a paper-thin sheet of ice balanced precariously on the tips of grass. The distinct jingle of a collar sends Scott further stumbling, rolling like a gator and getting up so fast he trips again, watching on all fours as a boy and a girl ascend the hill with Amsterdam shivering at their center.

"Amsterdam!"

The boy snaps to attention, looking down at the prone Scott and blowing a laugh at his shoes. *What the hell happened to him*, Scott thinks. Did Yuuyaraq get fucking crazy in the last five minutes? No, that magnitude of grime, pasted everywhere there is to paste, is earned over days. Weeks, maybe. Matted gold hair clings to the imperfections of his skull and the shifting of his clothes reveals harsh lines between dirt and skin. He walks with the slightest bow, holding the top of Amsterdam's collar in two clawed fingers.

"I don't know who this is," the boy vomits, practically, and the girl he walks with jumps to ease his concerns, brushing the back of his shirt. She sings, "Just another random guy…" and attempts to guide the three of them in a half circle towards the plane.

Scott shouts, head swiveling with them, "You have my dog!"

The boy stops all three of them on his own, jerking Amsterdam's collar. "Oh hold up you're Ricky's owner?"

"Please!" Scott reaches out pathetically. In only the boy's tone of voice he knew this was over. Some cruel power beyond what little he may call his own is taking his dog whether he wants it or not. Rod Serling may be crooning, off in space, about how poor Scott Holden's pursuit of isolation has unknowingly wretched from him his greatest friend and unearthed the frightening depths of his wish. Embarrassing and cold tears evacuate down the sides of his cold face, seeming to freeze over in thin strips. "That's my dog. His name is Amsterdam. He's not gonna live much longer. I want him. Please."

"Proceed to the plane," the man in sunglasses tells the hosts. "We'll remove him."

Scott curls up before these men could deny him the strain, whimpering at the ground, "I don't know what the fuck's going on I'm sorry Amsterdam." He focuses on the baritone jingling of Amsterdam's collar, chasing the sound as it falls to the jet engine's consumption.

Gloved fingers fall on his shoulder blades and the sound of Amsterdam's' collar regains. Scott's wet hands fall off his eyes, immediately met by those icy blue things inside his dog's. Amsterdam stands shivering, three feet from his dejected owner, looking half frozen to death but throwing his tail back and forth like it hadn't in years.

Blurry and out of focus, twenty feet out but more or less right where he was when Scott closed his eyes, the boys shouts over the engines, hand prone in the air where he let go of the collar, "*Hey take care of him man he looks a little old!*"

Scott doesn't return this. He lurches forward and tries hugging as much heat into his old dog as he can. He'd give him all the rest if he could. "*Hey there, budd—*"

"*Oh also he likes it when you scratch under his chin like this like how I'm doing so I think it* behooves *you to do that sometimes also.*"

"… I know he li—"

"*I mean like on him though not on me!*"

Whatever. Forget that guy. The girl he's with, zipping up her parka a little more, tells him, "come on, let's get on the plane. It's freezing."

"OH SHIT where'd you guys find my plane?!"

"... Where you left it, I guess?"

"Yo you went to that place with the garlic fries without me?"

"Let's just get you on the plane. And in a shower."

"Ayooo ahaha okay say it in front of everybody alright."

Gloved fingers hovering off Scott's back tell him those black blurry shapes fading into the plane means they're good. The aft stairwell folds up. Scott grips Amsterdam tighter.

Briefly, maybe accidentally, the loudspeaker of the plane barks, "We have Cameron. Taking off ASAP. Inform Mr. Aoki."

# (The) Koyaanisqatsi

***Olivia Achenbach, 21***

***3rd daughter of the Achenbach Family***

***CEO & Chief Brand Ambassador, Liv Lathish Soap Co.***

***Average Monthly Income (aggregated): $2,626,900***

***Girlfriend of Cameron Otterlake***

***Utah airspace***

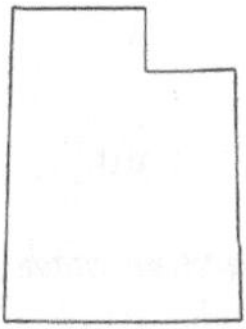

"2241 hours, pacific time. Ground team accompanied by Olivia Achenbach has secured Cameron Otterlake. Live snare was a success. Management has been informed to continue through tomorrow afternoon before prepping commuter aircraft for departure. Over."

*"Copy, Sharapova. SeaTac tells us refueling was delayed. Please confirm. Over."*

"Affirmative, Merchant. Cameron demanded money be drawn from his account and delivered to the craft. Ground team was ordered to acquiesce to all Cameron's requests which did not divert from intended course. Forty-minute delay. Over."

"*One more time. That's forty minutes to withdraw cash? Over.*"

"Correct. First chair's telling me it was forty-three. Over."

"*And he didn't say what it was for? Over.*"

"He did not. Olivia tells us it's possible holding cash calms him down. Over."

"*Copy. Fuel deposit is sufficient to land in Aspen without interruption. Proceed. Over.*"

"One more thing, Merchant: Sharapova security told us Cameron took a phone call. Cockpit cleared for that information? Over."

"..."

"Didn't pick you up, Merchant."

"*We were not informed Cameron made a phone call. Did this occur at SeaTac? Over.*"

"Negative. This was five minutes ago—first chair says it was seven."

"*Seven or five?*"

"Seven. Over."

"*Copy. Sharapova should not be capable of delivering satellite communication while airborne. Was Olivia present for the call? Over.*"

"Olivia was present. Security will ask her a few questions. Over."

"*Copy. Get in touch when you have details. Over.*"

"Copy. Over."

On the topic of how Olivia Achenbach singlehandedly achieved her level of wunderkind success, she didn't. But some of that impressive and maybe infuriating annual income can and should be attributed to her own quite natural business moxie, and it would be needless erasure to discount that hundred thousand just because of her parent's company and their other company and their other other company and the couple hundred properties and the Ivy League school. Everyone gets there somehow, and unlike her more or less boyfriend currently in the shower, Olivia remembers a time before private jets. What Olivia Achenbach doesn't yet know is she will live to forget the time before private jets. Let's not tell her.

"*You put too many soaps in here!*" that pretty much boyfriend shouts above the water. A smart showerer would think to muffle the showerhead, but the smarter individual would already know that impossible, as the *Sharapova* obviously packs a cubical, multidirectional water system showering from three sides and the ceiling—falling gently and densely from a grand, encompassing sheet.

"*Try the cinnamon coconut!*" Olivia suggests. Overstocking his personal shower may have been a mistake. She knows how he gets about too many options. Would clarifying that he shouldn't eat it belittle him? She worries about her tone sometimes. Suggesting one thing but delivering something else more disconnected and cutting. Cameron's scatterbrained for sure, but eating soap? Get a grip. He just drove a shitty little dirt bike from, apparently, Wisconsin to Alaska. He's not braindead.

Olivia takes the liberty of picking a fresh outfit for him. Easy to do since most of the clothes kept on the *Sharapova*, if not all, were picked by Olivia in the first place. All except that ugly sweater she thankfully has not seen in a while. As she sets the folded pants atop her pile she hears Cameron cough for some reason.

A rogue patch of turbulence makes the *Sharapova* shiver and it takes Olivia too long to believe the whole plane wasn't about to come down. She doesn't yet love airplanes. Private jets, a labor under delusion, she imagined would feel safer.

Another thing she remembers, and another thing she will forget, is her first time traveling by air. She was seventeen. Too old to have still never flown, the American was so bold to think and actually believe. Then, too fast to have happen all at once, her father was on solo business flights and returning with nothing but brighter and brighter smiles. Outside of a family friend's Cessna, he hadn't been on a plane either. But not long after that the whole Achenbach family was on a plane to Walt Disney World, then London, then Nassau, then Tokyo—god, they weren't even building miles on an airline credit card. There was no need.

Her first time flying on the *Sharapova* she remembers Cameron saying the plane is pretty old (a decommissioned passenger jet purchased for the Otterlake private fleet in 1996, nearly scrapped before a toddler-aged Cameron took a liking to the propped tail engines). A birthday gift, apparently. One assumes the pilots and crew were also birthday presents. When the two boarded in Alaska, Cameron broke common professionalism by calling the captain Steve and the copilot Rian. An impressive quantum of chumminess, or disrespect, seeing as their badges neglect first names. Then again the Sharapova seems reequipped for *only* Cameron's needs. Apart from the shower is a queen-size bed divided from the rest of the craft by shoulder-high vinyl partitions. For god's sake, there's a walk-in closet. Cameron's taste in aircraft fixtures is in lockstep with Polly Pocket.

A flight attendant Cameron had greeted *Suzy* while rummaging through his things sneaks past Olivia, stopping at the kitchen in the back to check on a bubbling basket of what will soon be garlic fries. Olivia hasn't had garlic fries in years.

As Olivia's thinking maybe a fragrance is due, remembering that awful tarmac-treesap cocktail she'd found him sporting, the cockpit door slides open with a mechanical growl and her least favorite of the two security guys comes her way. Mick just *sucks*. Doesn't take off his weapon for any reason, as if an action movie is gonna break out thirty-thousand feet in the air. Chews gum, too, which is just nasty if you ask her.

"Merchant would like to know who Cameron called."

"Okay, well, I don't know who that is."

"Callsign for Eugene Otterlake, first cousin once removed to Cameron."

"Well, I don't know what they talked about, okay? It didn't make sense."

"Could you tell me anyway?"

"I could tell *Merchant*."

If there's anything Olivia does not like about her boyfriend(?)'s family, it's all the discretion. Being as loaded as they are maybe it's essential but this doesn't make things any easier. In the early days of their relationship nearly everything she and Cameron had said to one another was monitored, probably recorded. When it came time to see each other in person she was shuttled around in unmarked jets, mingling with Cameron in Mykonos and Ibiza around someone else's schedule like these were playdates.

Aspen will be good for both of them. He's never been to the Achenbach compound before and she's never seen him more than twenty feet from men in earpieces.

"… Cockpit, please," Mick signals with his hands like a waiter.

"After you."

"*This is Merchant. Over.*"

"Hi, Eugene, it's Olivia."

"*Please end your comms with over. Over.*"

"Okay, well I'm not gonna do that. You guys were asking about that phone call Cameron had and I just wanted to tell you I don't know what it was about."

"*You don't need to know what it was about. We need to know what was said. Over.*"

"Am I overstepping if I ask why? *Over*?"

"*Cameron is in a delicate state of mind at this present moment. For the security of the Otterlake family and himself it's best we communally understand his trajectory. You've already been made aware of this. Over.*"

"I'm here. I'm watching him. He's doing better than when we found him. Plus he tried making a phone call in the air. Like I doubt whoever he was calling got anything anyway."

"*It would be a great he—*"

"Or if who he was calling got anything to him."

"*... It would be a great help if you could cooperate with us. Nigel has graciously approved Cameron's temporary relocation to the Achenbach residence in Colorado. We cannot collaborate only one-way. Over.*"

"... He said something about tweets. He wants somebody to tweet. I don't know. He talks to the TMZ guys, doesn't he?"

"*Copy.*"

"Copy what?"

"*On the comms I'd ask you to confirm—*"

Olivia hangs up.

Cameron got dressed in the aisleway, one imperial skip from the walk-in closet, asking his pretty much girlfriend where she had gotten the clothes from. She got them from the walk-in closet, but, for risk of making Cameron feel dumb, she tells him a story about shopping in Milan. Nonetheless, he mishears this and thinks she's talking about the movie *Mulan*, and as he fails to tie his shoes no less than three times he recounts some dope parts from *Moulin Rouge*, a different movie. Bless his soul.

Verbally, Cameron Otterlake remains unchanged by his adventure. Body language, however, something Olivia prides herself on clocking inherently and accurately, has taken a dive. He's looked her in the eye twice since leaving Alaska, when they first reunited and then when she said the word *shower*. Her attempts to prompt eye contact have since failed—loudly plopping down in the calf leather chair opposite his, waving a hand like a preschooler, standing directly in his way as he paced the aisle of the *Sharapova*, reopening the windows (he doesn't like redeye flights; he doesn't like not seeing the ground).

"… So…" Olivia raps her fingers together, watching Cameron gorge himself on garlic fries, served to him on Danish porcelain with an artistic wisp of aioli. "Who'd you call?"

"—My cousin told you to ask me that—" Cameron says in a pocket of empty mouth. "—The other place did these wetter."

"You said wetter?"

"Yeah I mean like they were wet."

"Maybe I wanna know who you called. I don't think I've ever seen *you* call somebody else, y'know?"

He nurses his place with a burdened aloofness. Dodging Olivia entirely, Cameron's eyes—glowing, a terribly bright teal like that dog he nearly took—retrace the panel lines in the interior roof. He swallows. "Y'know this is pretty much the only place they can't hear us."

"... Okay. Who is *they*."

"Just the people in my family who like to watch me and don't know how the internet actually works."

"Old people."

"Yeah I mean like old people yeah."

What Cameron struggles to say is the *Sharapova* is old enough that its wi-fi antenna was a retroactive feature. Revisionist enough that someone could hypothetically climb on top of the aircraft, break open the plastic housing, and sever satellite communication after landing in Wisconsin. And since the pilots commune exclusively with the Otterlake flight control via UHF radio, this modification has still gone unnoticed, apart from a purported router failure marked for the plane's next scheduled service.

"You mean we're alone."

"Ayo?"

"No I mean... it seems like you're not alone that much."

"And I'm still not really if you think about it."

This may be an inappropriate time to bum a fry.

"… Look, if you're at worried I was *brought along*, I promise I wasn't," Olivia starts. "I came along. Landing with your plane, and me being there, and us going to Aspen—this was all my idea. Most people, y'know, when they take a surprise vacation, it's because they're having a crisis. Am I allowed to worry about you?"

Cameron has no response to Olivia placing her hand on his. He's making his thinking face.

"Because I do. Maybe your uncle or cousin told me to ask you about phone calls or whatever—your family asks me to do a lot of things. But will all due respect to the surname, I'm not with them. I'm with you, and I choose you, Cameron, and I want you to know I'm in your corner. If we're alone, you can talk to me. There's clearly so much you wanna talk about, with someone, so if you'll let me into your *sphere*, here," (she hovers her hands at Cameron's head) "I think it would make both of us feel better."

Nodding, sparing considered eye contact for the first time since boarding, and topping off his garlic fries, Cameron says "I think maybe my dad died at the same time as my mom and everyone's lying about it because they don't trust me to inherit their stuff."

Olivia seems to choke on food she didn't have. "Uh—m-my condolences?"

"I called a friend I made in Wisconsin to get whoever runs that stupid twitter account tracking my plane to report it going one way even though it's actually going another."

"Cameron—"

"Oh and I could use my phone up here because a guy I saw in a dream left this box at my house that lets me do that without anyone knowing."

"Okay—"

"The thing I asked for in Seattle wasn't actually cash. You should go up to the front there and tell Steve and Rian I have a bomb."

"This is Sharapova. Over."

"*Sharapova, word is the craft has pivoted from Aspen, traveling due northeast. Is there a problem? Over.*"

"Negative, Merchant. Still riding the same airway. We've made no course correction. Over."

"*Copy, Sharapova. Seems like an error on the part of our contact. Proceed. Over.*"

"Quick confirmation for me, Merchant? Is this contact removed from traffic control? Over."

"*Affirmative. Our surveillance grid borrows intel from a vindictive social media network utilizing a satellite backend to report private flight patterns. Over.*"

"Copy. I'd ask if the family could trust myself and my co-pilot with all present flight intel. Over."

"*Always, Sharapova. Over.*"

"Thank you, Merch—hm? Rian why is the door locked—"

"*Sharapova? Something wrong?*"

"No problems up here, Merchant, just having issues with miss Achenbach…"

"*Copy. Radio down if anything comes up—*"

"—Merchant, we may have a code 467. Repeat, code 467. Over."

"*It's your job to remember what those mean, Sharapova, not mine. Elaborate. Over.*"

"Olivia's telling us Cameron Otterlake was delivered an unidentified explosive device along with his cash. Over."

"*Copy, Sharapova. Rest assured his delivery was checked prior to takeoff and the cash was delivered via armored truck by the Otterlake family's private security service. At no point in transportation was there any point where an explosive could be added to the package, nor does Cameron, to our knowledge, know anybody who could procure one for him. He's lying. Over.*"

"Copy, Merchant. We appreciate the assurances. Please understand, however, that we are obligated to follow US aviation procedures and approach the threat with some seriousness. Over."

"*Copy. Do what you have to, Captain. Did Cameron make any demands along with his threat? Over.*"

"We've been instructed not—"

"*Another flight diversion—was that you, Sharapova? Over.*"

"Huh? Negative. We're following the mandated route. If you'll permit me, Merchant, I think your contact may be feeding you misinformation. Over."

"*... Copy. Would US aviation law forbid you from bringing Cameron to the comms? Over.*"

"Affirmative. Over."

"*Stand by.*"

US aviation law prioritizes the safety of passengers. While the three security agents and two flight attendants would normally classify as staff, the Otterlake private aviation fleet evades certain federal employment taxes by classifying said staff as independent contractors rather than salaried employees. Under this jurisdiction, and compounded by present conditions, the commission would consider these individuals passengers, and as such seven of the nine bodies on board the *Sharapova*, save Cameron sitting in his chair at the back of the craft and Olivia acting as liaison, cram into the flight deck and lock the door.

Olivia steps nervously around the guns Cameron ordered the security agents to remove, unload, and disassemble into the little gun pieces like how when you take a mechanical pencil apart[sic]. He's left the bag full of cash in the center of the craft, which despite assurances from Eugene and Mick (hesitantly) that nothing's inside the bag she still finds herself biting the inside of her mouth as she steps over.

She asks, sarcasm badly masking anger, "should I have added my being in your corner doesn't extend to taking hostages?"

"Taking what?" Cameron yells from the shower.

"Hostages! Like the ones in the cockpit!"

"*Ahahaha* oh yeah that's what the front part is called."

"Could you take this seriously, please? Do you have a bomb for real?"

"Nah but I'm about to," he appears from the curved sliding door, double-fisting aerosol cans of dry shampoo and leave-in conditioner. "Hey, did you know most people don't get to bring these on airplanes?"

"Yeah, because they explode?" Olivia agrees before peppering in a "no, no, *nonono*," as she watches Cameron place the cans on top the kitchen unit's electric stove. "Can we talk about this?"

They most certainly can. Why Olivia remains so polite, borderline encouraging, may be chalked up to her sweet Nevadan upbringing (though she was born in Arizona). She clings to the yet-discounted possibility that Cameron is in a rather extreme version of his iconic manias. Rare is anyone or any government agency or strings of hundred-dollar words which can talk him out of what he's already declared a good idea. There remains large vaporous holes in Olivia's understanding of how Cameron Otterlake grew up. Likely still is he's never been conditioned to ask for anything or then accept a No. It's not her place to say, but the possibly late Lord and Lady Otterlake made a grave error in raising him if complicity would ever be required. What is complicity, after all, if not being told No in a thousand tongues.

"Please walk me through this," Olivia starts up again, injuring herself to a smile. "I feel like I'm missing a step here. Your dad *might* be dead—and Cameron I'm really sorry if he is—so your next move is to blow up the plane. Like… with people on it."

"Oh no I'm not gonna blow it up for real I just wanna do something else."

"Yeah, I figured. So I should go to the cockpit and tell them there's no bomb?"

"Ahaha yeah if people are scared probably yeah."

"No, *no*, *wrong*, we don't want them to know there isn't a bomb. You lose your bargaining chip. Right?"

By complete accident, Olivia has said *we* and, as far as her boyfriend is concerned, permanently implicated her in this clumsy hijacking. She's never hijacked an airplane before and thinks maybe, intrusively, she ought to prepare some demands of her own. Aggressive wants don't come easy for the comparatively humble lake girl who still presently remembers hot dogs nestled in sliced white bread. Coming up with something worth co-signing hostages threatens to overheat her brain. She may hurt herself thinking. She envies Cameron, who had stepped away to the kitchen pantry, reappearing with a bag of salt and vinegar potato chips for some reason.

"How do you know your dad is dead?" she tries again.

"You're gonna want one of these before you hear this shit:" he shakes the bag in her face.

*Fine*, she thinks, and she has a chip.

Pacing, Cameron says, "hey did you know a Duke uses both hands to seize all life's necessities and pleasures?"

"… Sorry, who does this?"

"Oh, you wouldn't've gone cuz they don't let girls be down there unless you're naked I think. But yeah me and I guess Nigel and I guess Quentin and I guess everyone else who has money can go down and use this thing called *The Mortar dun-dun-dun* and they can look at people. On cameras. So I used it to look at Nigel which you do—"

"—Please slow down—"

"—by just saying like *Nigel Otterlake* and then it shows it but all it showed was a video of a tree."

"How do you know this… thing works like that?"

"Oh because I used it to look at this guy I know his name is Evan but he was jerking off so I closed it real quick. Him and me skateboard sometimes."

Olivia does recall, when the two of them were visiting London and his awful British friends, Cameron's security guys at one point scuttling him off to somewhere she wasn't allowed to follow. Somewhere inside that Arthur guy's city block he calls a house. She's seen enough of the Otterlakes to know there's things she cannot see and likely would not believe. "The tree means the person you're trying to look at is dead."

"Yeah like I tried Walt Disney and it did the same thing and I'm pretty sure he's also dead." It seems like Cameron's father being dead only occurs to him right this moment. "He's dead!"

"And I really am sorry, Cameron, but what are you hoping to get by hijacking the plane—"

"Y'know what else is fucking crazy is Nigel had diabetes and Quentin had diabetes so I also probably got diabetes somewhere cooking." He spills chips on the stove for easier grabbing and makes himself mad through unknowable cognitive associations. "FUCK I got diabetes probably!"

"It's not their fault you *might* have diabetes," Olivia gestures to the cockpit door. "Let's not make this a tantrum."

"Come on you know how bad this actually is?"

"Bad in a way *we've* made it, or a different way?"

"Quentin made Nigel and Nigel made me I've got a disease in my blood baby I'M GONNA GET DIABETES."

"Okay?"

"That's not okay what the fuck you're pretty much my girlfriend why are you okay with that?"

"Because a lot of people have diabetes?! You're like the last person in human history that should be worried about getting, like, Insulin."

Fear of death has finally struck Cameron Otterlake. He

slaps his arms. He's mad at his own blood.

"Hey, *hey*," Olivia steps in, grabbing his wrists. "You'll be alright. Do you know how your dad might've died?"

He nods his head but looks unprepared to speak.

"Okay, well, your grandad died in a helicopter crash—I learned about it in school, it happened near the ski resort. Point is, he was, like, eighty, and it wasn't diabetes that killed him. I bet it didn't kill your dad either. If he is dead, it was probably some other thing."

Somehow this calms him down. A little. "They said they don't want me inheriting their stuff because I'm stupid or some shit which is BULLSHIT because I'm getting really good grades at Harvard right now and—"

"I thought you were paying someone—"

"—AND I just drove really far without dying which is cool because Nigel always hated me driving and thought I would die."

"Wanna know what I think?" She pulls him away from anything immediately dangerous on the stove, seventy percent of the way to a hug. "Hey. Hey. Wanna know what I think?"

It cannot be discounted, the way Cameron stops vocalizing but continues to move his lips in lockstep with the superhighway of his mind, that unless she's about to help him build a bomb, he does not wanna know what Olivia thinks. Not maliciously. There's not a square inch of her he dislikes. His inconsideration of her feelings about all this is nothing more or less than being Cameron Otterlake, a young man blind of everything but his pupils. In the long term, this thing they have will not work. His effective girlfriend is old enough to develop this consciousness yet clings to the fantasy of pulling her effective boyfriend from a mind he's been programmed for since birth. It will take another few decades of being Olivia Achenbach, third daughter of the Achenbach family, one of the hundred wealthiest families in America, for her to begin understanding the boy who thinks only in the one-two of wanting and getting. But by then she would find herself counted among the individuals who need help.

"*Cameron, it's me,*" buzzes the captain's intercom. "*We land at Aspen in fifty-five minutes. Just a quick heads-up depending on what you wanna do, here.*"

"Could you like run it around the block?"

Silence.

"I don't think they can hear you, Cam," Olivia pulls the aerosol cans off the stove, jamming them in her duffle bag on the bubbly, amorphous sofa. "But I'll ask for you. Don't blow up the plane while I'm gone."

"*Nigel John Quentin Otterlake was wounded by the sudden loss of his beloved wife and mother to his child. He has since diligently fulfilled his duties as Otterlake family patriarch, albeit removed from the public eye. Despite his heartbreak, he is living a healthy and prosperous life in private and wishes not to be disturbed. Over.*"

"Okay, yeah, but you understand that really sounds like he's dead."

*"Offering proof, which I'll remind you given your current familial status I am under no obligation to do, would be a gross violation of Nigel's boundaries and personally disrespectful of me as his first cousin. Over."*

"I'm not asking you to tell *me*, I'm asking you to tell Nigel John Jingleheimer-Schmidt Otterlake's *son*, who is in the back of this plane right now—and oh yeah, does have a bomb. He outranks you, doesn't he?"

*"Were emergency protocol to permit Cameron inside the flight deck I would tell him the same thing I told you, with perhaps a personal anecdote he, and not you, would be entitled to hearing. Over."*

"When's the last time they've seen each other?"

*"If our radio correspondence is having some hiccups, please let me know, because I've made it quite clear there is a majority of private Otterlake family discourse you are not entitled to. Over."*

"Well, somewhere in that private discourse have you ever thought maybe this dumbshit secrecy is why Cameron's… inside the cockpit hey Cameron what's up."

"Hey babe is this what you talk into when you wanna talk to someone?"

"Sir, this—"

"Wassup Steve! Hey sorry about the bomb thing I'm just kinda pissed right now."

"Don't worry about it, sir. For what it's worth, however, this is a grave violation of aviation—"

"Hey who is this who am I talking to?"

"It's Eugene Otterlake, sir. Callsign Merchant."

"Eugene!"

"*Speaking. Over.*"

"Hey sorry about the bomb thing I'm just a little pissed right now but don't worry I don't wanna blow up the plane."

"*We're willing to cooperate with your demands within reason, sir. Over.*"

"Awesome yeah okay so first thing's probably gotta be like… babe what were we talking about a second ago back that way."

"Your dad."

"Yeah! What's up with Nigel man I don't hear about him 'cept for birthday cards and shit."

"*Nigel John Quentin Otterlake was wounded by the sudden loss—*"

"Nah but really though because when I was down in *The Mortar* thing I looked him up and all I got was a tree."

"*I'll warn you, calmly, that what you're asking for is beyond your authority, sir, as protocol concerning Nigel Otterlake was agreed upon by Dukes on committee. I am, however, authorized to disclose more regarding Nigel Otterlake once you've fostered a son. Over.*"

"I don't want a kid though, also I'm way too young to be having—*ehhhhhh* but apparently Nigel made me when he was nineteen and I'm not nineteen—"

"Cameron."

"Oh yeah. Eugene man you're cool but I think it behooves you to be real with me right now. I got spray cans cooking on a stove right now."

"What?!"

"*I can speak candidly with you, sir, but nobody else. Ask the crew of the Sharapova to leave the flight deck.*"

"Merchant, this is Sharapova—it would be an undue risk leaving the helm unattended so close to descent—"

"EVERYONE OUT!"

"*Are we alone?*"

"Yeah Steve put the thing on whatever it's called where the plane goes and you don't do anything with it."

"*That's called Autopilot, son.*"

"Yeah! That's what it's called. But yeah I think they went to go take the spray cans off the stove. But yeah what's up Nigel it's been a minute."

"*You know my decision was impersonal, son. I would never leave you alone in the world had I thought you weren't ready—*"

"So like what's up with the tree thing like when I tried to find you on the TVs and it just had like a tree."

"Micah 4:4. *What you had seen while visiting* The Mortar *was an honorary skeuomorphic dating back to when the majority of Dukes were faithful men.* Everyone will sit under their own vine, and under their own fig tree, and no one will make them afraid, for the Lord Almighty has spoken. *In the case of a deceased Duke, the tree will indicate their passing, but I merely requested my removal from all Dukes surveillance.*"

"Oh okay."

"*Is that all?*"

"No like I just didn't know you could do that is all. Is it about mom being dead?"

"*In some ways. In others, well, I think you already know. You're feeling, at this time, much the same way I felt at your age. An avalanching cognizance that your life is not really your own.*"

"Wait it's not?"

"*I understand this episode of yours began in London. At any point prior to your Dukes visit, did you feel this ghostly sensation that something is wrong? You had to get away, and where did not matter so long as you felt safe?*"

"Kinda sorta I dunno."

"*Let's try something else. I'll tell you a story about myself, and you'll listen. Hm? Like when you were young.*"

"*Cameron?*"

"OH I thought we were starting right now, yeah I'm listening."

"*Somewhere in your brief escapade through the sticks, you may have realized that not only is our financial status in a galactically different place than ninety-nine percent of people, but as a result, so is the way we think. Living the way we do is more than comfortable, but I'm not so convinced it's healthy. I did not realize until it was perhaps too late how unilaterally money influences who we are, what we value, et cetera—that means 'and so on,' Cameron. Your grandfather believed in destiny; Otterlakes deserve where we are, and by extension other people do not."*

"Oh yeah Quentin told me the same thing."

*"Of course he did. When I began feeling what you do now, your grandfather told me I had a decision to make. He believed people of wealth had a responsibility, and either I accepted what was mine, or I step aside for someone else to take it. He meant you when he said this, though you weren't born yet. The titles of Otterlake patriarch is not up to meritocracy; it is wholly determined by blood. It is not a post I can simply abandon, though I've pulled myself as far away as I can manage."*

"Wait but why was it just you then, like why didn't you take me and also mom before she wasn't dead?"

*"Try not to think less of your mother, Cameron, but she agreed with your grandfather. You have to understand; she had more altruistic goals concerning our wealth, for which abandoning her post was not an option. What those were in the long-term, sadly we cannot know. But everyone made their decision."*

"No one asked me what I wanted though."

*"You were very young and likely don't remember, but you chose to stay with your mother. In the interest of disclosure, and because you're a grown man whether you think of yourself that way or not, I authorized your advanced surveillance. It was something that would have happened one way or the other, poised to inherit the family wealth as you are, and I needed to know whether that was something*

*you wanted.*"

"Oh."

"*Is it?*"

"Not really."

"*I didn't think so.*"

"Man Nigel I dunno what to do at this point y'know like all your friends found me anyway so like… yeah I dunno what I'm gonna do now."

"*Are you asking me seriously? You're an Otterlake. You don't have to do anything. Now step aside; your pilots have to land your plane.*"

"Okay! So! Your dad *isn't* dead."

Olivia's words plop wet on the carpet, ignored. Cameron goes through the backpack he had collected earlier, shifting away films of carefully folded tarp and bisectional rope and otherwise doesn't respond. Maybe Nigel's been dead for a while.

"I think it *behooves* you to go to Malibu," he mumbles.

"Malibu?"

"At my house in Malibu I got a bunch of those chinchillas you wanted. They're just running around the place right now but I left out the carrots and mangoes so they should be fine."

Truthfully, Olivia cannot remember ever talking to

Cameron about chinchillas. It's a little gerbil rat thing she's about as fond of as any other gerbil rat thing. He didn't have to go out of his way to buy an undisclosed plural, sweet as that may be. And, true, Olivia cannot remember asking, but Olivia will live to forget a lot of things. What she really cannot remember is drifting to sleep on the Otterlake superyacht *Calypso* some months prior, ragdolled on their unending fourth deck sofa, failing to find the edges no matter how far she stretched her hands and feet, radiating sunlight from her several hours spent on the highest platform, closer to the sun than she'd ever been, Olivia mumbled poor German and half-asleep dreams, topics ranging from scalped coconuts with the straw sticking out to her dream pet as a little girl. She did want a chinchilla. Two chinchillas named Amanda and Monchie. They would have one of those tall palatial cages, several floors, with the colored tubes and the wheels, and the plastic roaming balls for playing with the dogs who are now dead, and actually maybe the girl one will have a different name, but she'd pull one out every couple of weeks to wrap them in a towel and clip their nails because you're supposed to do that, and eventually Stevie and Monchie would have babies and her sisters would take care of the babies, and regretfully none of this can happen now because the best place in Olivia's house to put the chinchilla chateau would be where that Polish wardrobe is gonna go. The only reasonable spot for that cage now is the back of her mind, marked permanently for relocation, to the place where all the old Olivia Achenbach's stuff has been locked away and forgotten, to be brought out only for the taut, buzzed, sunpoisoned engagements where being Olivia

Achenbach and being herself eclipse.

"Thanks." That's all she's got.

"You should maybe go to the front part now," Cameron waits to say. "The cockpit."

"*ETA, Sharapova. We're still getting mixed signals. Over.*"

"Copy, Merchant. We're ten minutes from descent, on the money. Is the ground crew prepared? Over."

"*Affirmative. Bomb squad and ground crew are prepared to receive your passengers and deliver from airstrip to compound. Over.*"

"Copy. Out of curiosity, Merchant, where do you think we're going? Over."

"*We're seeing you due south over Albuquerque. Over.*"

"Copy, Merchant—oh, I see."

"*See what?*"

"Cameron made a change to our heading, Merchant, we've been southbound for twenty minutes. Over."

"*I'll let the ground te—*"

"Be advised, Achenbach has reentered the flight deck. Over."

"Does she have orders from Cameron? Over."

"I have an order, actually—oh, excuse me—hey, hi, it's me. How about you all leave Cameron the fuck alone? *Over?*"

*"You won't be hearing anything we haven't already told you, ma'am, with all respect. But I'll answer what is within your rights to know and what is within my bounds to say. Over."*

"You guys are really dumb, you know that? Gone fishing—what my dad says. You clowns with your agendas and not so careful planning. You don't have a single resource that isn't available to the rest of the world; We've all got cameras, we've all got… goddamn… Wikipedia. You're monitoring Cameron at all times? You really think that? You don't even know for sure where this plane is right now. When Cameron rightfully assumes what you've entitled him to, and if he fucks it all up, it'll be entirely your own fault because you guys have no idea how outgunned you really are—"

"Captain!"

"Let her finish, Rian—"

"Cabin depressurized!"

Olivia hangs up.

As nobody but the pilots classify as crew for this present moment, checking the cabin is something only Steve and Rian are authorized to do. That said, when the cockpit door is unlocked and ripped open by the violent, incoming wind, everybody but the copilot piles out—very nearly sucked out—grabbing onto furniture and stable fixtures while fingering at the ceiling for deployed oxygen masks. Against a wind violent enough to rip makeup off the face, occupants of the *Sharapova* look to the aft in horror, to a wobbling, deployed airstair, screaming against aerodynamics and leading to an absence of light. The bag of money, the wrinkled backpack, and Cameron Otterlake are gone, whipped away to howling Hades and rendering unto the *Sharapova* a personal hurricane of aerosol cans and potato chips and kitchen utensils and onlookers without words.

Upon landing, though graciously allowed to the family compound in nearby Aspen, Olivia Achenbach will be questioned by Colorado state police and Otterlake family security regarding her involvement in Cameron's latest vanishing. Whatever motivation she supplied she will not remember, because the question occupying her ever-constricting mind will be why she didn't jump with him, away from security agents named Mick and authorized family information and more money than there is paper. This may be the final year of her life she can still know to dislike these things—being an Achenbach by current terms, being an heir. The final year she can remember wanting chinchillas.

# (The) Peroration

***Jacob Pulkkinen, 30***

***Technically homeless***

***Average monthly income: $210***

***Income this month: $400.54***

***Las Vegas, Nevada***

*"When you call my name, it's like you said a prayer…"*

*"I'm on my knees, I wanna take you here…"*

Jacob Pulkkinen, swinging his car keys on a pilfered lanyard from this weekend's Anime Takes Vegas convention, adorned with Disney-eyed characters you couldn't pay him to recognize, falsettos through Madonna's *Like A Prayer*, a song he's heard recently enough to know the words if not to a sufficient accuracy.

*"Six o'clock already I was just in the middle of a dream…"*

*"I was kissing Valentino by a crystal blue Italian stream…"*

It's not that he's confused Madonna's *Like A Prayer* and The Bangles' *Manic Monday*; he's just arbitrarily elected to start singing the latter. Somehow, he knows the words perfectly.

A roommate from before Jacob's rent spiked to unpayable figures has invited him down to Vegas. Possibly to live, maybe just to try his four hundred dollars' worth of luck. Wherever the desert wind may still blow lost men to the rest of their lives. For a young guy (thirty is still young) the manufactured excitement of Vegas should be the reset he needs. Some honest, artistic stuff is apparently happening beneath the gross Yankee sewervomit. But the pawn shop from Pawn Stars popped up sooner on the Google Maps result, so that's where Jacob spent his morning. In a long queue. They weren't even filming an episode. He doesn't know for sure if the show is still running.

But Jacob did recognize the make and model of their back door alarm. A respected German manufacturer considered in some circles to be top of the business security pile, and in other circles a sparkling electric sign in the Vegas tradition promising free action. So tantalizingly crackable. They never know what's gonna come through that door.

It was the roommate who is currently attending Anime Takes Vegas and can still afford to live in the same apartment from a few months ago, not Jacob. Those two are friends in only convenient places, predominantly where it concerns money. One or both could be counted on for something enterprising. How they didn't end up in Vegas sooner is the real question, if one that will remain unanswered as that ex-roommate currently has panels to attend and Jacob has pavement to pound.

Nevada is hotter than anyone could have prepared him for; Hardly twenty minutes under the sun and he's sweated through the ratty bomber jacket he for some reason took from the car thinking maybe he'd need one. What he needs is air conditioning. The heat can't be good for Raoul.

Him and the blue rat were solid. As essential as a good coat with a lot of pockets. The number of dates and free drinks and warm rooms to crash begotten by a sideman chinchilla have been as good as the income he's lost. Once the guy is trained to crawl up drainage pipes and unlock doors from the inside it's over. Until then, Raoul is a brother. The glovebox in Jacob's car was gutted of all receipts and Wendy's wrappers to make room for a little chinchilla pen with all the fixings Jacob had read about online. They love to roll around in sand. Kick it everywhere. Jacob didn't mind. He's got his own things and it's not like the car could look any worse.

Oasis arrives, then, in the form of Rolling Greens, a cannabis dispensary truck parked illegally in the lot of the Planet Hollywood resort. The ID guy is so overcome with joy to see Raoul pop from inside Jacob's jacket he forgets to do his one job and lets Jacob board uncarded. As soon as they're inside the retrofitted, air-conditioned school bus, Raoul's olive eyes relax and he shakes cool wind through his fur.

Rolling Greens has just enough width for a couch, a glass counter, and a shimmy's worth of customer space. The tumultuous reality of operating a marijuana business ceases to matter as all thirteen functioning eyes inside Rolling Greens center on Raoul, the guest of honor. Jacob plops his pet on the counter and Raoul does that great thing where he rolls around, slapping his feet on the glass. *Can they pet him? Yes. Raoul's super friendly. Yeah, that's his name.*

"What can I get you, man?" an employee asks without eye contact, scratching Raoul on his big head.

"Mm," Jacob tries, fails, too parched. "Some water for me and the guy," he succeeds, pointing at Raoul.

Incredible wingman, Raoul. A liter of Fiji Jacob wasn't even asked to pay for *and* some cups. Clever Swiss engineering severs a Dixie to something chinchilla accessible.

The employee says, and Jacob is glad it's not about paying, "Cops didn't harass you about your friend, did they?"

"Huh? No, no, I didn't see any."

"We've had to move twice in half a week," he goes on. Really Jacob doesn't care and has no intention of buying—what is that—*Talos Guide You 10g*, but anything not concerning money is welcome. "We were over by the Louis V building and they wanted a permit. So we move over to the Criss Angel banners and the same fucking guy tell us we need a permit. We don't, by the way. And yesterday we get served a fine that a guy just skates by and pays off so, I dunno, thank God. Saw some squad cars doing laps this morning though, so I thought I'd ask."

"You said a guy skated by and paid your fine?"

"On a skateboard," the employee smiles at the thought. "Wasn't even pushing, either, like the guy had a magic genie skateboard. Real cash, too, out the pocket. Crazy town."

"Lucky guy?"

"Maybe. What'd you say this little dude's name was? Rudy?"

Cameron Otterlake never learned to survive because he's never had to. His is a mind unencumbered by squishy human necessity. Twenty years without motivation have rendered the otherwise affluent young man a feral child. Whether he is happy is dependent on whether he is free, which will remain the question until he is dead, remain the question until Otterlake means nothing, until all the money is left to the repossessed elements, frayed and distressed, rounded at the corners and resembling tender only as cave paintings resemble their maker. It was Cameron Otterlake who paid the fine, and Cameron Otterlake who hops from penthouse to penthouse, his choice in hotels coordinated with the song playing in the lobby, a pattern the concierges have only begun to notice, it is Cameron Otterlake who can stand at the floor to ceiling windows with his face oiling the glass, look over the tops of idiotic buildings and trace a finger across the horizon, a splitting of Earth and space, it is Cameron Otterlake who can choose which will belong to him.

Braden Thompson, 2024